The Second Life of Ava Rivers

A NOVEL BY

FAITH GARDNER

RAZORBILL®

RAZORBILL®

An Imprint of Penguin Random House LLC
Penguin.com

RAZORBILL & colophon is a registered trademark
of Penguin Random House LLC.

First published in the United States of America by Razorbill,
an imprint of Penguin Random House LLC, 2018

LIBRARY OF CONGRESS CATALOGING-IN-PUBLICATION DATA IS AVAILABLE
ISBN 9780451478306

Printed in the United States of America

1 3 5 7 9 10 8 6 4 2

Interior design by Corina Lupp

For Micaela, my sister,
And Ramona, who might as well be.

1

MY SISTER, AVA, disappeared on Halloween.

We were dressed in angel costumes. Homemade halos hovered over our heads, cheeks glitter-smeared with Mom's makeup, limbs draped in dripping cake-white chiffon. It was a rare decision we could agree on.

We were six.

Ava and I were fraternal twins. We weren't the same. And I was apt to point that out when she was still here—the little and not-so-little ways in which we were different. Ava was blond, I was auburn. Ava had dusty-blue eyes, I had hazel. Ava was loud, and I was quiet. Ava adored cartoons, I devoured books. Ava had boyfriends all through kindergarten, I had only kissed pillows by the time she disappeared.

But later I would just remember how we were the same. Our matching mood rings, our pigtails, our dolls, our room with the line duct-taped on the carpet to designate sides, our noses, the seashell-shaped vanilla perfume bottle we shared, the way we cut up Mom's old magazines and made strange faces out of models' lips and eyes and bangs. Our hair, wisps and waves that burst in clouds around our faces.

Ava's disappearance was the crack in the Rivers family. I wish I could explain to you how we were before, but I can't, because the before is so filmy and shadowed by the after. I can only tell you our family's happiness was wonderfully unremarkable; our love was unfamiliar with the clutching claws of regret; there were no maybe-ghosts rattling our windowpanes or perhaps-angels at our dinner tables. I had a good childhood. Hot Junes and ice cream truck chases and dancing in the sprinklers. Loud Christmas mornings and Saturday pancake feasts and tickle fights.

It ended too early.

2

EVERYBODY BLAMES THEMSELVES for what happened. The blame is a loop that never really goes away. My parents blame themselves for hosting a party that night and telling our older brother, Elliott, a not-so-responsible twelve-year-old, to take us trick-or-treating in our neighborhood. Elliott blames himself for putting us on his bike—me on his lap, Ava on the handlebars—and riding us over to his friend's house on the other side of Ashby Avenue. I vaguely remember that ride, the way the air picked our hair up and reached with cold fingers down my neck. That badass feeling, so honored my brother would take us with him to go to hang out at his friend's house, passing gaggles of goblins and bunnies along the street, the sky blue-black as the deep sea except for a few unspectacular stars. When he parked his bike on his friend's lawn, Elliott told us to go up the block for more candy. Loud music was coming from inside the apartment building. It was a party. Teenagers—back then, they might as well have been gods—smoked cigarettes out front. I wanted to stay with my brother, but whining only pissed him off.

"Get out of here," he told us. "This isn't for kids. Just go trick-or-treat down the block and come back in a while and we'll head home."

I don't remember exactly what happened after that, but I remember I felt uneasy, being in the dark alone with my sister in a neighborhood that wasn't ours. Even though the party seemed so mysterious, the teens so untouchably cool without their costumes, we did as he said. The angels walked into the night together, down the sidewalk, knocking on doors for puny candies. But it wasn't fun anymore. It was getting cold. My costume seemed childish in this light. I wanted to go home.

This is where I blame myself.

After looping the block once we went back to the party, but Elliott wasn't there, just a few teens out front drinking sodas and snickering at our costumes. I whispered to Ava that we should head home. It wasn't that far. We had come straight down California Street. We could walk straight back in the other direction, and eventually we had to cross Ashby and hit our street.

Ava was the ambitious one. She wasn't ready to leave yet. She liked the unfamiliar houses and yards, while I just wanted to be back on our block where everything made sense. She ran ahead of me. She wanted to play hide-and-seek. But my legs hurt and I was tired. I parked my butt on someone's lawn and shoved candy in my mouth while she skipped down the street, taunting me to come with her.

"Count to a hundred!" she shouted as she ran up the sidewalk, glancing back over her shoulder. "Bet you can't find me!"

I didn't count. She was always trying to force me into playing games I didn't want to play. Soon all I heard were cars roaring like ocean waves. I waited for her to return. I sat there eating candy and shivering until eventually I walked home alone, halo in hand, calling her name like a question into the air, crying, swinging my stupid pillowcase full of candy.

After that, the night becomes a blur.

Hazy memories of a house full of costumed, half-drunk adults freaking out over news that a kid was missing. Bride of Frankenstein leading a search party. A pirate calling the police. Cops everywhere, the nonstop spinning red-blue-white lights coming in through the window and crawling along the ceiling as I lay in bed, alone for the first time.

Her last words forever haunt me. She was right. I never found her. Nobody did.

3

AVA'S DISAPPEARANCE WAS almost twelve years ago—the divider between then and now like a duct-tape line on the carpet designating HERE and THERE.

There are still no answers. There are "leads," "theories," and "tips." Investigators, TV specials, websites, memorials, anniversaries. There are the names of serial killers in the area during that decade who abducted little girls within miles of Berkeley. There are the steep crags of backyard creeks, there are runaway rumors, there are psychic visions of violet VW buses and mass graves. Police reports. Missing persons. Billboards, bus benches, flashing pictures at baseball games, enough fliers to swallow the town in neon pink. But there is still no trace of Ava—as if she walked straight into death's tunnel that Halloween and left not a speck of angel-glitter or a golden thread of hair behind.

4

HOPE TAKES SUCH a twisted shape when someone is gone without explanation.

Years ago a hiker and her dog discovered the remains of a child off a trail at Diablo, a mountain about twenty miles inland. Shallow grave, heaped in dead pine needles, tiny skeleton curled in the fetal position in the dirt. A "friend" posted the news article to my mom's Facebook wall—also an odd thing that begins occurring when someone disappears into thin air, everyone's an armchair sleuth—and my mom lived on the news for weeks as the investigation into the remains ensued. She called our PI every day for updates first thing in the morning. She started remodeling the downstairs bathroom with sponge paints and wallpaper trim dotted with seahorses. She bought window boxes with preplanted pansies. She scrubbed out the fridge till it sparkled. But then the forensic lab results came in and it turned out to be a small eight-year-old boy. Mom hung up the phone when the news was delivered, and her eyes shone and she yelled at Mexico and Canada, her pugs, for barfing on the runner. Mom's chipper attitude and household projects fell to the wayside. The downstairs bathroom has only one sponge-painted wall and a few stenciled seahorses, and the bucket of periwinkle paint still sits behind the toilet. Mom disappeared again into a string of Pilates appointments and charity work, her face hardened back into that determined, unreachable expression. More than once I saw her go into her SUV in the driveway just to sit in the driver's seat, dabbing at her eyes, screaming a muffled scream.

She had been so excited at the prospect of an answer, a funeral, a burial, a door closing, a goodbye.

Dad's the worst, though. www.FindAvaRivers.com and the corresponding social media pages are his full-time job. One that doesn't pay as well as when he was the head of marketing at a media firm. Every day there's a new tip, a new shiny lie to follow. A girl with no memories showed up at a hospital in Wichita. A woman strung out on drugs was spotted at a campsite in Oregon. The basement—Dad's home—is stacked with books covering the sex-trafficking trade. Memoirs of girls locked in bunkers for years, with highlighted pages and fluorescent Post-its. When those ladies were discovered padlocked in that Midwestern man's house a few years back, Dad actually pumped his fist in the air at the news, like yay, like hooray. "Can you imagine? Ten *years*," he said, his eyes aglow.

He lives on that hope, that jacked-up hope that Ava's not dead, she's only been a slave for over a decade.

Jesus Oprah-watching Christ, my family.

I don't mean to sound bitter. I don't ever express my feelings about this stuff to my parents—they've had enough heartbreak for several eternities. Regarding Ava and her fate, I almost prefer Elliott's naked hopelessness. Because whatever happened to her, it ain't rainbows and unicorns, that's for sure.

Everyone's got their hunch, their theory, in the Rivers family.

Everyone's got their false leg of hope to lean on. What about me, Vera Rose, her not-so-identical twin? What do I believe? I prefer the sci-fi angle. Alien abduction. A rip in this dimension. Time travel. I prefer to joke about it if I can, because the truth is, we don't know what happened to Ava May Rivers, and I'm afraid we never will.

I wasn't always like this. I used to scan every horizon for a certain cloud of dirty-blond hair. I used to think, lying in bed, that every car I heard purring to park on the street was someone coming to bring me back my sister. I trusted my parents when they said she would come home. Then I grew; I started looking into their eyes when they said it instead of listening to their words. I let myself wonder, what if she *doesn't* come home? I thought of her dead somewhere, and though it disturbed me, it seemed all too possible. After time, that thought became inevitable, then a sick relief.

And the wheel, it turned.

And the wheel keeps on turning.

5

EVERY YEAR MID-JULY I dread my birthday because it's her birthday, too.

We have this tradition that involves gathering, with many balloons, in a park near where Ava disappeared. Sheet cake and a picnic bench and a shady oak tree. We brought enough balloons today that I contemplate tying them to Mexico and Canada and watching the fat pugs float away into the blue yonder. *Hahaha, when pugs fly*, I think to myself. But I don't crack a smile. The mood is somber, multicolored Sharpies whispering against card paper, brows knit and brains hard at work. We fill out mini note cards to attach to the balloons. Notes that say things like:

"We miss you, Ladybird. Love, Dad."

"Not a day goes by, Ava. Mom."

I draw a cartoon of a stick figure in a hot dog suit, waving.

We release the balloons into the air one by one and watch them drift upward, as if depleting the world's helium resources and releasing latex doomed to choke birds somewhere is going to get the message to Ava somehow.

It's still better than the "remembrance ceremony" the year I reached double digits, though.

That year we had thirty or so people here at the park to memorialize Ava. My mom had this beautiful idea to release butterflies into the great beyond, one per person. She ordered these monarch butterflies, and they came in fancy white boxes. We brought them to the park and distributed them to everyone, one by one, and said some secular prayer-type message of hope for Ava, and everyone opened the boxes so the butterflies would flutter their collective wings and rise heavenward. Only there was a problem. Something must have gone wrong in the shipping or the butterfly storage process, and everyone opened their boxes and . . . the butterflies were dead.

Talk about a downer of an already big old downer of a situation.

But wait, I'm not done.

An hour later, when everyone was putting on their coats and grabbing their purses and saying their final sorries and goodbyes, the boxes began moving, and all the butterflies suddenly awoke at the same time and flew up, up, and away. It was sort of magical. Plenty of tears were shed. Still . . . since that first year, my parents have gone with balloons instead of butterflies.

The crowd thins on an annual basis. It used to be extended relatives, kids and teachers from our elementary school, neighbors. On the important anniversaries—one, five, ten—there were news crews. But now it's just family, minus Elliott. Which is basically family these days.

I know it shouldn't be about me, it shouldn't, but even with dozens of balloons it's not exactly the most uplifting way to spend my eighteenth. We sing the happy birthday song to my question mark of a sister, and I wonder when anyone is going to mention the fact it's also a certain someone's birthday as well, ahem, ahem. I comfort myself by checking my phone and noting the somebodies I barely know who took the time to post on my wall today. Madeline, my ex, texted *happy bday* with three red hearts. I keep opening up that damn message and staring at it as if it's going to make some difference in my life. Like all the other texts she's sent, I ignore it. After the balloons are on their mission to Mars and Mom has neatly packed away the note cards and Sharpies, Dad heaves a sigh that's like a window shutting and turns to me, petting my hair.

"What do you want to do for your birthday, Ladybug?" Dad asks, as if my birthday isn't today and we aren't already doing something.

"Nothing," I say. "Cake's good."

Dad sips wine from a paper cup. Trust my mother to bring a seventy-dollar bottle of wine to the park and my father to grab Dixie cups. But seriously, it's good to see my dad in something other than sweats. He even shaved and put in his contact lenses. My mother is busy on her shiny phone. Up in the sky, the balloons are rainbow pinpricks in the blue. *In two months*, I think, *I will be living in Portland, Oregon, and my life will be green and growing and new. I hear it's different there in the fall. I hear they have something more like seasons.*

Across the lawn, some young hippie types are having a barbecue, reggae on full blast. I smell the skunk from here. I squint my eyes at a guy in bell bottoms and big old-lady sunglasses resting on his 'fro. Even from thirty feet away, his staring problem is obvious. It's probably the balloons. Then again, his eyes are very fixed down here on earth, specifically on me. A strange man's gaze usually chills me. But everything—the tree-spotted park, the shouts of partygoers, the shuffle of my family's nonconversation—becomes a green blur and white noise. The guy points at me. I point at myself. For one second, it's as if there are only the two of us in this world and it's quiet and full. Happy birthday to me.

That's when I realize I went to elementary school with that guy, to junior high and high school, too; that guy's slept over at my house. Once upon a memorial he used to come release balloons with us, but now he's all grown up and probably stoned and having a blast, and here I am with my family and our sad-ass tradition.

Ava had a million friends, but her one best friend who was like her inseparable conjoined twin was such a usual sight in the house he had his own monogrammed placemat and napkin the way the Rivers kids did. He was a firecracker with a puff of amazing blond-tipped Afro hair and freckles on his brown face, who played piano and was a total Stevie wunderkind type and even his name made you go, yeah, this kid's going places. Maximus Presley Spangler—aka Max.

Max Spangler has a name you almost have to say like that—*Max Spangler*, surname and all—no matter how many times he's thrown water balloons at you and called you a smelly poo-poo face.

At the annual birthday balloon-a-palooza, Max used to write notes that were superlong poems and spent all this time drawing classy borders on the cards with several colors of Sharpie. The last time he showed up, he was fourteen, I think. It was our freshman year. He didn't stay long. He had buzzed his head and grown so many inches I barely recognized him. We exchanged polite small talk sans eye contact. I saw him around the halls in high school, passed a smile back and forth now and then, but no words. And maybe this is crazy, but that look he gave back then—stuck on me, mouth corners turning down, glass-shine in his brown eyes—made me wonder if he wished hard it had been me and not Ava.

And now there are our juxtaposed barbecues and an impromptu staring contest. I'm slightly mortified, but he waves me over.

Me?

Really?

Lil old me?

My parents are opening a card and gazing at it together. FOR YOUR SPECIAL DAY, it says in glitter. Mom oohs and Dad grunts, unimpressed.

"Look," Mom says. "Ozzie sent you a gift card. He's sorry he couldn't make it today."

"I'll be right back," I say.

Maybe it's the wine I gulped out of Dad's cup a few minutes ago, but I'm a little bold at the moment. I mean, soon I'm going to be thrust into a new, stranger-filled habitat, so I'd better learn to schmooze it up like a normal human, right? I stride across the lawn toward Max as he loiters among his boho gang. Someone is doing a headstand for no apparent reason. A white girl with dreadlocks is dancing—poorly, I might add. Bongos are being played. It's a group portrait of Berkeley stereotypes. Max stands there grinning with Mars-red eyes.

"Vera!" he says, and gives me a hug like this is normal, when actually we went through about ten-odd years of school together without exchanging multiple syllables at a time. I accept his embrace awkwardly, patting him once on the back.

"Nice glasses," I tell him.

"Oh," he says with a goofy, hyena-like laugh. He takes them off his head. "They're my G-ma's."

"That's cool she let you borrow them."

"Yyyeah . . . she's dead."

"My condolences."

"She's been dead for a long time, actually, since, like, fifth grade," he tells me, putting the glasses back on his head. "So, you know, it's kosher."

"Glad to hear."

"But I found these old specs in our garage and I've been rocking them."

"Suits you."

This, I think, *is why I usually avoid social interaction*. But no. I refuse to give up. This is the new me, the new girl I'm going to be in Portland. I'm going to start conversations even if it means randomly discussing dead grandmas' sunglasses with boys I hardly know.

My parents squint at me from their picnic table. Even from this distance, their suspicion reeks.

"So what's the haps?" Max asks. "You having a . . ."

"Party," I finish.

From here you can't see the cake, and the balloons are all up in the atmosphere now.

"Yeah, I'm sure it's hard to tell," I go on. "Pretty pathetic, right? Three people."

"Intimacy's tight."

"It's my birthday."

"Happy birthday!" He turns around and yells at his friends. "Yo—this is Vera. It's her birthday!"

The bongo guy bangs maniacally for a moment, I guess in celebration?

"Rad," someone says.

"Um, thanks," I say to Max.

My parents are now whispering to each other from the picnic table as they gape at me.

"I should go," I say. "Back to the 'party.' You know, it's her birthday, too, so that's why we did the whole balloons thing."

Max nods slowly.

"Ava," I remind him.

"Yeah," he says.

His face changes, a shadow passes over it, his smile disappears.

"Right," he says. "That."

That—my forever missing sister. The bummer bomb thrown into every interaction ever. I can't wait to live a life far enough away from here that no one ever sighs and gets all sad-faced and says the word *that*. Like *that*.

"See you around," I say.

"Man," he says, shaking his head, suddenly sober.

I start to walk away, but he tugs my sleeve once.

"Sorry—I mean—we should hang sometime," he says.

I turn, surprised.

"Um . . . sure." I tell him my number, and he punches it into his phone. I consider letting him know I'll be gone in two months, but think, *Why bother?* He won't call.

I get back to my parents and they're all questions. Do I know those people? Who was the boy I was talking to? It would take too long to explain it was Max, who they knew as a wee one, and they might even embarrass us all by trying to go say hi to him or something totally unnecessary like that. Dad chastises me for associating myself with "such inelegant bongo players."

"Are there any other kinds?" I joke.

"Touché," he says, patting my back.

I blink to watch an airplane pass the shrinking spectacle of balloons, and when I look back, Max's back is turned to me. He's got his arm around some long-haired dude with a didgeridoo. I hear laughter. I smell barbecue. And I realize how thirsty I am.

Dad gulps the last of his wine, crumples his cup, and tosses it in the trash while I pour myself a splash. He sits on the bench and opens his guitar case. His fingers find their places and he strums, watching the sky with squinty eyes. He sings lines about real life and fantasy and landslides and reality. His voice is so sincere and sweet, the guitar's every string plucked so perfect, even the birds still themselves to listen.

My Dad, like Elliott, is a gifted guitar player and can sing as well as any radio star. Dad doesn't do it often anymore, but when he does, even my mom stops what she's doing. I try to imagine my dad when my parents first met—that shoulder-length hair in their wedding picture. And my mother, sans makeup, letting her freckles show. They are holding hands in that picture, and it breaks my heart. So simple. A thrilled clasp as they stood before the future unknown. The last time they held hands was so long ago that I had a sister.

I chime my tone-deaf voice into Dad's song, belting the next line about being a poor boy and not needing sympathy. I add a falsetto Cockney accent just because why the hell not.

Dad laughs as he sings the next line and my mother says, "Oh Vera," for the zillionth time in her life.

Oh Vera, oh Vera, oh Vera.

"Elliott call?" Mom asks me when I look at my phone.

"Yeah," I lie.

Because he will. I know my brother. He will call. He will.

She shoots me a steely-eyed X-ray look that means, I know you're lying, Vera Rose. She gives me a side hug and whispers happy birthday. But she's not entirely happy. And it's not entirely my birthday.

I love them, I do. But next year when I'm in Portland, I'll be at my birthday with friends I haven't even met yet, with people who have no idea who Ava is. And how free I'll be then. How me I'll be.

We pack up. The stoner barbecue has left a mess of beer cans on their picnic table. Max is nowhere to be seen. Look up—neither are Ava's balloons.

6

ELLIOTT CALLS AFTER midnight. Let's not get into technicalities, though. I'm still awake in bed, playing a game on my phone when it rings. I sit up. It's a number I don't recognize, which I know means it's my brother on someone else's phone.

"Yo," I say.

"Well, happy birthday, little sister. Is that Vera-Bo-Bira-Nana-Fana-Fo-Feera I'm talkin' to?"

He sounds, shall we say, *festive*. I can always tell how drunk my brother is by how southern he sounds. He's not from the South; he's from California, like me. But he has these characters he falls into—he's been known to adopt a cartoonish French accent at the dinner table, leaves me voice messages in a weird Irish leprechaun voice, and acquires a southern drawl when he drinks. Only a couple of beers and we're barely into Texas. But I can tell right now he's probably near a twelver in. Right now he's good old Mississippi drunk.

"Guilty," I say in a high southern belle voice because, well, my brother's characters are contagious.

"If I had ma old git-fiddle, I'd pluck ye a lil ditty," he says. "But I sold the doggone dag-nab thing."

"Wait—seriously? Are you being serious?" I ask, sans southern belle.

19

"I did," he says, dropping the accent. His voice gets closer. "These jerks keep upping my rent, you know what I'm saying? First they're like, 'You can sleep here for free,' and then they're like, 'Actually, we need money.' Because I'm living with a couple of druggies."

"You shouldn't live with druggies."

"Maybe they're not. I don't even know what they're into."

"But you sold your guitar."

"Not really *sold*, because it's like, it's in a shop and I can get it back. And I will get it back, after this paycheck."

"How're you going to play with the band now?" I ask.

My brother's funk-metal band, Vomitstain, truly lives up to its name. I wish Elliott would just play sweetly sung acoustic Ramones covers the way he used to in secret at home. Unfortunately I don't control the world.

"Band's dag-nab broke up," he says.

"Shame."

His voice becomes normal again. "How's your birthday?"

"Eh. You know. Park, balloons to heaven, sheet cake with plastic sprinkles. I swear those sprinkles aren't supposed to be consumed by humans."

He speaks seriously now. I can hear the puff of a cigarette. "They still doing that?"

He's not talking about the sprinkles.

"Yep. Come, now, don't act so shocked." I pick at my polish, black glitter that has chipped away to tiny islands in the middle of my fingernails. "I'll bet you're bummed you couldn't make it."

"I sure am," he says with a sigh, my sarcasm soaring over his head. *Whoosh*. "Too long a drive."

Heh. Two hours *is* too long a drive . . . if your license is suspended. He's in Los Banos now, which literally translates to "the bathrooms." This conveys just how desirable a location it is. Flat, treeless land dotted with chain restaurants. It's a couple hours away, which might as well be another continent. It's not just two hours and a suspended license that keeps us apart. I'm afraid of freeway driving. His relationship with my parents is shadowed by his paranoia. Booze, pills, sketchy girls.

"It's too long a drive."

My brother is drunk and repeating himself. That sentence, in my life, is like saying, Oh, look, the sun is in the sky again. But it could be worse. These days I try to think optimistically—he's only drunk. Gold star for Elliott.

"But it was a good birthday?" he asks.

"It was fine. Mexico ended up eating the cake and diarrheaed all over Mom's car seat on the way home—kind of a party pooper. Hey, I wonder if that's where the expression came from."

"Mexico," Elliott says wistfully. "That lil fatpile."

"Mom's pugs really are the most disgusting creatures in history. They're like mini furry pig-walruses."

In the silence, I hear people in the background on my brother's line. Cheesy jukebox tunes ooze. Glasses clink. Men holler.

"What'd you do for your birthday, anyway?" he asks. "The big one-eight."

"Other than get sad about Ava with the family in the park? Oh, I bought a load of porno and cigarettes and lottery tickets. Registered to vote. Joined the marines. Fun stuff."

His voice gets muffled. "Just a second, just a second—don't get your panties in a bundle, man."

"I'll let you go," I say.

His voice gets closer. "Sorry."

"You can get going. It's late. I'm tired."

"I wanna talk to my sister," he says. "I feel bad I didn't see you graduate."

He's talking about an incident weeks ago when I put on a very expensive muumuu gown and a square hat no one in their right mind would call fashionable and listened to my name being called and walked on a stage to receive a piece of paper from a dinosaur in a three-piece suit. It was no biggie, really. Millions of humans do it every June.

"I wouldn't have gone to my graduation if I hadn't had to," I say. "So stop getting all emo about it."

Portland was so vibrant and sharp and rained on when I visited—the bookstores and coffee shops and strangers everywhere—it was almost like everything was in focus, like I put on a new pair of glasses and only then realized I'd been half-blind.

"Don't be a college dropout out now," he says. "Don't be a dummy like your brother."

"Try my best."

"You should buy one of them Tasers," he says. "I'll send you one for your birthday."

"Sure," I say.

Because sending someone a Taser is actually a perfectly

acceptable gesture in my family. I have pepper spray in multiple colors. We live in a reality of always possible monsters that many other people have the luxury of ignoring. Also sure because Elliott's big on talk and not so much on follow-through. If he even remembers his promise next conversation, color me impressed.

"One of these days I swear, I'm gonna come see you," he goes on.

Someone starts yelling in the background on my brother's end. Elliott yells back, "Beat it, okay? It's my sister's birthday."

"Elliott," I say loudly. "I have to go anyway. It's cool."

"I love you, sis," he says, his lips sounding so close to the receiver I pull my head back. "I love you so much."

"I love you, too."

"You're just—you're so special to me."

"I know, bro, I think you're super-duper and we'll talk soon."

"I mean it. I love you."

"Love you, too," I say. "Night. Be safe. Talk soon."

"Happy birthday, Ava."

Those two syllables, those three letters—a word, a knife. I suck in air. I wait for him to realize his mistake.

I can't wait forever.

"Yeah, thanks," I say finally.

I hang up. I stand in the middle of my room. I recently steamrolled everything into my room's corners and vacuumed, so my steps sink into the perfect carpet like footprints. I erase them one by one, rubbing my foot across them to make them disappear. I look in the mirror. There I am: short, almost-black hair; heart-shaped face; wide, hazel eyes. Mom's cheekbones and arched eyebrows. Dad's button nose. For a long time after Ava disappeared, I felt like I couldn't tell if I was growing up or staying the same. I didn't know if I was pretty or ugly, fat or thin, tall or short.

Once upon a time, I was one of two. I knew exactly what I was then. I had a comparison.

I go online before I go to sleep. I count the birthday wishes, even though I know it's petty. It's not that many. It shouldn't matter. *Thanks, nicefaces!! Birthdays are the best days.* I stare far too long at the picture of a cat with a birthday hat on my page that Madeline put there, as if the silly image might offer some clue into my buried heartache. I see my dad just posted something to the FindAvaRivers group three minutes ago. It's a picture of today's balloons ascending skyward.

Happy birthday, Ava. You are with us every day. In our prayers, in our hearts.

Sigh. Poor Dad. He should be asleep. I go downstairs to refill my water glass in the kitchen sink—Mom bought some new purifier, and it takes me way too long to figure out how to operate it—and I stop by the door that leads to the basement. I crack it open to head downstairs, but then I can hear my dad talking.

"Sure, well, you can order it in ebony or chaparral *or* you can order a custom and I'll tailor it any way you want." He laughs. He sounds so gregarious. He doesn't sound like a guy who just uploaded a picture of wasted balloons for his vanished daughter's birthday. He's switched into the *Other Life* world where he is not Ben Rivers, unemployed man living in basement, father of the disappeared. He is Sergio Ontario, owner of a high-end men's fashion store by day, singer-songwriter by night. I know exactly what he looks like right now without even having to go downstairs to look—he's got his headset on, ogling the enormous computer monitor, cigarette in hand.

I close the door gently, so he never knows it opened.

7

I'M GOING TO become an elementary school teacher. I've wanted to forever. Children are pure, delicate faces open and bright as flowers. There are wicked people out there and bad weather you can't help. But a teacher can be a lighthouse. You are all worth love. Words are your best advocates and friends. Never trust a stranger.

8

FOR NOW, I'M a part-time princess. A few days a month, I put on a blue-yellow taffeta dress and a red ribbon in my bobbed black doll haircut and simulate Snow White. Get in my beater car, drive at my usual granny speed, and take every back road possible to a children's party within a forty-mile radius. Since graduation, I've been working as a contractor for a company called Funmakerz. It's funz. Who can be in a bad mood after hanging out with a bunch of gussied up, sugar-drunk kids?

Today I'm going to a five-year-old's birthday party in the Uplands, which is essentially Berkeley's Bel-Air. Mansions. Plotted elms. Impossibly green squares of lawn. Why children's parties start at god-awful times like eleven in the morning, I will never understand. To drive the knife in deeper, the slave drivers at Funmakerz insist I get there half an hour early. I slept through my alarm. My stomach is growling. I forgot to brush my teeth. And on my way out of my car, the only POS-mobile parked on Uber Fancy Lane, I spill coffee on my dress.

"Shit!" I yell.

I look up and see about a dozen tiny pigtailed heads staring at me through the picture window.

"God, I hope they didn't hear that," I whisper as I arrange my face into a smile and give a little princess wave. My hand will stay right there and cover the coffee stain. I pick up my skirt and tiptoe across the lawn—which must have been recently watered because *squelch squelch* (damn it)—and ring the doorbell.

The door opens. A smiling mother with bags under her eyes opens her mouth to speak to me, but I am overwhelmed by a sea of tiny hands. My ears fill with excited screams.

"I heard someone here was having a birthday?" I say, widening my eyes.

"Me!" screams a blonde with a long French braid.

It's like a girl at an Elvis concert circa 1956. She can hardly contain her enthusiasm—I wouldn't be surprised if she peed her party dress. I give her a hug and wish her happy birthday. She smells like cinnamon and cake.

"Me too!" yells a dark-haired girl in a tutu with zombie-chocolate lips.

"You too?" I ask.

The mother smiles, nods. "They're twins."

"Oh," I say. "I . . ."

All shiny eyes point up at me. I force the smile to stay on my lips and look down at the two girls, who stand in front of the tiny crowd. They hold hands. I can see the resemblance in their faces now, in the way their different-colored hair hangs, in their thick eyelashes and the shapes of their lips. A prick begins in my throat and travels slowly to my nose and threatens my eyes. I don't finish my sentence.

"That's wonderful," I say instead. "How lucky you are."

I lead everyone into the living room and sing about how someday my prince will come, and never mind the stinging.

The father pays me with a check. He asks me my name and when I tell him, he pens it slowly into his checkbook and then looks up at me to do a double take. "Rivers—any relation to Michelle?"

"She's my mom," I say.

"Thought I saw a resemblance," he says.

Which shocks and flatters me. I'm always flattered when people think I look like my mom, even when I don't totally see it. My mom is half Mexican, half Iranian, and 100 percent stunning—high cheekbones framed by inky waves that would make a hair commercial jealous, and brown eyes that burn with a fiery intensity. Even the wrinkles age and worry have given her seem somehow elegant on her.

"I own a diner on Fourth Street," he goes. "She brings flyers by every month."

"Ah," I say.

His face changes as he tears the check out and hands it to me. He looks at his own little girls, running around the backyard in their party dresses. "I just can't even imagine," he says. "I'm so sorry about everything you guys have gone through."

"It's okay," I say, even though it never is.

I look down at the check. He gave me way too much. I'm embarrassed to take it but don't know what to say.

"You and your folks take care, now," he says, patting my shoulder like I'm sad and injured. "Come by the diner anytime and tell them Lalo says lunch's on him."

As I've grown up, I've learned there are monsters in the world, and you never know who they are, yes—but there are so many more kind people. It makes me feel bad in this inverse way that's hard to put into words. I appreciate strangers' compassion, but more than that, I wish I didn't deserve it or need it at all. I wish I wasn't a magnet for generosity—I wish I was just a girl.

9

SOON I WILL be in an IKEA-fresh dorm room with zany characters who are majoring in art and philosophy and queer studies. I'll go on hikes in the forest and date tattooed ladies and gents with peculiar hair. My parents, my brother will be names programmed into my phone. I'll forget what color eyes Madeline has. I'll have classes with complicated titles and my professors will give me A-plusses and I'll never once wonder if it's because I'm related to Ava Rivers.

10

MY MOM TAKES me out for a movie night, which isn't a regular thing. I'm leaving soon, and suddenly my parents have been pretending to be a family again, ordering takeout and suffering through it together with the little TV on in the kitchen. Hello and goodbyeing instead of ignoring each other as we pass through rooms. They say they're going to miss me, and the worst part is I believe them.

The movie theater's carpets look like clown vomit. I know because I've been studying them for minutes now as Mom tries to find out what kind of animal the hot dogs are made out of and whether or not they were fed hormones. The poor cashier just keeps saying, "Uh." There's a clearly not-amused couple behind us. And my mom won't stop, *she keeps going*. Now she's asking the poor cashier about the calorie counts in Sour Patch Kids versus Twizzlers and whether they're made with "cane sugar or high-fructose corn syrup."

"High-fructose corn syrup's *terrible* for you," she tells him. "There's this documentary about it—let me write down the name for you—"

The dead-eyed, overworked twentysomething does not appear interested in the sweet syrup of my mom's conversation or the info she's penning onto a napkin. I leave the line and pretend to be riveted by my movie-postered surroundings. I stop to admire a man-sized cutout for a movie about a Nordic god, my eyes begging him to zap me away with his paper lightning fork. I should be appreciating this though. Mom time. When was the last time my mom and I went out alone? Probably when she took me bra shopping in sixth grade.

I kid. Kind of.

She's empty-handed when she approaches. "So many artificial *dyes* in everything."

The couple that was behind us in line turns around to eye us. One whispers to the other and I think, *They know who we are.* The guy at the drinking fountain we pass, standing up and wiping his chin with a glance—he knows us, too. I can't help the paranoia, especially when I'm out with my mom, who has been on local TV so many times and who wears her lipstick so bright and is so damn beautiful you can't forget her.

Wasn't that woman on Unresolved Crimes?

Wait, I think that's the lady who ran for city council . . .

It's that girl who was kidnapped—Ava Rivers—it's her family.

I can hear them thinking. And even in the dark theater, when the credits begin blasting bright, Mom's presence beside me on one side's like a moon, and the negative presence of my twin sister on the other side's like a sun. Both burn.

11

BERKELEY'S NOT A small town, but when you're semifamous it might as well be. There are many ways to be famous. Not all are good. Our family has been in the paper, featured in blogs and on local news, highlighted on nighttime crime shows and daytime talk shows. My dad does the PR end from the basement, emailing producers and reaching out to anyone with press releases who will hear our story. My mom is the face. She flyers the town on the weekly and meets with our PI, Ozzie, for coffee to discuss any new tips called in. Ozzie looks like a bear of a man, ex-LAPD with the clichéd cop 'stache and all, but behind his persona he's a bit of a new-age softie. He meditates. He bought my mom an aromatherapy set. Once, after he drank a bit of bourbon many Thanksgivings ago—a few years after Ava went missing, right after his wife left him—Ozzie told me ghost stories. He and my mom go way back, to high school. Apparently they dated. Ozzie still looks at her with the adoration of a puppy-eyed teen sometimes, after all these years.

About four years ago, when I was a freshman, I was so excited to start over. I got a haircut and some new clothes. The public high school is way bigger than my private middle school was, and there was a good chance some people might not know that I was Ava Rivers's sister. But then the tip came in on the hotline—some anonymous prick said he heard some so-and-so boasting that he had killed Ava Rivers years ago and buried her in the high school football field. The day before the homecoming game, tractors ravaged the entire stadium and rumors spread around campus like some rampant disease. They were looking for the dead body of that little girl who disappeared all those years ago. By fourth period, everyone had connected me to her—oh, *that's* her sister?—my teacher gave me these pitiful smiles and students whispered and pointed. When I passed the football field at lunch—green grass razed, police dogs sniffing the freshly upturned soil, news vans and reporters flocking to report on the dig, students pressed up against the fence watching—I felt like I couldn't hold the contents of my stomach in a second longer. I was lucky Ozzie was there, the only familiar face among the uniforms and scanners and cameras and microphones. He put his arm around me and steered me away from the scene, made me walk the other way.

"Tip's a load of BS," he told me.

"Okay," I said, exhaling in relief.

"They're just chasing their five o'clock story."

At that moment, a woman popped out from behind a building and asked if I was Vera Rivers. She had some kind of audio recorder in her hand.

"Are you a human being?" Ozzie asked her.

It was such an odd question, the woman knit her painted eyebrows.

"Yes . . ." she answered.

"Then act like one," he said.

She backed away.

He walked me to the library and told me to go hang out there until lunch period was done. "Besides, the library's the world's best-kept secret," he said, surprising me, because he never for one second struck me as a bookworm. "It's the only place where anything's possible and everyone will leave you alone."

I tried to tell him how much I appreciated everything, but he, as usual, brushed it off. Ozzie ignores any and all effort to thank, compliment, give credit. It's like everything he does is owed.

Ozzie was right. They didn't find anything. The tip was completely bogus. After that I ate lunch as far away as possible from that football field, in the corner of the library, sneaking my sandwiches in a cubicle and escaping into books. High school wasn't bad. People were really nice to me. Sometimes I wondered if they were too nice. I was quiet, although sometimes people commended me on my dark sense of humor. I sat in the back of class and took excellent notes. I was friendless, but friendly. Never let anyone get too close. Never knew how. I had three loves—one lasted days, one lasted weeks, one lasted months. But more than anything I read a lot of books.

12

SINCE I GRADUATED, on Sunday nights I try to pick up dinner for Dad and me to have some time together. Mom is always out, the woman of a thousand acquaintances and obligations, but I worry about my dad. He never leaves his basement. To even see him upstairs these days is a shock. I know he keeps busy with Ava stuff and *Other Life* stuff and when I visit him, he seems cheerful, but I don't think his day-to-day is anywhere near healthy. I've tried to ask Elliott to come by and spend time with him but Elliott's always got an excuse. Deep down, I know Elliott just hates this house and hates Berkeley and hates everything that reminds him of our childhood. He acts like it's my parents who don't want him around, but it's exactly the opposite. Elliott can convince himself—and other people, too, sometimes—of pretty much anything.

Tonight it's Wexican food. You know, corporate white people faking Mexican food. I step down the wooden steps and into Dad's low-roofed, cream-colored hovel. There are stacks of books every-where, an unmade futon bed, a rowing machine that seems to be serving as a dryer for his boxer shorts, and a very bitchy-looking obese tabby cat in the one window, which is covered with a floral sheet yellowed from cigarette smoke. I sit and unsheathe the plastic bag and paper wrapping and tinfoil and reveal tonight's bounty.

"God, this burrito is delicious," Dad says, wolfing it down like he hasn't eaten in days. He has some stubble growing in. It's getting harder to see his blond hair in all the gray that's taking over. "Where'd you get it from?"

"Jalapeño," I say.

"Don't tell your mom," he says. "She hates those fast food chains running out the local businesses."

"Okay, I won't," I say.

I pick at my burrito. Bastards put lettuce in it even though I asked them not to.

"Do you think you're going to come visit me?" I ask.

"Where?" he asks through a mouthful. Then he realizes and says, "Mmmm." Chews and swallows. "I keep forgetting it's coming up so soon. I'm so proud of you."

He didn't answer my question. Which kind of answered my question. I think my dad's actually come to the point where he's afraid of leaving the house. My dad, who used to travel for business, who won awards for his ability in advertising, who used to leave early and come home late, is phobic and lives in his pajamas. It didn't happen overnight. He cut down his hours, he took a leave of absence, he freelanced instead. For a while he was certain he was going back to work full-time. Now it's so many years later and he never did. Never will, I fear.

What is going to become of him when I'm gone?

Sometimes I get flashes of anger. It's not at Ava, of course, poor Ava—but it's because of her. It's not fair. I wish we could know the truth already. It's been almost twelve years—twice as long as she'd even been alive when she went missing. I wish we could all move on and Dad could be like the dads of other people I know, who are thinking of retiring and getting into sailing and entering a new stage of life when their kids leave the house. He's beyond frozen in time. He's paralyzed.

"I worry about you in Portland, though," he says, crumpling his foil into a little ball. He ate that burrito in record time. "It rains so much—it's easy to get depressed in a place like that."

"I'll be okay," I say. "Everything's green. It's not depressing."

"Just promise you'll get help if you start feeling that way, okay, Ladybug?"

"I will," I say.

Will you? I wish I'd said instead. Will you get help? Then I get a surge of fearlessness, of say-anythingness. I am leaving soon. I am free.

"Will you?" I ask.

"What?"

"Get help if you need it?"

"Of course." He laughs, as if this is funny.

"Here," I say. "Eat my burrito."

"You're not hungry?" he asks, amazed.

"Not as hungry as you."

"Well, I won't let good food go to waste," he says, opening it up and devouring it. "Man, these are just the best burritos I've had in a long time."

It makes me happy to watch him lost in something simple and purely pleasurable for a moment. On his desk behind him is a book called *Inside the Mind of a Child Predator* and an ashtray overflowing with cigarette butts. On the ground I count at least a dozen empty Cup Noodles. On his bed the new flyers are spread out—updated, with that computer-aged picture of Ava where she's my age and looks like an avatar from one of his *Other Life* games. A forensic artist volunteered to do it for us. See? All it takes is a well-publicized tragedy to prove there are Good Samaritans aplenty.

"Have you seen this?" he asks excitedly as I peer at the flyers. "Your mom got a spot on the six o'clock news to share them."

"Cool," I say.

"Who knows what kinds of tips this will bring in," he says. "This picture might jog a lot more memories than the first-grade picture."

"If—"

I stop myself. I was about to blurt, if she's alive. I can't believe I was just about to say that.

"It's been so long," I say.

"Feels like it just happened," he says.

I think that's the fundamental difference between me and my parents. My eternity is their blink.

13

"**DID YOU SEE** the news last night?" Mom asks the next morning when I come down for breakfast.

"I did," I tell her.

"How'd I do?"

"Great."

"How did you think that violet jacket showed up? Too violet?"

"It was just perfectly violet, Mom."

"Oh, I love you I love you I love you," she says, bending down as her pugs grunt and shuffle in excitement.

"I love you, too. And your violet jacket."

"Your dad is already wading through a bunch of new tips," she says, standing up. "He said the inbox was overflowing this morning."

"That's great."

"Oz thinks it might be more trouble than it's worth," she says lowly. "You know how it is with those tips. Up the reward, and everyone calls in with a bunch of dead ends." She sips her coffee. "I mainly did it for your father. You know how excited that computer-generated-picture idea made him."

"You weren't excited?" I ask her.

"We'll see," she says.

She pours the rest of her coffee out and says, "Got to run." Kisses my forehead and leaves the room, her dogs running after her.

14

WHEN I WAS in sixth grade, my mom was contacted by a famous psychic who had her own TV show. She was a white woman named Cassie with a Long Island accent, long tacky fingernails, and a platinum mullet. Cassie wanted to do an episode on my family since Ava's case was so high-profile. Her story had recently aired again on national news for the fifth anniversary of her disappearance; there's always renewed interest around anniversaries.

My mom was thrilled. She knew that Cassie had worked for the FBI at certain points and helped to reunite people with their loved ones. Mom flew to New York. I remember waving goodbye to her at the airport. Her grin was huge, her eyes flashed with hope and life. She brought one of Ava's favorite stuffed animals—a ragged button-eyed lamb—for Cassie to "read its energy." When Mom came back from New York, she was like a different person. Something had left her expression. Even her posture had changed. Then I watched the episode weeks later, and I understood.

"You sweet woman," Cassie said, after touching the stuffed lamb for some time. She sighed and held my mom's hands over her crystal ball. "You sweet woman, I'm so sorry, but your daughter is no longer with us in this world."

"No," Mom said.

"She's moved on," Cassie said. "What I'm seeing is a tree."

"A tree? What do you mean a tree?" Mom cried.

"Her resting place," Cassie said. "She's on the other side now. I'm hearing her saying, 'Don't worry, Mommy. I'm okay now.'"

"No*no*NO—"

You don't know suffering until you've seen your mom scream-weeping on daytime TV.

15

I WOULD NEVER say this out loud, but I remember hardly anything vivid about my sister. The past I see when I shut my eyes was built with family photographs. I've studied pictures so many times, trying to imagine life back then, at moments convincing myself I really am remembering. But I think my memory is imagination and images, nothing more. We were just too young.

I do remember telling people we were twins and seeing their eyes widen because we looked so unalike. I remember thinking people liked her better because she was louder and knew how to make people laugh. I remember that there was something secret to being a twin—an amazing fact that would make other people react in surprise, a bond we shared alone in the room when we spoke in tongues all our own and finished each other's sung sentences. I remember wishing I was the goofy one with the mane of blond curls, but being happy I resembled our mother the most. I remember going to the drugstore together and buying matching mood rings on our sixth birthday and promising we would never take them off—and I didn't, until years after she went missing, when my ring finger got too big for it. It stained my skin green and lingered like a scar. I remember all this, but it's blurry. It could be a story I read somewhere for all I feel.

16

ONCE UPON A time, Ava and I shared a room.

On one side, a canopy bed with violet mosquito netting; on the other, a bunk bed with *Peanuts* sheets. One end had a chock-full bookshelf. The other had paint stains on the carpet and dirty skirts strewn like debris. In the middle, a line of gray duct tape. I still live in this room. The duct tape has long been pulled but it's still imprinted there in the middle like a permanent memory.

In a blink, the space was all mine, but her belongings haunted it. I lived with the silence of her paint stains and her neatly lined-up shoes. Her bed, disheveled, still unmade, seemed to hide her ghost. My parents kept her side of the room pristine for nearly a year as their hope wouldn't budge—then it became some sort of monument, an archaeological site dedicated to Rivers life before the disappearance. Finally Elliott convinced them to pack up Ava's things and move them out. I was eleven. I spread my clothes out on the closet's rod. I moved my bed and finally enjoyed the view—our back lawn stretched long and green, an enormous ash tree reaching for my window. Lastly, I pulled the duct tape off the carpet, wadded it up into a sticky mound. Guilt sickened me as I shoved it down into the trash, but I told myself it was only duct tape. It wasn't my sister.

That was how I ended up with the biggest room in the house.

Elliott's dim, blue-walled room became the exercise room, where the only thing that seems to actually get any exercise is the dust that dances from corner to cobwebbed corner. If I had to bet, I'd say my room will soon be an office. Airy, light-filled, inviting—a place you imagine yourself but never really end up.

17

ELLIOTT CALLS ME from a new cell phone number. He's always getting new cell phones, and by the time you've programmed his number in he's disconnected it or lost it and it doesn't work anymore.

"Um, like, hi, is this, like, Vera?" he asks in a dopey surfer voice.

"Chya, bra," I tell him.

He tells me he's fixing up motorcycles now. I didn't even know he could ride one. I tell him I'm leaving for Portland in two weeks.

"You excited to get out of the house?"

"Yeah. A little worried about Dad though."

"He be aight," Elliott says. I can't tell if he's being ironic or if that's how he really talks nowadays. You just never know with Elliott.

"I wish you'd come visit before I go," I say. "It's been, like, years since we all ate dinner together. Who knows the next time we'll do it again."

I hear him light up a smoke. "I'm not allowed there—you remember."

"Stop being a martyr, they both love the crap out of you."

"When we got in that fight, I remember—" (The "fight" was actually Mom asking, curiously, "Are you on drugs?" after Elliott went on a random, paranoid rant about chemtrails at Thanksgiving dinner years ago, and Elliott responding by throwing our organic turkey through the sliding glass door and yelling, "You guys all look down on me!" before storming out the door.) "I remember Mom said, 'DON'T COME BACK.'"

It is aggravating how many times Elliott and I have had this conversation. It's like reading from a script at this point.

"You're getting the punctuation wrong, and that changes the meaning entirely. She said, Don't exclamation point. *Come back* exclamation point."

"If they want me to come over, they can call me," Elliott says.

"Dad emails you."

"I forgot my password."

"Mom would call if she had your number."

"*Don't* give her this number," he says.

Usually I keep my feelings to myself but right now, I'm so tired of having these same conversations. I'm so tired of nodding or agreeing when really I want to yell or shake someone. My tongue has permanent bite marks in it. When I imagine my future—which is green, green as Oregon—I imagine a new me there. One who says whatever's written in her heart, even if it hurts.

"Bro, you do this to yourself."

How good it feels, the unadulterated truth hot on my lips.

"Over and over and over again," I go on. "You just have to be the victim. Doesn't it get tiring? Don't you feel sometimes like you're ready for a new role, a new game?"

"You don't get it," he insists. "They hate me. They blame me for Ava."

He says *Ava* like she's an event and not a human being. Which she kind of is at this point.

"But they don't," I say calmly. "You're full of bullshit, Elliott."

It is the first time I have firmly contradicted his warped truth in my many years alive. I tingle like I just discharged a weapon.

Believe me, I've tried for years to gently tackle Elliott's lies. Problem is, he actually believes them. I don't know if it's the drugs he's done over the years or if it's just the way he's wired. Like most things, it's most likely a mix. Anyway, I've learned to speak to him using careful logic and to not get upset by his ever-ridiculous responses. But this is the first time I've called him out.

And of course he glides right over it.

"I'll visit you up in Portland," he says. "Pot's legal in Washington, right?"

"Portland is in Oregon, and yes, pot's legal."

"I wonder if you can just buy a pound and drive over the border with it."

"Please don't turn a college visit into an opportunity to go to prison." I say it jokingly, because hey, we both know it's all talk. He's never coming to visit me.

"I love you, little sis," he says. "How are things over there?"

"Mom was on the news the other night," I say. "This forensic artist worked up a picture of what Ava would look like now, and they're sending it to all the local stations."

I can hear him breathing, smoking. "What's she look like?"

"I don't know, she looked like a computer game character."

"Can you send me a picture?"

"Sure."

"You can send it on the phone as a text," he says. "I can get pictures on my phone."

"Welcome to the twenty-first century," I say.

We say our I love yous. Elliott's surprisingly undrunk, although it's late and he's oddly chipper and talking about lifting weights now. I've always got to wonder.

I go downstairs and take the flyer that's been sitting on the dining room table for days. I hold it up in the light and take a picture. I can see how the image grew from the seed of her first-grade portrait. The eye shape. The nose. She's just so different. The connection is lost.

I send the photo.

18

JESUS FIREWORKS-EXPLODING CHRIST, I am going to Portland in a week. My future is so close I can taste it in my mouth, and it's rich and honey-sweet.

I paint my room white. My life is draped in plastic fog. Even though I loved the dark walls and the quotes I inked on pages of paper in beautiful penmanship and tacked up, I'm not sad to erase myself from this room. My childhood wasn't all loneliness, but there was a lot of wishing in here. I spent my childhood wanting so badly to grow up, to be free, to be far away.

I've lived my life in a hurricane eye of mourning that I plain do not feel sometimes. I look at my room and know I lived here with someone else once upon a time, but it's been so many years alone now that I can't sense it. I can't sense it in the way my parents sense it. In a way, it's been a rift between us—their constant obsession with finding Ava, and my resignation to never knowing her. I'm eighteen years old and acquaintances still apologize to me and give me the pity stare.

I still remember the first night Madeline spent the night in high school—Madeline, who I met in Greek Mythology, the first girl I ever kissed. We ate dinner with my parents, and the whole time they were gushing about some tip that Ozzie was chasing to New

Orleans. When we got back upstairs, Madeline said to me, "It feels like there's a ghost in this house."

That's what I thought she said anyway. My arms goose bumped. When I said, "Excuse me?" she clarified.

"It feels like you're a ghost in this house," she repeated.

A hurt bloomed in my middle. I nodded my head yes.

Madeline was my best friend and then she was more, and then she sold an exclusive to the *Enquirer* last year about our family called "The Ghost in the Rivers House," betraying me and swearing me off intimacy. Eventually, thankfully, she ended up moving to Canada and I didn't have to see the painful sight of her beautiful face any longer. I still remember the way her hair smelled—cloves and vanilla.

19

ON A STREET corner near my house, latte in hand, I'm waiting for the light to change when I check my phone and see a missed call. Suspicious unrecognizable number. I listen to the voicemail and almost spurt hot caffeinated beverage out my nose when I hear Max singing a passionate song about me calling him back. It's stream of consciousness, confident as hell, and almost bursts my eardrum.

I tell myself my blood pressure is high right now because I'm walking home so fast. No big. It's not because some sexy weirdo called me. Maybe I shouldn't return his call. It would be easier that way, because I'm leaving soon, and I don't find the fluttery lungs-bursting effect attractive humans have on me particularly fun. But today I don't mind. Plus, I have to practice being brave—because that's who I am inside and who I'm going to be once I move. I'm going to look people in the eyes and I'm going to tell them what I think and, most of all, I'm going to let myself near them.

When I call him back, he asks me if I want to go for a walk and I say yes and he tells me that he thinks walking is a religion and I say that might be going a little far but okay. We meet at the corner of our old elementary school, which is only a few blocks from my house. We stand underneath a mural of hand-holding, butterfly-chasing children. Neither of us says anything about how this was once our school and it's pretty much the last place either of us said more than a handful of words to each other. There's a ghost between us, but we don't mention her.

The sunshine spills everywhere and turns every tree and leaf gold. I take in the sting-you-with-its-blue sky, music drifting from open doorways, college kids lazy on porch swings with chatter and beer bottles, the friendly walkers we pass who say hello. Max tells me his mother thinks their hot tub is contaminated with mold and he spent the day trying to convince her that this wasn't true. We meander through downtown and construction zones, past campus, up into neighborhoods with picture windows, elaborate landscaping, and luxury cars. Max beatboxes and scats randomly, not caring if people we pass hear him. We talk about books. He's surprisingly well-read, but he's all into beatniks and I give him a hard time about it. He teases me because I love Dickens so much, calling me a seventy-year-old woman trapped in a teenage body. I laugh. Apparently he paints and wants to be an art teacher. The cutest freaking thing.

We end up walking up a huge hill, and I complain freely the whole way. Max tells me to "chill" my "funk," he has something to show me. We reach the huge rock formations pushed up into the sun, climb up the stairs carved into the immense rock, faded orange and rough as a tiny planet, and sit at the top and catch our breath. The sun has just started to sink over the skyscraper-infested hills behind the water, San Francisco's TV tower jutting up glorious into the screaming sunset at the hilltop across the Bay. The water glitters blue, wisped with sailboats, strung with bridges, and all the cars sparkle on the streets and in the roads.

"I forgot how beautiful everything is," I tell him.

Our hands are right next to each other on the rock. I put my pinky against his, my blood pulsing wild. I can feel my life beginning—*my* life, not just a life I was given, but one I made.

"I forgot, too," he says.

He watches me. I see something special in his eyes, something like water, deep and always moving.

"I'm moving to Portland in a week," I tell him.

I swear I see a disappointed flicker in his expression, but then he just breaks into a smile and congratulates me. He pats my hand and we get up and walk back, through the darkening streets, until we hit Ashby and go our separate ways, promising to keep in touch. I know we won't. It's just one of those things you say when you don't have the right words.

20

IT'S MY LAST Friday. Next Wednesday morning, my plane leaves and angels will sing. We're supposed to have an official family dinner tonight. As in, my choice. As in, leaving the house. I choose Italian even though it makes my mom cringe (*"Carbs!"*) and my dad pale (*"Outside!"*). I get fancy, in a black poofy dress and heels—my goodbye dress, I think—and wait at the kitchen table. Long shot of the century, I texted Elliott to come earlier but he responded, *k @ jkyd pickn u jkbx wif laur*, which I honestly don't know what to make of except I'm sure it means he's not coming and anyway, if I'm being honest, Elliott can be a little loud and embarrassing in public, so it's for the best.

At ten till, Dad comes up the stairs. He hasn't brushed his hair. Sinking, but kicking myself for my surprise at this moment, I realize he's about to make an excuse to not go to dinner and pretend it has nothing to do with something that begins with "agora" and ends with "phobia."

"My *ears* have been *ringing* all day," he says.

"Bummer," I say flatly.

"I read on the internet it could be a ruptured eardrum or blood flow problem. I *have* been feeling dizzy, now that you mention it."

"I didn't mention anything."

"Acoustic neuroma."

"Excuse me?"

"It could also be an acoustic neuroma," he says.

He's holding his fingers near his ears and wincing, as if he really needs to demonstrate.

"Which I hope it's not," he goes on. "Because that's a tumor."

"I don't think you have a tumor," I say. "I just think you really don't want to go to dinner."

There she is again—Portland Vera, rearing her knife-sharp honesty. I get a nice shot of adrenaline as I watch my father's mouth try to locate a proper response.

"Vera" is all he manages.

Mom comes into the house, dogs barking at her feet. She's carrying a ridiculous amount of Pottery Barn bags that she puts on the floor.

"Redecorating," she says breathlessly.

"Let me guess—for my room?" I get up and peek in the bags. The colors—coral and gold—literally remind me of barf. "Did you *try* to pick the grossest colors?"

She leaves the room to go into the master bedroom, which is behind her through a short hall. She comes back out magically in a different scarf and rebrightened lipstick. "Okay," she says with a clap. "I have to be at the child abuse ice cream social by nine, so let's go."

"Number one, they should really rethink that name," I tell her. "Child abuse ice cream social? That's awful."

"It's not the full name. That's just what I'm calling it."

"Number two, Dad's got a tumor and he's not coming to dinner."

"A tumor?" she asks incredulously.

"It's not a tumor," he says in an Arnold Schwarzenegger voice. Then he checks his humor, going grave again. "Um . . . tinnitus. My ears have been ringing all day."

"Probably all that loud pagan music you've been blasting at odd hours."

"It's Celtic," he says. Then he turns to me, almost pleading. "Vera, I really don't feel well."

"I'm sure you don't," I reply.

"Let's get going," Mom tells me.

"Wait, you have to be at your . . . thing . . . at nine?" I look at my phone. "It's eight fifteen right now, Mom. We don't have time to sit at a restaurant."

"It's fine, my speech isn't until at least nine fifteen."

"You're giving a speech?"

"I'm accepting an award. As an advocate. It's fine—let's go."

"Mom." I fake a laugh. "Just go accept your award."

"Vera," she says. "I told you I would take you to dinner, so let's go, I'm taking you to dinner."

VERA DINNER—penned in the narrow space between CLEARANCE SALE and CHILD ABUSE ICE CREAM SOCIAL.

"I didn't want it to be like this," I say.

"I am really sorry," she says. "If we leave right now we can do it. Maybe you can call the order in ahead so it's ready when we get there?"

"Really." I laugh. "Let's just—we'll do it some other time. Maybe next time Elliott can come."

"That would be so nice," Mom says. "Have you been talking to him? Did he see me on the news?"

"Yes, and no."

Mom comes over and rubs my arm. "Listen, I'm sorry it was like this."

"It's fine," I say.

"My ears are just—*rrrrrinnnggggg*," Dad says from the doorway to the basement. He's taken one step down and looks like he's shrunk.

"We got it, Ben," Mom says loudly.

"I'm going to lie down," he says.

Mom feeds her dogs. "You look very nice," she tells me.

I bite my nail. Usually I wouldn't say anything, but I'm warm with anger right now. And soon I'll be gone. So for once, I speak my mind.

"You know what?" I say. "You're too busy, Mom. You're too busy and you're missing the things that really matter for a bunch of BS you'll never remember."

She gasps and makes a small *uh* noise, as if I slugged her or something. Although her reaction makes me wince, I don't blink or turn away. Behind my back, I clasp my hands so hard it hurts.

"Oh, honey," she says.

Her eyes fill with tears. *Ugh*, I think. I made my mom cry. The last thing I want is to make her cry. But I bite my lip, don't apologize, don't take it back.

"I'm so sorry," she says, coming over to me and putting her hands on my face. "My sweet baby girl, I'm so sorry. You're right.

Why do I do this? I'll do better, I promise. We'll take a whole day before you go—a spa day, how about?"

I don't have the heart to tell her there's no room for a spa day now, and I hate mani-pedis and touchy-feely strangers. I smile and nod.

"I'll get an app," she says. "A time-management thing. I'll do better, Vera, I will."

She means it, she truly does. But she won't follow through. And even if she did, there's not a lot of time with me left to manage. Her lips quiver, begging forgiveness.

"It's okay," I tell her.

"I love you so much." She pulls back and waits for me to echo the same before she leaves the house again, slamming the door, sealing in the silence.

The stack of weird computer-generated Avas is still there on the table. I pick one up. I don't know what it is, but I get a feeling like the faintest fingers lifting my hair and I suck in air, tickled by something between spookiness and promise.

Downstairs, Dad laughs, pauses, and then says, "Well, Judd, thinking about upgrading the dressing rooms but am wondering if the return will be worth the investment."

I hurt. I hurt in my eyeballs, I hurt deep in my throat. But you know what? It doesn't matter. Because soon I will be gone.

21

MY LAST STINT as Snow White is on a muggy gray Saturday at a park near a reservoir in Lafayette. After princessing, I hit a drive-through immediately and wolf down two cheeseburgers that squirt ketchup on my lap. Usually I'd be pissed at myself because now my costume will require dry cleaning, but guess what? It doesn't matter anymore *because Portland*! When I get home, I stub my toe on a stack of Mom's Amazon Prime boxes. Normally I would grumble about it, but it doesn't matter anymore *because Portland*! Inside, I almost step in Mexico's or Canada's vomit on the hardwood kitchen floors and I'm tempted to yell at them for being gross, but who cares *because Portland*! There's nothing extraordinary about today except that soon I'll be elsewhere. It's blissfully normal. It's not a square that you look at on your calendar and say, hey, everything's going to go topsy-turvy today.

Life's a prankster.

I check my phone and notice I have two missed calls from Mom. I yell, "Dad?" to the house, but hear nothing. *Huh. That's weird. Don't panic. He's probably napping.* I go down to his basement just to check—but he's not there.

"Dad?"

Sergio Ontario is paused on the screen. He's in his underwear sitting on a bed, and I feel as if I've violated some code by seeing him that way and knowing that Sergio prefers purple leopard-print thongs. Dad's cat sits on the windowsill glaring at me through slits for eyes.

"Wow," I say. "Stink eye central."

At this point, my heart has picked up a little speed.

"Dad?" I yell throughout the house.

I'm thinking something bad has happened. Some kind of accident. Heart attack. Dad *never* leaves. I sit back on the basement stairs with my phone and listen to my mom's voicemail message.

"The police think they found Ava!" she screams. "We're on our way to Kaiser in Fremont right now to see her—come as soon as you get this."

What the *what*?

No. No. She didn't just . . . I have to listen to the message again. As soon as it's done, I start uncontrollably shaking.

"Oh my God!" I scream so loud the dogs go running.

My fingers aren't working. I try to call my mom, flustered, pressing the wrong buttons. Finally I get through.

I yell, eyes spilling over. Suspicious brain, gullible heart. "Really? Really? How do you know?"

"Vera, she looks just like the sketch. Several people recognized her from TV when she was brought in. And you won't believe this—she was still wearing the mood ring."

The mood ring!

The mood ring she wore when we were kids—with the silver band and the ever-changing dot of glass on top. The mood ring she was wearing when she got sucked up into the ether.

"Jesus," I say.

See? my heart says to my brain. *See?*

A dam. A dam unleashing in my chest. Holy shit. We've had leads before. We've had skeletons and remains and photos of found children sent to us online. We have never had a flesh-and-blood living girl multiple people recognized off the bat with the proof in a mood ring.

In all the years she was gone, I never once let myself fully imagine what this would be like. I have to look in a mirror to be sure I'm not dreaming—but there I am, a shocked, flushed-faced Snow White with a purse trembling in my hands.

"Are you with her?" I ask.

"We're on our way to the hospital!" Mom says. "The FBI are meeting us there, and then we get to see her!"

She's shrieking every word.

"I can't believe it!" Dad hollers in the background.

"We're supposed to meet the agent at the trauma ward!" Mom says. "Call Elliott right now, you have to get hold of him!"

"Elliott! Yes!"

I call Elliott, saying, "Elliott Elliott Elliott," as the phone rings in my ear. Trying to use ESP to get him to pick up. But not only do I get voicemail, it's a random woman saying, "Yo, it's CC, leave a message, BEE-ATCH."

Beep.

I hang up.

I don't even know if I close the front door behind me. I run to my car and start it up. I turn the music off, find the address in my phone, and drive. My heart chokes. *Trauma ward*, I keep thinking. *Trauma ward, trauma ward, trauma ward*. Could this be real life? *Really?*

22

I'M IN A daze of questions as I navigate traffic. Usually I'm an anxious driver and I avoid freeways whenever possible, but right now every road is just a tunnel I'm getting through; I don't care about anything except getting to that hospital in record time. Hospital . . . Fremont . . . trauma ward . . . I should have asked more questions, like is she okay? Of course she's okay, though. What does "okay" mean again exactly? She's alive. I wipe away tears and just keep saying, "Oh my God," to nobody.

I'm ecstatic, I am, but it's mixed with an odd panic. What if this is just another false lead? And if it's not—which it really seems like it's not because this feels so different from all the other times—who the hell is this person I'm about to go meet? She and I shared a womb, but we're not really sisters anymore. And how broken of a person must she be? Where was she all these years—is it as ghastly as the stacks of books on Dad's floor promise? I don't know if I have the strength in me to confront that. I thought she was gone long ago. I never truly let myself believe she was alive until now, partly because the burden of such a horror—slavery, kidnapping, a life inhumane—is downright suffocating. Tears fall, and I have to will myself to breathe in, out, in, out, like I've forgotten how. I don't know if I can do this. A part of me is afraid of her, and afraid of what this means. I'm a twin again. One of two. I might not have loved my life every moment, my family might need a lot of help, I might dream of escaping constantly—but it's my life. And I'm used to it.

And I am terrible for even allowing these thoughts to flow through my mind as I drive. But I can't stop them. I'm a mess.

I finally get to the Kaiser and park in some emergency space—because if this isn't an emergency, show me what the hell is. I run inside the automatic glass doors, passing old people in wheelchairs and pregnant ladies and nurses, and make my way to the info booth, where a red-haired white woman watches me with curiosity.

"I need the trauma ward," I say.

"You all right?" she asks, looking down at my Snow White dress and up at my face, her eyebrows raised.

"It's not for me—it's my sister—"

"You part of the family of the missing girl?" she asks excitedly.

"Yes!"

"Oh, I'll walk you there myself," the woman says.

She leaves the station and takes my arm, walking me down long shining halls, past the pharmacy, into an elevator.

"There was a news crew asking about it a few minutes ago," the woman says.

"Oh," I say.

"What a miracle," the woman says. "I remember when Ava Rivers first went missing years ago—I had a five-year-old at the time."

I don't know what to say. I'm wild with disbelief. This seems like it's really happening. The woman is talking to me like Ava Rivers has returned. It's so weird that everyone knows who my sister is and what we've been through. I'm so overwhelmed with emotion and nerves, my eyes are filled with tears as the elevator floor numbers blink-blink-blink and the door *ding-ding-ding*s.

"Down the hall," the woman says, pointing, as we step off the elevator.

Like she really needs to point. There are—not exaggerating— two dozen reporter-looking people, and the halls are packed with law-enforcement types. This must be real. It's never been like this before. The red-haired woman stands back by the elevators and watches as I hurry forward. I look back and see her eyes, hungry, a woman watching a soap opera. I keep going, into the thickness of blue uniforms.

"I'm Vera Rivers!" I say to one of the first cops who notices me, who opens his mouth and looks at me as if he is about to say something. "I'm—my sister—where's my sister?"

A couple reporters on the sidelines snap photos of me. A woman with a microphone says, "Are you with the family?" I ignore them. It's so overwhelming and bright and loud and crowded. "Surreal" doesn't even begin to cover it. I'm stunned, I'm curious, I'm weighted with dread, I'm a braid of contradictions. A few cops turn around and the first one I spoke to takes me by the arm and leads me past a barricade and past some locked hospital doors that a doctor has to beep open for us. We turn a corner and the cop leads me through a hall.

Farther from the swarm of press and cops in the lobby, it's quieter in here; the beeping of machines in the rooms we pass is calming. He leads me to a closed office door and knocks once.

"More family," he says.

A shaved-bald guy opens the door. He has an FBI badge hanging around his neck. Ozzie's there, too, in a button-up shirt, his hair gelled back. He comes and squeezes my hand and then pats my shoulder—somewhere halfway between a handshake and a hug, which about sums up our relationship. He introduces me to the shaved-bald FBI guy, who seriously looks like he could be younger than me. Ozzie is positively abuzz. It's not in his expression, which is impenetrable, like most law enforcement. His eyes just sparkle, his face radiates.

My parents, sitting at a table with Coca-Colas—which I have never seen them drink before in my life—both stand up. I run to them and give them a simultaneous hug. The three of us shudder with joy.

"So crazy out there," I say.

"Someone leaked it to the press," Mom says. "Never mind them."

"This is really happening?" I ask.

"This looks like the real thing," Dad says.

"Oh my God, have you seen her?" I cry.

"Pictures—and through the door," Mom says, her voice shaking. "She's all grown up."

"Is she okay?" I ask.

"We're getting briefed right now," Dad tells me as we pull apart.

I sit down with them, wiping my eyes. Ozzie offers to get me a Coke and leaves, and the FBI dude shuts the door. He introduces himself and I immediately forget his name because honestly I don't even really care, I just want to see my sister and know what's happened and what's happening next so badly I could vomit.

"So . . . when can we see her?" I ask.

"In a little bit," FBI dude says. He sits up straight and politely folds his hands on the table. He's nervous. Possibly more so than we are. "I was catching your parents up."

"She was hit by a car," Mom blurts.

"But she's okay," Dad adds.

"Just a concussion and some scrapes and bruises," FBI dude says.

"Okay . . ." I say.

"She's . . . kind of out of it—we're waiting for the results to come back from the blood test," Mom says.

"It's possible she was on something when she was hit by the car," FBI dude says. "The woman driving said Ava was in a stupor. The woman turned a corner in a parking lot and ran into Ava."

"Where's the woman?" I ask.

"At the station giving a deposition. She feels terrible—she drove her to the hospital this morning."

"She hit her outside a Starbucks," Dad says excitedly, like this information matters.

"So . . . the woman had her?" I ask, confused.

"No. We haven't been able to iron out the details yet, but the girl we think is Ava says she was 'dumped,'" FBI dude says. "We can't get details, but she's said, 'He dumped me,' multiple times. She had a backpack with her with some snacks, some clothes."

"He 'dumped' her?" I ask. "After all these years?"

"That's how it appears," FBI dude answers.

"Who is 'he'?" I ask.

"We haven't been able to establish that yet."

"And how did you find her?" I ask.

"An ER nurse here recognized her from the news segment that aired on TV when she came in, initially," FBI dude informs me.

"From the forensic artist's picture," Dad adds.

"Anyone can see it's her," Mom says. "Thank God for that forensic sketch."

"Wow," I say.

If I ever doubted their relentless PR strategy, I stand corrected.

Ozzie comes back in with a Coke. I hold it in my hand, chilling, the sensation a comfort proving this is real.

"Ozzie, did you—did you know about any of this?" I ask.

He heaves into his chair and adjusts it, so squeaky it makes everyone flinch.

"I did not," he says simply. "I had leads in Fresno years ago. Not Fremont. This is goddamn surprising."

He has a way with words, he does.

"Right now we're simply working through the details," FBI dude tells us, clearing his throat and looking at a notepad he has in front of him before continuing. "She says last she remembers she was locked up. She keeps talking about an attic and someone named Jonathan—she says he dumped her—but I don't think she knows where she was exactly before this or how she ended up in the parking lot. Right now we're just trying to get her stabilized and we're not pressing her too hard. If anything comes up, please tell us when you're done visiting with her."

"Sure," I say, bracing myself. "Are we going to go see her now?"

"I need to share the details of the case so far so you understand what we're dealing with," the FBI guy says.

Lean in. Pulse a stutter.

"She's been examined by a doctor and we've confirmed quite a bit of evidence of physical abuse that looks to have happened a number of years ago now—broken radius, some scars on her back, cigarette burns on her skin."

"And what else?" Ozzie asks without blinking.

"Oh, God," Mom says, gasping for just a moment and then regaining composure.

Ozzie scoots his chair closer with an excruciating squeak and puts a hand on her arm. On the other side, Dad holds her hand with a tight white fist.

"Results of the pelvic exam this morning confirm sexual abuse," FBI guy says.

"To what extent?" Ozzie asks.

The looks on my parents' faces—pragmatic, unemotional—like, We're going to tackle this without falling to pieces, goddammit.

"According to the doctor, the scar tissue definitely shows signs of repeated rape that probably started at a young age," he says.

Even Ozzie's face falls a little.

"Okay," Mom says.

Her eyes are watering, but she just keeps nodding like she is working so hard to accept the reality of this.

"Okay," she says again.

"Thank you for sharing this with us," Dad says.

And then, a lapse in his facial expression as he sobs for a moment into his hands. Mom looks away at a wall and I put my hand on Dad's hand. "She's going to be okay, Dad."

"She's very happy to be here," Ozzie says after giving us a respectful moment to recover. He wipes his eyes with a handkerchief, but his face remains professional, emotionless. "She's been asking about her family."

"Can we see her, then?" Mom asks.

After a few more details, some coaching on how to react to different reunion scenarios, and a serious warning to not tell the press anything for fear of jeopardizing the case, FBI dude nods. "All right then. Follow me."

We spring up, and he leads us down the hall.

"Doctor said she'll be discharged this evening," Ozzie tells us. "They're going to wait until then in hopes the press thins out."

"We'll escort you guys to a hotel and have agents accompanying you tonight," FBI dude says.

"Why a hotel?" I ask.

"To help you keep your privacy," Ozzie says. "High-profile cases like this, you're going to have the press slobbering after you like wolves."

We stand in front of a door that's nearly shut. 4C. I can hear a TV and a beeping machine. I am trembling. Trembling so hard parts of me I thought couldn't physically tremble are trembling. My eyelashes. My hair.

"I'll stand outside to give you your privacy," FBI dude says.

"You coming?" Mom asks Ozzie.

"I'll meet her later," he says. "Give you guys some time."

"Thank you," she says.

She holds her hand up to Dad and me, like, Give me a minute. She wipes her eyes and takes a giant breath and breathes out. Dad squeezes her arm. I can't help thinking, *This is the last time I am your only daughter. After this, everything's different.*

"I think this is it, honey," he says softly.

"I know," she whispers.

She gives me a nod, like, Go for it. And I push.

The knob creaks. The door *eek*s open.

She has a puffy white bandage wrapped around her forehead. The fluorescent light catches her long electrified curls in a burst of gold. She's in a hospital bed, sitting up, IVs highwaying off her arms into drips and machines. I almost cry out when I see the mood ring on her pinky, the silver band so old and worn it's nearly black. She is pale and malnourished but her features are the same. All I can think of is that photo on the flyers on our dining room table—that computer game–girl picture—and how Jesus graphic-designing Christ, it really is her. Down to the mole on her cheek, the cowlick in her hair. The sight of her softens me. I don't know what I was expecting—a girl in pieces—but she's whole and there's a brightness to her despite her injured state that makes me breathe a sigh of relief.

My bones know it's her, but my eyes can't believe this. The last time I saw her we were tiny. We were different humans then.

"It's you," Mom says. She's the first one to the side of the hospital bed. "Oh my God, sweetie—it's you—I'd recognize you in a second—"

"Mommy?" Ava asks, a little confused, like she doesn't believe herself.

"You recognize me?" Mom asks. "You remember me?"

Ava gives a timid little nod.

"Ava!" Dad says, eyes shining, going to the other side of the hospital bed.

"Daddy?" she says in a scared, childlike voice.

"You remember," he says, all choked up.

"Ava?" I ask, the urge to burst into tears an itch I will not scratch.

"You're my sister?" she asks, like she just can't believe it.

"Yeah," I say. "Vera. Your twin."

"Holy crap," she says tearfully. "You look like a princess."

Everyone but Ava laughs. I should explain why I'm dressed like this, but I can't talk. Can't stop staring. Soon Mom reaches out and hugs Ava, so gently, just hugging her poor stuck-with-needles arm like she worships it. And Dad leans in and pets Ava's hair. Ava's face twists, looking like the child she was, overwhelmed.

"It's really you," Mom says.

"You're all . . . grown up," Dad says.

"My family," she says. "I have a family."

Ava and Mom hug, then Ava and Dad, then it's my turn. Her lake-colored eyes—worn, exhaustion-shrunken, but so familiar. Like staring into a mirror in a dream. They lock with mine. She smells like rubbing alcohol and disinfectant when we hug. I can feel her bones. I pull back and try to drink in her every detail. Those striking dark eyebrows. That olive skin. There's a scrape on her cheek and bandages on her arm.

"I'm really scared," she says to us.

We tell her anything and everything she's feeling is fine.

"My head feels messed up," Ava says, touching the bandage. "I keep forgetting my name. Then the nurse has to tell me again—and I don't remember. I got hit by a car—what was I doing outside? I don't know how I ended up here."

"We'll figure all that out later," Mom says. "What matters is you're here, you're with us now, and you're safe."

Ava nods. Finally, she says, in her low husky voice that is all her, that I've never heard before exactly but that I'm fast getting used to, "I think this is really good." She keeps nodding, like she's trying to calm herself down. "I think I just finally woke up from the nightmare."

I don't know what she means, but it hurts to hear, fills me with anger I don't know where to direct, pangs with twelve years' worth of longing, but the joy—hallelujah—is so much louder than all the pain.

23

SO MANY PROFESSIONALS come this afternoon to talk to Ava. She's poked, prodded, tested, questioned all day long. The only truths that matter to me are: She's my sister, she's been through hell, and she wants to go home. I'm so anxious to get her there, I could jump out of my skin.

Whenever one of the doctors shows up, Mom, Dad, and I go back to the tiny blank room with the Coca-Colas again to give her space. They're all nicefaces to us and come by the room for introductions and to explain what they do and ask if we need anything and to tell us how happy they are for us. The miracle has spread joy to everyone, even strangers and hard-faced experts and law enforcement. The news is infectious and electrifying. I lose count of the people we meet. Sergeants, doctors, more FBI, a victim advocate, a transition specialist, the head of the Berkeley PD, and a psychiatrist. That pubescent FBI dude whose name I now see on his badge is Jean-Paul Johnson sticks with us the whole time we're in the little room and gets food delivered. He asks us if we'd like him to relay a statement to the media circus, and Mom says to tell them we're going to take a day or two to reconnect with Ava and we'll give a statement once she's home.

So far, Ava's only asked if we know where Jonathan is. That's the first clue toward a person or a reason for all this. *Jonathan.* The name turns my stomach, even though she can't tell us if he was who "dumped" her, how she got in that parking lot, or where he is now.

Every time I pass by the locked door to the ward to hit up the bathroom, the reporters ogle through the window and police have to keep pushing them back. It's gross, actually. I always liked reporters and newspeople before this—they wanted to help us, they wanted Ava to be found. Now they're just a bunch of bloodthirsty dogs let off their leashes.

One of them gets in a couple hours before discharge, a man with a crooked nose and a camera who went so far as to dress in scrubs to pass himself off as a medical worker. He waltzes into the hospital room while we're with Ava and offers to pay us for an exclusive interview. I recognize the name of the magazine. I see it in drug-stores with pictures of celebrities in bikinis with arrows pointing to their cellulite. Dad threatens to kick his ass—I've never heard Dad say anything so menacing before—and Mom frantically presses the nurse button and says she's going to sue. Ava watches on blankly, even as the reporter in scrubs uses his camera to snap a picture of Dad standing protectively in front of Ava's hospital bed, brandishing a jar of cotton balls like a weapon. We shout in unison, and then the nurse comes in and pulls the reporter in scrubs away and yells, "Security!"

If Elliott were here, I'm sure he would not have hesitated to bust the guy's teeth in. I've seen him do it for way less heinous crimes. Where the hell is Elliott, anyway?

Mom closes the door. We all stare at one another.

"Wow," Ava says.

The TV drones on nonstop in the background as we sit together.

MISSING GIRL FOUND ALIVE AFTER 12 YEARS

AVA RIVERS DISCOVERED ALIVE IN CALIFORNIA

BREAKING NEWS!

#AVARIVERS

Click the remote. Same show, different channel. They keep repeating the noninformation over and over again, flashing between her first-grade portrait and a blurry current photo. It's been less than an hour and the picture the guy took of Ava, with Dad in front of her with cotton balls and crazy eyes, is on every news station.

"I look insane," Dad says, shocked.

"Are we famous?" Ava asks, eyes bright.

"Unfortunately," Dad says.

Mom goes and glances out the window. "They're lined up down the street. I don't know how we're ever getting out of here." She crosses to the mirror above the sink and finger-combs her hair. "I mean, I *could* give a statement."

"Michelle," Dad says. "We said we'd wait."

"What?" she says. "Ask them to respect our privacy and to let Ava be with family right now."

"Exactly, honey, let's just be with Ava right now."

It took twelve tragic years and a miracle resurrection to hear my dad call my mom "honey" again without irony.

"You're right," she says.

That also took twelve years.

They look to Ava for her input, but she's closed her eyes and appears to have fallen asleep. She's holding the remote to her chest with a bandaged hand, the mood ring bright violet. We gaze at her for a long time. We whisper about the parts of her that look different than we expected—her hair didn't straighten like mine and Elliott's did. Instead it curled even kinkier. She stayed blond while Elliott went brown. But her dark eyelashes and eyebrow shapes, her mole on her cheek, the little bow above her upper lip are all exactly her. Her proportions are identical to the little girl we last saw. The curve of her chin, the stretch between her eyes, the nearness of her nose to her lips. Funny how we're not just our features, we're the areas between.

I'm not sure when this will start feeling real. There's something in me that can't trust what's happened today—like any second I'm going to wake back up to the reality where my sister is a giant black hole instead of a person.

24

WE FINALLY HEAD to the hotel that night after a long, ridiculous escape from the hospital through a back entrance and then a ride in an unmarked van. Police cars and Ozzie in his Prius drive along with us. I can't tell whom they're protecting us from at this point—the press or the villain who's allegedly responsible for Ava's state. My mom, my dad, and I sit in the back, and Ava sits in front. She's been quiet all day, dazed, except every once in a while she turns to us and says, "You're my family?" or "Why is there a bandage on my head?" or "Am I in trouble?" The doctor warned us she'd be like this— repeating herself, a little bit out of it—because of the concussion and the traces of drugs in her system. The tests showed Zolpidem, a sedative. But she's going to be okay.

Facts keep rattling around in my head. There aren't many yet. Here's what we know: Ava was locked up by a monster named Jonathan, and for reasons unknown he drugged her and packed her a backpack and kicked her to the curb in a parking lot, where she was apparently then hit by a random car. In the hospital, a nurse recognized her from TV. More staff noticed her. They alerted the police. And here we are.

But honestly, there are so many unanswered questions and this day has been so endless and surreal, I don't even have the brainpower to analyze the information on the drive to the hotel. It's all swarthy clouds and the diamond chops of whizzing street-lights. By the time we get to the Best Western off the freeway and into our room and dig into the bags of toiletries and sweats provided by the FBI, we collapse, Ava in one bed, my mom and I in the other, my dad with a makeshift sheet bed on the floor between. Ozzie lingers outside somewhere, self-appointed reporter patrol. Jean-Paul Johnson is there in the room next door and asks us more than once if we want an additional room, but we don't. Ava says she doesn't want to be alone. Dad and I get up again, stepping out onto the balcony. He smokes cigarette after cigarette and tries to call Elliott's number again, but now it's fully disconnected. I can't believe he's missed this, or hasn't turned on a TV or a radio all day to figure it out. I mention as much to Dad, but he just shrugs. His eyes look younger to me right now, but his wrinkles seem deeper. We hug. He lets me take a drag of his cigarette once before I head inside.

Ava asks Mom if she can sleep with the Home Shopping Network on.

"Sure," Mom says cheerfully. "Anything you want."

"I always sleep with it on," Ava says, and drifts off in an instant.

Even though I've never been this exhausted, I can't sleep. I'm humming with the knowledge that my family is whole again. My sick curiosity about Ava's blank years gnaws at me. I can hear Dad going in and out of the room, the sliding glass door to the balcony opening and closing while his secondhand smoke drifts in, and Mom kicks the blankets off and pulls them back on, and my sister snores as the man on TV yammers on about spectacular dish soap.

25

THE NEXT MORNING we wake up early, and the four of us—plus Ozzie, plus Jean-Paul Johnson—go downstairs to eat at the breakfast buffet. Mom of course is coiffed for the gods. Dad's got bedhead that you'd think must be on purpose—I mean, it's pretty much a monument. I haven't even washed my face. Ava removed her head bandage this morning. A violet bruise remains; it hurts to look at. I keep admiring her cheekbones and reminding myself we are twins.

We are *twins*.

Present tense.

We're all in Cal sweats we slept in courtesy of the FBI as we stand at the buffet, fixing our plates.

"We look like a family of school-spirited dorks," I say.

Ava stares back at me blankly, putting a box of Lucky Charms on her plate with no milk.

"These are Cal Berkeley sweats," I say. "It's a university."

"Oh, I thought it was, like, a California thing," she says.

There's no one else up this early to enjoy the breakfast buffet. Or they're not allowed—Jean-Paul Johnson instead sits on the computer at a table in the corner mumbling nervously to himself, and Ozzie stands in the doorway like a bodyguard. Our family sits at a table in the middle of the room. Ava's across from me. The gap in years is something I can't hurdle. She's my sister and also someone I just met. But her eyes. Her features. Déjà vu.

"We do look like dorks," she agrees after a moment.

She and I crack up. For the first time since we were kids, we giggle together. Mom and Dad watch with proud, faraway expressions.

Then the four of us talk like normal people—about how I graduated, and how Dad has been really into keeping up a website we built for Ava, and you remember your brother Elliott, well, he'll be here soon, and Mom is on the board of all these charities . . . There's a long silence. Dad asks, gently, "Ava, do you have any things you want to do?"

"I just want to go home," she says. "And for my brain to stop feeling so fuzzy."

Mom nods and puts her hand on Ava's.

"Did I have a dog with me?" Ava asks, sitting up straighter. She has this amazing volcano of crimped blond ponytail on the top of her head.

"We have dogs!" Mom tells her.

"I think she's saying she had a dog . . . where she was," Dad says to Mom.

Ava squints at something indiscernible. "Where's my dog?"

"Do you remember anything else new, Ladybird?" Dad asks. "Because we want to find this guy and keep you safe."

Ava has been eating Lucky Charms piece by piece, digging through the tiny box and singling out the marshmallows. Her teeth are yellow-gray. Last night, when she busted open the toothbrush from the kit the FBI gave her, she confessed she couldn't remember the last time she brushed. "I'm scraping off universes," she said. "And it hurts good."

My sister, oblivious poetess.

"I remember the attic a little better," Ava answers Dad. "I had a dog."

We pause, listening, watching her face light up with the memory.

"My dog's name was Madonna . . . a Chihuahua." She shakes her cereal box, brow scrunched. "I wish I could remember better. They said it'll come back—my mind's not right. I still feel the drugs . . . I hope Madonna's all right."

"What happened to you on that Halloween?" Mom asks, not able to help herself. Although she's in the same sweatpants and sweatshirt we are, her hair is neatly braided and she's bejeweled and lipsticked. I couldn't help noticing Jean-Paul Johnson as he couldn't help noticing her in the elevator on the way down. And Ozzie, well, I definitely saw him bend in to smell her hair.

"Halloween?" Ava asks in complete confusion.

"Stop," Dad tells Mom sharply. "Let her be."

We eat. Out the picture windows, it seems like any ordinary day in the nothing-special Best Western parking lot with suburban sprawl splashed behind it. But then there are the cop cars and unmarked vans parked near the pool. Look harder—six news vans out there with their cranes—and listen for the helicopters. We're trying to ignore the mayhem, picking at our breakfasts.

"I wish they had scrambled eggs," Ava says. "I've been wishing for fluffy scrambled eggs with savory ketchup for a long time."

Fluffy. Savory. Adorable.

"French toast used to be your favorite," Dad says.

Mine too. We used to ask for it every weekend morning to eat with our cartoons.

Ava smiles without showing her teeth, shyly, eyes sparkling. "If this is real I'm real happy," she says. "But I wonder if I'm just on another trip."

I chew my pancake with its fake syrup and think, *Girl, I wonder the same thing*. Days ago I was packing for Portland, I was hanging out with Max—feels worlds away to me now. I check my reflection in the window glass again, superimposed over the parking lot and all its quiet cops, and think, *Yeah, there I am. Here we are. Real.*

26

AVA'S MEMORIES OOZE back hour by hour as the concussion heals and the drugs leave her system. She'll stop, mute the TV, stare into space. She'll put down her food. She'll stop walking and grip furniture for support. She'll stop mid-word. Freeze. A facial storm brews. Sometimes a new detail will leap off her tongue or a tear will roll. Other times, she swallows, quiet, and will not say.

27

TWO DAYS LATER, this is what we know so far and what Ava's given the police and the FBI: She was locked in Jonathan's attic for years. She thought she was married to him, but it turns out the man had just printed out his own marriage certificate and told her he was an internet-certified priest and officiated them himself. Ava said she always thought it wasn't true but wasn't sure. She said it was hard to tell lies from truth with Jonathan.

"He could be real convincing," she said.

The memories multiply, and she shares them during her nearly constant sit-downs with the FBI and police. But details are lost—and it's not all her concussion's fault. She doesn't know where she was, not a state, not a city name, nothing. Her windows were apparently boarded up, no view. She gives details about Jonathan (who has no last name): "kinda fat," "goatee," "fortyish maybe," "white dude." Fanatical. Mood swings, on and off pills. Sometimes, she says, he was nice to her and bought her things. The FBI says when they ask about the other times she mostly gets tired and doesn't want to talk anymore.

They can't figure out the timeline of how long she was with Jonathan. Ava's memory is still so vague. They're concentrating on trying to get any details she can remember about him, or the house and its features, if she heard trains or bird cries or other identifiable sounds, commercials on TV that might pinpoint location, anything to steer them anyfreakingwhere.

It's an inch in so many miles of madness. I know loneliness and quiet aches and long nights with a wild mind and books so good they crack me open and make my insides scream with joy-hurt and beautiful girls and dudes who will never look back at me. I don't know what it's like to be kidnapped, imprisoned, raped, manipulated, abused. I am not equipped to understand this kind of nightmare. Now that she's back I realize I never fully let myself imagine Ava's torture, though it seems familiar, like it's been there as a blurry possibility I entertained in the deep, dark depths of my heart.

When Jean-Paul Johnson briefs us the morning we leave for Berkeley, thirty-six hours after we got into the hotel and many exhausting interviews later, hearing even those scant details makes my eyes feel like they're bleeding.

Already, somewhere, law enforcement is working in full ass-whooping force, hunting for fat, white, fortysomething Jonathans.

28

THERE'S NO WAY to be prepared for an exhausted homecoming where you're greeted by a train of news vans and a bunch of strangers with flowers and stuffed bears and signs that say WELCOME HOME, AVA RIVERS. No way.

"It's like we're on reality TV," Ava says as the FBI van pulls up to the curb.

"What in the—" Dad mutters.

The three of us make a run for the front door, paparazzi shouting and snapping pictures. Mom lingers outside to give a statement to the press on the sidewalk in front of the house. I only hear the beginning of her speech. The woman doesn't need a megaphone.

"I am Michelle Amini-Rivers, Ava's mother, and to say we are thrilled to be home is an understatement. . . ."

Inside, Dad and Ava and I share a moment of complete stunned silence in the foyer. Outside, there is applause.

"Did you expect it to be like this?" I ask Dad.

"I didn't expect any of this." He puts an arm around Ava, who is still swimming in her Cal sweatshirt. "Welcome home."

I really see the place suddenly as I stand next to this wide-eyed stranger I once shared a womb with. The big-bellied Victorian teeming with colorful Tiffany-style lamps, half-wizened houseplants, and Persian rugs. The dusty black piano. The Ernst prints and framed postcards.

"Remember?" Dad asks.

Ava nods slowly.

"Pardon the mess," Dad says.

Then he starts crying. Then Ava, then me. It's Dad's fault. He gave us the sobs like a sickness.

We wipe our eyes and walk Ava through the house. She touches the dusty built-in bookshelves in the hall. Pauses long in the doorway of my mother's room, different from the rest of the house, shining, nothing-colored, and magazine-ordinary.

"Well, this room is probably completely unrecognizable to you since the remodel," Dad says.

"It's nice," Ava says.

Dad doesn't point out nothing in the room is his anymore.

We move on upstairs, to my room all half boxed up. There, Dad squeaks out the word "sorry" and fights tears.

"Dad," I groan, looking away so I don't catch them again.

"I'm okay," he says hoarsely, and keeps on.

We move to the guest room, another eerily, lifelessly decorated blip in the house. Elliott's old room, exercise machines with price tags, blue and shuddering with dust.

"Looks different without all the punk posters on the wall, right?" Dad asks her.

Ava emits a small *hmmm* that I think is supposed to be a laugh.

"You remember all this?" Dad asks once we get to the kitchen and stand at the sliding glass door looking out onto the backyard.

"I think so," she says. "My head's still . . . weird. But yeah."

Dad stares at the yard through the glass door like a man with a movie in his head. I come and stand next to him, whispering, "Dad."

"Yeah," he says with a possibly World Records–heavy sigh.

Mom comes back inside. "How inspiring to know how many strangers care that you came home," she tells Ava.

"Or maybe we're just ratings to them," Dad mutters.

"Don't be so cynical," Mom says. "These people really do care."

Ava yawn-speaks. "I can't believe it."

"Are you tired?" Mom asks. "You want a bath? Hungry? We can order takeout."

"Can I just go lie down and watch TV or something?" Ava asks.

"Sure. You want to be alone? I can set up the guest room."

Ava hesitates. "But you'll still be here downstairs, right?"

"Of course we will!"

"And we're setting up a security system," Dad assures Ava. "I'm calling them to come over today. I don't want you to worry."

Ava chews a fingernail with a confused expression.

"Since they haven't caught him," Mom goes on. "If that's what you're worried about. Is that what you're worried about?"

Ava weighs this info. You can see her brain working behind her eyes as she thinks this through. "I don't think he's going to come get me. I don't think he wanted me anymore anyway. That's why he left me there."

"Well, we want you," Mom says with a shiny gaze. "And we will protect you."

We group hug. It's weird. We've done this more than once already today. We're like a sudden team, us Riverses. I didn't realize how much I missed it.

"I'll show you to the guest room," Mom says. "Ozzie's coming back in a bit. You know how thrilled he is? A dozen years working pro bono—he deserves an award."

"Pro bono?" Ava asks.

"It means free," Mom says.

"That's really nice," Ava says, surprised.

"A lot of people care about you," Dad says. "Haven't you noticed?"

Ava nods and starts crying. "I keep feeling like I don't deserve this."

"You deserve this," Mom says, strong and unflinching, holding Ava's arm. "You absolutely deserve this. No one, *no one* deserves this more than you."

She walks her upstairs. I follow them and linger in the hallway as Mom escorts her to the guest room. I can hear them behind the ajar door.

"Are these pillows okay? They're not very fluffy. I'll order new ones. Are you sure you don't want something else to wear? Vera probably has something. Or do you want to just tell me what size you are and I'll order some clothing for you? Are you sure you don't want a bath?"

I can already envision Mom turning today's miracle into tomorrow's shopping spree. Time to stop creeping in the hallway. Also, I'm biting my fingernails, a habit I gave up in seventh grade. I have to pull my hand away from my mouth and force my body down the stairs and remind myself that Ava's home for good now, there's no need to be crazy. That's Mom's job.

What's to become of me now? a tiny voice in me dares to ask.

I go down to Dad's basement. I knock and hear a muffled "Come in." The cigarette smoke is fog-thick. He's perched on the edge of his bed, head in his hands. I touch his shoulder, and he takes his hand away from his face. There are tears running down his neck. I sit next to him and hug him and catch the crying disease.

After these wet-happy moments pass, we dry our eyes and I take one of his cigarettes out of his pack and light it with his Zippo. Usually he would halfheartedly discourage me from doing so, but right now I could probably tell him I robbed a bank and he'd be okay with it.

"Is this real life?" he asks, running a hand through his thick gray-brown mop of hair.

"I think so," I say. "How about you punch me in the face so we can be sure?"

"Don't say that."

"Sorry." I exhale smoke through my nose. It burns. "Are they going to find the guy who did this to her?"

He squints his crybaby blue eyes at the light. "Hell yes, they will. You see how big this case is."

"Mom says the FBI was already showing Ava pictures of men back at the hotel room."

He lights a cigarette.

"Why FBI?" I ask. "Why not the police?"

"Right now they're working together. If there's the possibility of trafficking, it becomes too big for the police."

Trafficking. That word is a lie. It sounds too harmless, some minor infraction involving stop signs and red-yellow-green lights. That word is too weak for how vile a crime we're talking here. But I don't let myself dwell on it. It's all blankness. There are so few answers or truths yet, ugly or otherwise. Right now we're operating in the dark.

"She's so . . . sweet," he says, his voice rising with emotion. "You can see it in her face. She seems younger than she is. Naïve." He sucks his cigarette, hard. "I want to know where she went . . . but then again, I'm scared to." Smoke oozes from between his lips. "I just want to know that every person responsible for what happened to her will never live a free day again."

"I can't believe."

"Part of me wants her back with no questions."

"Doesn't work that way."

"I know that, Ladybug. I'm just telling you what I want. I don't ever expect to get what I want."

I get up and pace slowly, chewing my cheek, and stop at Dad's wood-paneled wall above his desk. The dusty wedding picture, except for a few smudged fingerprints around my mother's face. Ava's baby to toddler to kid pictures arranged in a sunny circle. If you follow it clockwise, you can see her grow. It used to bother me that there were no pictures of me down here. A lot of things used to bother me, but I learned to live with them. I was different than Ava. I didn't need shrines or websites. I was alive.

I can't even begin to think how everything will change now that she's here. *Stop biting your nails*, I scream at myself. My fingernails, chewed to the quick, are still painted red from the princessing earlier. Seems like eons ago already.

"I worked a party earlier this month," I tell him.

"Good, good." He gets up and stubs his cigarette into this ashtray shaped like a foot on his desk. I can tell he's not listening.

"It was weird," I say. "Because they were twins. Fraternal twins. One brown-haired and the other one blond. One loud and hammy and the other one nerdy and quiet."

"Huh," he says, refocusing on me. "Is that how you see yourself? Nerdy and quiet?"

"Don't you?"

"You're studious . . . but you're not a stereotype. You've got a sense of humor like a hot poker. And I'm sorry, but sometimes I see flashes of me in you. You inherited my goofballism."

I smile. "Not a word."

"That's your studious side talking." He smiles back. "Ava . . . she was different than you. Loud, high energy. She wanted to be on the move, she didn't want to sit and concentrate and think the way you do."

It's been years since he took this tone. Meditative, peaceful, nostalgic.

"But in one way you were always the same." He points his finger at me. "Hearts too big for your little bodies."

I touch my chest, as if that'll tell me if my dad's right.

"I feel like I've spent my life wondering where she is," I tell him. "Now she's two rooms away. I have a million things to ask her and to say."

"We're going to have to be strategic," he says. "Not suffocate. Not bombard her with questions. She's overwhelmed, you can see it on her face. And the concussion thing, and the memory issues . . . it's really thrown her on top of everything else."

I nod.

"Trauma," he says with the frankness of a doctor. His expression crumbles into a fatherly grimace of pain. "God, you have to marvel at the human spirit. How can anyone . . ."

"Therapy."

"The best in the field. We'll get her through this." He rubs the silvery fuzz on his chin. "Let's be happy for now."

His voice breaks, the word "happy" halved.

We hug long and hard. It's like a dozen hugs rolled into one.

"My girls," he whispers into my hair.

When we pull away, we both wipe our damn eyes. As I float upstairs, he says, "Hey."

I don't know what I'm expecting him to say. But not: "Remind me I want to take a picture of you in your Snow White dress."

"Okay," I say after a beat.

"I don't want you to feel pushed aside."

"I don't!"

"I need to remember to show you I'm here for you, too," he says. "I'm interested in your life."

The way the words come out, it's as if it's being rehearsed. I don't have the energy to break the news to him right now—I've already felt pushed aside for too long for it to matter now. Plus, she's home. As in, mere feet away from us—human, not angel. I just want a piece of her.

29

THAT FIRST NIGHT, she screams in her sleep. I fly up and into the hallway and stumble toward her room, lids half-sealed, dead-tired shut.

"Get off me!" she roars with shocking force.

I grip the doorway and enter, sitting next to her on the bed.

"I can't move!" she screams, higher. Her dark blond hair explodes from beneath the pillows and blankets. I perch on the edge, shaking a sheet-covered shoulder.

"Hey," I say gently. "Hey."

"Please stop, please just stop, no, no no, no, *no*," she cries.

"Hey," I say, louder. My heartbeat's a catastrophe. "Ava, you're dreaming."

She sits up, eyes alarmingly wide. It's dim in here, lit by the hallway's slit of light, but I can see her fearful stare-shine.

"It's me, it's your sister, Vera," I say.

She claps her bony fingers over her mouth, shaking. She draws her knees up into her chest. She pants.

"You were screaming," I say.

"I thought I was back there," she says, breaking.

I reach to give her a hug, instinct.

She shrinks back and yells, "Don't touch me."

Instinct.

I hold my hands up in the air.

"I'm sorry," she says.

She sobs. I think I understand the feeling of being gutted, I do.

"I had a bad dream," she says. "I'll be okay. It's okay. Please, sorry . . . I'd like to forget about it and go back to sleep."

She asks permission a lot and is often all too thankful. It breaks my heart.

"I'm right down the hall," I tell her, getting up.

"Can you just . . . leave the door open?"

"Yeah."

I linger outside in the hall. Her snores come quickly, and there's no more crying. Actually, strangely, there's snickering, and then she sings a song. I recognize it, stepping closer in the dark to listen. It's a jingle from a laundry detergent commercial.

"Follow your nose

To the cleanest-smelling clothes

Courtesy of F-L-O-W . . . FLOW!"

"Um," I say.

In bed, a new sound escapes me—something halfway between a whimper and a laugh.

30

THE NEXT MORNING I go downstairs and discover Mom and Dad crouched near the living room window in awkward, wide-eyed silence.

"Shhh," Mom says, then looks back out the window with that hawk stare. Even from this distance I can see that vein ticking on her forehead. I consider slipping a Xanax into her bubbly water. Dad, for some unknown reason, is sporting a neon yellow bandana.

"What's going on?" I come in for the huddle.

"Your dad was sitting in here watching TV," Mom says, "and some scuzzy photographer came onto our property, taking pictures through the window."

"They arrested him a minute ago," Dad whispers.

"I always miss the drama," I say. "Where's Ava?"

"She has no idea, don't say anything." Mom points to the kitchen, and now that I listen for it, I can hear Ozzie talking to Ava in a low voice.

A cop comes back in to brief my parents on the arrest that apparently just happened, and I go stand around the corner in between the kitchen and the living room and pretend to look at a back issue of *Mother Jones*. My sister is in there sitting at the table.

My sister whose profile looks the same as it did when we were kids. My sister who changed in size but not in shape.

I am wallpaper, I am want.

And I can't stop myself from eavesdropping.

"You look nervous," Ozzie says.

Creak of a chair. "I feel like I'm in trouble or something."

"Why would you feel that way?"

"I don't know, all your questions, the way you stare at me and write stuff down."

"I want to find Jonathan, like everybody else."

A sniff.

"I want to help you remember things—so we can help you," Ozzie goes on.

"What if I don't want to remember things?"

"Can't say I blame you. How about, for fun, just to get the memories going, you think of something from before you got kidnapped? Something good, something with the family?"

She sighs, long and measured. "Hmmm."

"Take your time."

The blood in my ears thumps like a clock.

"Yeah," she says softly. "I don't want to talk to you anymore right now."

Chairs screech. I put the magazine back and step into the living room. Ava walks in and smiles, her hair up in a huge bun. She looks different than the night before—pinker, healthier, eyes whiter, better rested.

The cops skedaddle. Ozzie takes the longest, complaining to my parents about that guy Jean-Paul and how he clearly got flustered by the media circus. Ozzie mutters the word "rookie" more than once and says only amateurs get thrown off by idiot reporters.

"The trespassing should never have happened," he says. "I'll make sure it doesn't happen again."

Then he moves on to asking my mom's advice about orchids near the front door. Orchids. How to grow them. Right now. Our house has orchids in every windowsill, and do you know my mom's secret? She lets them die and then buys new ones. But she tells Ozzie something about fertilizer as he stares at her red, red mouth and lingers with his hand on the knob. Finally, he leaves, saying he has some ideas to "flesh out" about Ava. The door slams behind him—Ozzie slams doors, it's just his way, like how he stomps instead of walks—and we Riverses are alone. TV fills the tired quiet.

Ava flips through the TV guide and marvels at how many channels we have. The whole family sits in here together and the room feels smaller. Mexico and Canada growl at Ava, and Mom tells them, "She's your sister, stop that." She says the same thing when Mexico opts for a different approach and humps Ava's ankle. Dad comes to sit beside Ava with the family photo album and shows her pictures as she half watches a cooking show about bacon-flavored cupcakes.

I sit on an ottoman a careful distance away, trying not to seem like I'm ogling Ava when I totally am. In fact, my every cell is screaming, LOOK AT ME LOVE ME I AM YOUR TWIN. Her face, her furrowed brow, relays a studious curiosity as Mom explains the pictures to her in a voice usually reserved for dogs and babies. I vow not to condescend when I finally get Ava alone.

"That's the swing set we used to have." Dad points. "Remember?"

"Kind of . . ." Ava says after a moment. "It was red?"

Her voice is so hoarse, low, and different than I would have imagined. I might remember Ava's voice as a child's—silvery and full of sugar and song. I definitely remember it from videos.

"Yes!" Mom's face is a lit bulb. *Pop.* "Remember how Vera got her finger stuck in it and stood there crying for hours before anyone noticed her and then we had to have that neighbor guy with the saw get her out?"

Not my favorite memory, but it gets Ava to look me in the eyes. And I get a faint half smile. So it's fine. We can stroll down bad-memory lane all they want.

"And then the swing set ended up getting recalled," I say. "Thousands of children had their backyard fun dismantled and driven to the city dump, all because of me."

Ava smiles wider and keeps her eyes on me. It's like the sun after so much rain.

"I think I remember the swing set," Ava says. "Swinging on it."

Dad does this clap and then fist pump thing usually reserved for men who watch football games. "Good job!"

He flips to another page.

"This?" asks Ava, pointing.

"Elliott," Mom says.

"My brother?"

"Yeah," Dad says. "He looks weird here—this was in his punk phase. He doesn't look like that anymore."

"Where is he?" Ava asks.

The silence is long and awkward. How to explain the slipping throughout high school, the dishonorable discharge from the army, the string of sketchy jobs and stripper girlfriends and pills, the stint in jail for forging prescriptions, the bitterness, the paranoia? The fact he now lives in The Bathrooms, California, and the last time we gathered as a family he threw a Thanksgiving turkey through the sliding glass door?

"He lives far away" is all Mom says. She turns to me. "And I can't believe you haven't gotten ahold of him."

"I've called him and talked to some 'CC' person twice who has no idea who Elliott is and says she just got that number," I say. "Clearly something happened with his phone."

Someone knocks on the door, and the four of us look at one another. Through the lace curtains we spy three news vans with subpar parking skills. Humans with cameras and microphones are oozing from the vehicles and making a beeline for our front door.

"Vultures," Dad mutters. "They want a statement?" He gets up. "Oh, I'll give them a statement."

"I'll go out," Mom says, shooting up. She puts a fingertip to her tongue and then smooths her eyebrows. She's been dressed for a press conference since she woke up this morning. As she strides toward the door, Dad peeks out the curtains and murmurs something about a restraining order.

"I could talk to them," Ava says, brightening. "It's me they want, right?"

"You don't want that, honey," Dad says. "They're not good people."

"We can hide out upstairs," I tell Ava. "Want to go to my room? Come on."

After a moment's hesitation, Ava stands up to follow me. Strange how something as easy as standing up and leaving a room together— exchanging a smile—seems like utter *magic*.

31

THE FEAR. THE blood-stopping fear when I walked home alone in my later years of elementary school, pretending not to be terrified by every stranger I passed on the sidewalk. The scream ready in my mouth any time a grown man made eye contact with me. The panic when I lost my mom in a shopping mall, afraid I would be gone, sucked up into the oblivion where my sister was. That one time my schoolmate's mom slowed her car down when she saw me walking home to offer me a ride and I yelled, "No!" and put my hand out in the gesture I'd learned at my kiddie self-defense course. I could see her eyes were laughing at me while she bit her lip and drove on. She didn't know. She didn't know the barbed sadness that made me the jumpy child I was. She didn't know the ghost I was tethered to.

Ava being gone was always this bombshell. Every crush, every new friend I made, I had to at some point explain the situation to . . . that is, if they didn't already know. And when I explained the void that was my twin sister—oh, you mean Ava *Rivers*?—there was this sad face those crushes or friends would make as they bit down on their lower lips and widened their eyes. I hated that look. Like I was disfigured by it. Like loss was this scar and everyone saw it.

It occurred to me this morning that I have a new story to tell.

32

AVA STOPS INSIDE the room, and her eyes flit from surface to surface—the floor, with its brown boxes still taped up. The naked wall. The pile of quotes I'd pulled off it when I was getting ready to go to Portland.

Portland. The word's a sinking stone.

"Are you moving?" she asks.

"Not anymore," I say after a sec. "I was supposed to go to college in Portland."

"Like that comedy show?" she asks brightly. "That Portland?"

"Yeah."

"How far is it?"

"About a ten-hour drive."

"When are you going?"

"I was supposed to leave . . ."

I do the math. Count. No. Recount. Recount *again*.

Holy mother.

". . . tomorrow," I say.

When I say it out loud, the truth sounds an alarm. I've pushed this out of my mind ever since Ava returned. *Portland.* It used to signal joy. Now it's surreal, overshadowed by crisis.

"Are you really leaving tomorrow?" she asks.

"Of course not," I say. "I honestly completely forgot it was happening until right now."

"Can I ask, what are all these?" she asks, stooping to pick through the ribbons of torn paper riddled with my best cursive.

"Just quotes I like," I say. "From books, writers, I don't know."

"What's your major?" she asks.

"Oh, I don't know yet." A lie. I haven't even started school but I picked out my major years ago. "But I think I want to be a teacher, so education, maybe a double major in education and English."

I say it all casual, like I just thought of it.

"I've thought about being a teacher," Ava says.

My tongue hovers, searching for a response. My dumb heart flutters. All these years later, separated by a vague tragedy we've yet to pierce the surface of, could we really be the same?

"Or maybe a detective like Leticia Munson," Ava says.

I have no idea who Leticia Munson is, but I nod.

"I don't know," she says.

"That's cool," I tell her. "You have lots of time to figure it out."

Ava tiptoes from the door to the window, arms folded over her chest. She's probably thinking, Jesus lawn-mowing Christ, is that a jungle, a dump, or our backyard?

"You remember this room?" I ask.

She turns.

"Your side was over there." I point. "You had the window. I had easy access to the closet." I draw the invisible line. "Duct-taped down the middle, remember?"

She smiles at the floor. "Yeah."

The silence is long and burns with my own second-guessing. I am so inarticulate right now, it's like I'm trying to schmooze at an excruciating party or attempting to charm an unattainable girl or boy.

"It's weird," she says after a moment. "It's almost like . . . there's all this *stuff.*" She makes big circles around her ears. Her ears look like they're never been pierced, even though we went to the mall and got them pierced together when we were toddlers. The holes have closed up, and now it looks like they were never there. "Right here, right behind me. Malingering or whatever."

I don't correct her.

"What kind of stuff?" I ask, immediately regretting it. Why, oh, why did I have to sound as cheesy as a school counselor?

Her face assumes a blankness, unalive and strange. "Him, the past, everything."

"Right," I say, my voice cracking with emotion.

"I mean, everyone here's so nice and patient, like all the FBI dudes and that therapist lady, Shelly—I really appreciate it," she says. "And they're nothing like police on TV, even their clothes— it's so weird, all of it—but I just, I just . . ." She breathes heavy and her face changes. "I don't know."

"Hey," I say.

"I feel so sick." She balls up her fists. She rocks back and forth, back and forth. "I just need—just *shhhhhut up*. Shut up, Diamond. Shut up, Diamond. Shut up, Diamond."

Diamond? What is happening? Ava is wigging out and I don't know what to do. Maybe I should run and get my parents. Or say something. I can't find the words; all my life I've relied on words, I use words to get everything I want, I love words more than life, and now words fail me.

I put a hand on her arm.

"I'm so sorry," I hurry to say. "You're okay. You're safe."

Everything goes still, like even the air has stopped to listen.

Deep breaths. Ava opens her eyes. "Sorry."

"Stop being sorry," I tell her.

My hand is still on her arm. I squeeze it gently.

"Really, you don't need to apologize, like, ever . . . I understand."

Understand? How can I understand? But Ava smiles weakly at me.

"I feel like I'm broken and I'm never going to be right," she says. "There I was, wishing I was free all that time, and now here I am and I'm a mess."

"It's okay."

Though is it? Every word that leaves my mouth seems like a lie.

"He called me Diamond," Ava says. "'Cause of my eyes. Sparkle, sparkle."

My posture changes when I hear this. "What happened to you that night?" I dare ask. "I mean, on Halloween? How'd you . . . just disappear?"

The dead-serious silence grips my throat.

"Dude with a van rolled up," she says, expressionless. "White van, no windows. Said he'd help me find my mom and dad. Told me to breathe the cloth he had in his hand. Next thing I know, I wake up tied to a bed watching cartoons."

"I want to kill him," I say, so much hate in me I feel new, not myself.

"Please don't," she begs, meeting my eyes. "There's enough hurt in this world already."

Ava is ten thousand times the person I am.

She gets up and crosses to my closet, half-open and revealing clothes I haven't packed yet.

"Can I look?"

"Of course." I throw open my closet doors. It's as if a nuclear bomb went off in a thrift store. A knee-high pile avalanches at our feet, my Snow White getup on top.

"Your style's cute," she says, touching my dresses. "It's different." She drops her hand. "I can't wait to get some real clothes."

The way she stares wistfully at my embarrassing pile is plain heartbreaking.

"You will," I say. "I'll help you."

"That'd be nice."

It's like I'm taming some strange animal by holding her attention. I have to keep this up. I don't want to lose her.

"I'll take you shopping," I say.

She nods. "It's more than clothes, though."

"Of course it is."

"I don't know anymore."

She leans against the wall next to the closet. Her delicate wrists, her elbows stick out sharply—then the silver asterisks that dot her arms. Cigarette burns. They tell some wordless horror story. Or I wonder if she did it to herself. She's in therapy and I'm sure Shelly must have noticed them and they must talk about them. But don't be so obvious, Vera. Don't gape, don't suck in air. Don't let that wave of fire spread all through you and singe your eyeballs. Tell that aimless wish for revenge to simmer down. Pretend not to notice. Look at her eyes fixed on yours.

"What was I like?" she asks softly.

Where to begin? At the beginning, when we were identical swaddled bundles we can't remember anymore? In pre-K, when we refused to wear the same dresses or sit on the bus together? In grade school, after our faces changed, when hardly anyone believed we were sisters, let alone twins?

The fights over space and shoes? The hushed, giggled talks on school nights after the lights were out? The time you saved me from a careening car on a street corner, gripping my hand until it hurt? Halloween night, when I sat on that lawn and let you go alone—when I let you march to your doom?

Our history is infinite. I don't know how to broach it.

"You loved singing," I say. "You had a lot of friends. Kind of a show-off . . . in a good way. Bold, big, always smiling and climbing trees."

Ava focuses on some invisible atom in the air.

"You were everyone's favorite," I say. "I'd be jealous—but then, you were my favorite, too." My throat aches. "You were my best friend."

I hate that I'm crying. I close my eyes and beg it to stop. It's not the tears that bother me—it's the stinging.

"Sorry," I say. "I haven't let myself talk about this in a long time."

"It's okay," she says.

I open my eyes. She's covering her mouth and letting the tears dampen her face without wiping them away. Her voice gets hoarse with emotion, and it's so endearing I want to scream. "I'm just so glad I'm here in this amazing house—and I have a family. And all these people like me and want to write stories about me. And everything's . . . everything. And I have you."

How to describe it? A sunrise. A glorious hope, gold, covering everything.

"Can we hug?" I ask. "Is that allowed?"

She nods. There's snot beneath her nose. I reach out my arms and hug her. She is bony, not cuddly. She doesn't hug me back. Her arms are limp. But she puts her forehead on my shoulder, and that's when I realize that in these twelve years, I became the taller one.

We're silent, besides the sniffling. I've wished, many times in life, I had a fast-forward button. Skip the awkward gangly adolescence, the pimples and frizz-disaster hair, the whispers in school halls, the pity stares. Get me through the pain—of missing-person hunts in nearby woods, my parents' muffled fighting behind closed doors, or petty heartbreaks of boys who didn't crush back or straight girls who plain ignored me. And Madeline, of course, whose name throbs in hate-shaped love when it comes to mind. Whiz past the boredom of classes, the dragging of senior year, the Shakespeare I had to wade through in theater, and how hot my cheeks burned onstage.

But for the first time in I don't know how long—ever?—I hold my breath and wish there was a pause button. A little click that could extend this wonderful moment into eternity. There isn't one though, so I have to let go of Ava and stand back and wipe my face clean.

"I have something to show you," I tell her.

Slitting open the top of a tiny taped-up box labeled JEWELRY with my fingernail, I open it and the two of us peer inside. I rifle through rhinestones, fake pearls, and plastic bracelets until I find what I'm looking for.

"Look," I say, palming the mood ring, the one that looks just like hers only cleaner, the band still silver.

Ava touches the one on her pinky. "You have one, too."

I slip mine on my pinky and hold it up to hers, side by side—twins again. "We bought them together, remember?"

"We bought them together," she repeats.

The knock on my door startles us. Mom barges in without waiting for a response. Her eyelinered eyes are wide and kidlike.

"The reporters are gone," Mom says. "Your dad came storming out in the middle of my speech, waving a guitar at them like a weapon."

"How very Dad," I say.

Ava snickers. *I made Ava snicker!*

"Some of the cameramen got footage of him. It's already getting aired on the local news."

"Tonight at eleven, crazy man in neon bandana threatens media with stringed instrument," I say in a newscaster voice.

"They called it a 'breaking development.'" Mom puts an arm around Ava. "Anyway, the coast is clear."

"Can I have something to eat?" Ava asks.

"Honey, you don't need to ask. Just go to the kitchen and get yourself whatever you want. Unless you want to order something?"

Mom escorts Ava downstairs. I take in the sights of all these sealed boxes in my room. My black lace curtains. My mirror with a lipsticked heart. My portable record player and splayed records on the ground that I was planning to leave behind. A ukulele I can hardly play, gathering dust in a corner. My pile of quotes. I try to imagine what this sum of stuff conveys to Ava at first glance, someone who is back from the dead, a blank-slate girl. The very question of who she is seems to have stirred an equal and opposite reactionary question in me. Who am I?

33

AVA GOES TO her first lineup. It's what you've seen on TV, but like most of life, more boring, more waiting, and more paperwork. She doesn't recognize any of the dudes and apologizes profusely. The police tell us to keep up hope, that the investigation's only just begun.

Ava and I drive up to Tilden Park afterward and go for a walk. Tilden's enormous, lush, full of trees and rich-stinking soil, and no one will find us here. She said she wanted to "see some nature," and this is about as naturey as it gets here. We walk a path around an emerald lake, the breeze hissing in the reeds, and we don't say much for a long time. Every once in a while, Ava will stop for something—a duck, a dragonfly, an oak shimmying its leaves—and she'll sigh, or say, "It's so beautiful," in a voice like it hurts good. A couple times she stops and closes her eyes and smiles in a blissful pause that I'm so lucky to witness. I see the possibility of her peace out here in the middle of the green.

I think of Portland once more, a paper boat in a brook, and let it float away. I'll defer enrollment. I'll cancel my flight.

Once we've looped the little lake once, Ava asks me if I'm okay. Which seems backward. But I look at her and answer.

"Of course," I say. "Are you?"

"It's so pretty here," she says. "Like a commercial."

"Yeah."

"You seem sad though . . . hope it's not my fault."

I smile at her. "No way."

"You should go to college like you were planning," Ava says. "College is, like, a big thing."

"I know."

We stop and sit on a bench.

"But . . . this is a much bigger thing," I tell her.

A middle-aged white woman in a long hippie skirt leans against the railing of the lake about twenty feet away from us and looks back at us more than once. I try to ignore her, focusing on the birds, who don't care who we are and never watch the news.

"I'm feeling really mixed up, too," Ava says. "Like . . . nothing in my head is making sense."

"It'll take time."

"Yeah. Shelly said to focus on what comes next. I'm making a list of what I want to do with my life . . . but . . . I don't know. Something about all this feels wrong."

"What do you mean?"

"It just doesn't make sense," she says again. "I'm . . ."

Ava's getting upset again, breathing shallow. The anvil on my own chest gets heavier.

"Hey," I say. "It's okay."

"Ava, everybody keeps calling me Ava," she says. "It's hard to get used to, it feels weird, all of this feels weird, and I think maybe—"

Ava stops talking because we both realize the lady in the hippie skirt is approaching us with caution, standing closer now with a wide-eyed expression, like she knows she's caught a glimpse of the rare North American Ava Rivers in the wild.

"Excuse me for interrupting," the woman says.

Neither Ava nor I respond. We just exchange a worried look. A look like, Really? Out here in the goddamned urban wilderness where there is one person, and even *she* won't leave us alone?

"Hi," the woman tries again, coming closer. "I—I'm sorry, I just— You're Ava Rivers, right?"

Ava nods once.

"I just . . ." The woman inches her sandals closer. She's got so many creases and lines on her face from a life of too much sun and/or emotion. Her voice shakes and she's clearly nervous. "You are so brave."

"Thanks," Ava says.

"I mean—I'm a survivor," the woman says. "I was raped by a friend of the family from the age of ten to fourteen. I never told anyone for years and years. I was so afraid and ashamed."

To me, a girl who's never been a victim of such horror, it's a marvel a woman can offer such a story to two strangers, and do so with dry eyes.

Ava's listening now, her sweatshirt-covered hand over her mouth.

"I'm sorry to tell you all this, I . . . I just followed your story on the news and I couldn't believe . . . I couldn't believe what you went through. I can't imagine what you lived through, Ava."

Ava, she says, like she knows her. It must be strange to be known so intimately by strangers. To have your darkest hours and years exposed for all to see. Sure, she hasn't given interviews or anything, but everyone knows what being locked up in a man's attic for years means.

"It made me feel less alone," the woman goes on. "I—I felt like, wow, what an inspiring person you are. You are the definition of a survivor. Your story really touched me and made me feel like . . . it made me feel hope. Not just for myself, but for everybody who goes through what we went through."

The woman's emotion shines in her brown eyes, and a part of me feels protective of my sister, like, Okay, lady, I'm sorry that happened to you but keep your sob story to yourself and leave Ava alone. My whole body tenses up. I'm so afraid this will upset Ava.

But Ava nods, shiny-eyed, and doesn't seem bothered by the woman's confession.

"I'll leave you two alone," the woman says. "Didn't mean to intrude. I'm sure you need your privacy. But bless you, you are an amazing, unbreakable spirit. I hope they find and punish whoever did this to you."

The woman does a little namaste bow and walks away, looking over her shoulder a couple times as if to make sure we're really real.

"I'm sorry," I tell Ava.

Ava cries into her sweatshirt hands quietly. She removes them. Her eyes are pink and wet and it's true, they really do sparkle.

"Wow" is all she says. "I can't believe . . . I don't know."

"What?" I ask.

"Hearing that, it makes all this worth it." She wipes her eyes with her sleeve. "Like, my story touches other people—I never thought about it that way. What if I'm here for a reason? What if all this is, like . . . like, I can help other people who've gone through hell the way I have?"

"That would be amazing," I say.

It would be amazing if there were a reason for all this. A reason for her misfortune, a reason for her captivity and abuse, a reason for her return. I'm skeptical at first as we steep in the contemplative silence. But then I remember reasons are human inventions.

As we walk back toward the parking lot, Ava smiles at her shoes. And I don't know why or how, but whatever happened back there with that woman, it seems to have brightened Ava.

34

IT'S BEEN GLORIOUS, the homecoming, but where the hell is Elliott? There's no way he hasn't heard the news, and I can't imagine any scenario where he wouldn't immediately come to see Ava. We're getting worried. I consider driving down to Los Banos to find him, but where would I even go? I have no address, no workplace, no full names of friends.

Finally, Ozzie tells us Elliott got ahold of him—I guess Ozzie's number is easy to find since he's a PI, and a PI is what Elliott needs right now. My brother is stuck in Tijuana after losing his passport. Ozzie's pulling some strings to get one expedited so he can come home. Elliott calls my phone and talks to Ava for the first time. I can't hear what he's saying, just his loud, crazy voice and Ava giggling as she paces the hall. Her giggling is infectious. Even though I have no idea what they're laughing about, I catch myself joining her from a room away.

Mom sends Ozzie a gift certificate for a steak dinner and a live rare orchid for his trouble.

35

THE VISITORS. JESUS basket-giving Christ, the visitors. Our kindergarten teacher. Every neighbor within a one-mile radius. Family friends who once hiked through hillsides with flashlights in searches for Ava, but who long ago dropped off the radar. Retired cops who worked on the case. Random church people from churches we never went to. The mayor of Berkeley and his partner. A lady running for Congress who has done favors for Mom. Schoolmates who never deigned to say hello to me in high school now stop by asking, "How are you *doing*?" and looking in my eyes like they *care*.

And then there's Max.

I answer the door one morning and Max is standing there, hands pulling on his peacock-blue jacket pockets, hip jutted out to the side. He dyed his hair and it's now an amazing red-brown Afro and he's trying to grow some kind of goatee that's not really working out for him. But he's still got it going on. Those eyes and lashes are the kind you could get lost in for a while. You could probably get lost in those plump lips, too.

"Hey," I say.

"Yo," he says. "How you doing, Vera?"

"Living the dream. You?"

"I'm kosher. Your pops said I could come by. I tried to text you, but . . ."

"I literally have not turned on my phone in days, I'm sorry."

He doesn't look at my eyes. He seems to be looking at my hair, which I blame on the fact that I cut my bangs myself last night.

"Well . . . come inside," I say after a moment.

I let him inside and he stands in the doorway in awe of the house, seeming to drink in every detail with his gaze. "I couldn't *believe* when I saw the news."

"Yeah, it's a freaking fairy tale."

"Is she . . . here?"

"Upstairs."

"Do they know anything? Like, have they caught the guy?" he asks in a low voice.

"No. But there's a manhunt going on. She's working with a forensic artist again later today, and when they get a better picture then it's going on the FBI's Most Wanted list."

"*Mental.*"

"Yeah."

"I wanted to bring something," he says. "But I was like, what do I *bring*?"

I gesture toward the corner of the room, where a mass of flowers in vases wither next to random stuffed animals, balloons, and gift baskets.

"Rrright," he says.

"You know what would be nice?" I say. "Food. Like, bring her a healthy meal. We're not going out that much because of the news crews."

"There was a van outside right now."

"They're always outside."

"I was at CVS and I saw Ava on the cover of a tabloid rag," he says.

"It's disgusting, actually. I hope it ends soon."

"I can bring a meal," he says.

He runs a hand along the piano and blows the dust off his finger. Taking a seat at the bench, his fingers run along the keys and he starts playing a perfect, moody jazz song that makes me want to melt.

"What is that?" I ask.

"I don't know, just making it up. I haven't played a real piano in forever."

Like I said, he's a prodigy.

"I've been cooking a lot for my mom," he says, stopping his song and standing up again. "She's . . . infirm right now. So yeah. I can, like, double up on something and skate it over."

"That'd be really sweet," I say.

When I utter the word "sweet," we finally make eye contact. His are bright brown and quivering with something—fear, nerves, emotion, I don't know. I'm about to tell him I'll go get Ava, but he asks me, "You still going to school?"

"Oh—not anymore," I say. "I submitted a request to defer. I might have to reapply again."

He nods. "I did the same."

"Really? Why?"

"My mom's . . . infirm, like I said. So yeah, I got into NYU but I had to back out last month."

I had no idea. He didn't mention this on our Indian Rock mini adventure. NYU. So fancy. Of course. This boy deserves Manhattan glitz.

"Bummer," I say. "I hope your mom's okay."

"Yeah, she'll keep existing."

He says it so robotically I can't tell if there's bitterness. I want to pick his brain and ask him more. There's something comforting about someone else who, after graduating in June, is going to be sticking around town because destiny interfered.

"She is *here*, right?" Max asks.

I don't know what I was thinking—that he was here for me. Foolish girl. Get it together.

"Yeah, sorry, she's upstairs. I'll go check if she's up for a visit right now. Don't be offended if she isn't. It's just been so hectic."

"I get it."

Upstairs, I knock on Ava's door. She answers. Her room is a sea of open cardboard boxes and bubble wrap tsunamis. There's a shiny new computer on the quilted bed and she's holding a shiny new phone.

"Look," she says excitedly. "Mommy bought it for me!"

"I can show you how to use that later," I say.

"I'm figuring it out," she says. "I took a picture."

She shows me a blurry selfie. I'm impressed. It took me like an hour to figure out how to take selfies on my first phone—not that I take many.

"I always wanted a phone," she says.

The infantile excitement is too cute. I mean, this is *elation*. Over a phone. A thing I let fall off counters and run out of batteries and curse for freezing up during Scrabble games. But to Ava, it's a jewel.

"Well done!" I check myself, reminding myself she's not actually six years old. "Max is here."

"Oh. Okay." She puts her phone on the bed and sits on the edge. "He was my friend."

She's saying it like she's telling herself a story.

"Your best friend," I remind her. "We showed you the pictures."

She nods.

"You don't remember, do you?"

"No, I do." She bites a nail. "Just not a lot. I mean, it was a while ago."

"There won't be a test," I tease her.

"Ha. Thanks, Veer."

We've apparently moved into nickname territory. Chalk up another victory.

"So you're up for it?" I double-check.

"Yeah, sure."

We smile. She follows me out of her room.

Max stares at Ava as she trails behind me on the staircase like she's Venus descending from Mount Olympus rather than a scared-faced girl who hasn't brushed her teeth or hair.

"Hey," he says, eyes lit up.

At the bottom of the stairs, he gets close to her. I can tell his instinct is to hug her, but then he checks himself and steps back, shoves his hands in his pockets.

"Hi," she says.

"Ava." He shakes his head. "Damn. This is just . . ."

"Hi, Max," she says.

They laugh for a second, tears flashing, shiny threats.

"Been a minute," she says. "Right?"

"Oh, man . . . you dazzle," Max starts. "I mean, it's just, you know, blowing me away to see you at *all*, to see you at *all* is just, like . . ."

His tongue will never find what he's looking for. To my amazement, there are some things words just can't do.

Instead of gawking at their intimate moment, I excuse myself—begrudgingly, I'll admit—and slip into the kitchen. I knock on the basement door.

"Come in," Dad sings.

Down, down I go.

"Hey," I say.

Dad's in the corner, at his desk on a rolling chair squinting at the computer. I can tell from here it's Ava's website.

"Whatcha doing?" I ask.

"Just going through the comments again," he says. "I've been attacked by spambots lately, gotta keep on it."

"How's Serge?"

"Serge?" he asks, turning around.

"Your *Other Life* guy."

"*Ohhh*," he says, making the word all long, like he's completely forgotten.

"Have you been neglecting your little computer man?"

"I've been kind of busy, Vera."

I know what he means. These long, lazy family days spent hiding from the cameras and well-coiffed people with mics feel busy somehow.

"Max is here," I say.

"Max Spangler!" Dad says. "That kid still play music?"

"'That kid' is seven feet tall and has a goatee now."

"She remember him?" Dad asks in a low voice.

"Seems like it," I tell him.

"Memory is such an odd thing," Dad says. "To remember Max and us and Elliott, but have entire days where she says she can't remember anything about That Monster."

"Well, like Ozzie told Mom, it's probably more that she doesn't *want* to remember him."

"I know," he says with bitterness.

The remembering and the not-remembering have both been—behind closed doors, away from Ava-ears, of course—points of contention between us and the police. The feds and the police want answers. Ozzie wants constant contact, grilling her with graphic questions. We want Ava to feel okay. It's hard because we want That Monster, as his household name has become, behind bars paying for what he did. But at the same time, the more anyone presses Ava for info, the more upset she gets. So it's a tricky balance.

Yesterday the alarm company came by and installed their most expensive system around our rickety Victorian. Cameras, automatic floodlights, wailing alarms. I have to say I slept better last night knowing. The pugs aren't exactly comforting protection against wandering monsters or sleazy paparazzi.

When Max takes off, he and Ava shake hands like business partners and he shoots me a bright smile on his way out the door. After the door thuds shut, Ava and I exchange a wild-eyed look. I can't describe what we're saying with words but it's like we shared some-thing warm—something from the past, future, and other world outside these walls and this tragedy that has become a news story confining us here. A boy. A visit from a boy.

36

AVA IS GOING to appear on the *Flora Daly Show*.

If you haven't heard of the *Flora Daly Show*, you've clearly been living beneath a stone for the past decade. Flora Daly has her own clothing line, magazine, charity, and book club. Flora Daly is a brown woman with layered hair who is timelessly, almost eerily unaged, a compassionate do-gooder with a talk show on channel 3 every afternoon.

Why Flora Daly? Why not any of the other ten thousand TV and radio shows—three-letter acronyms that all run together after a while, CBSNPRNBCCNN—that have approached Ava? Why not the dozens of classy glossies that solicited interviews? Ava didn't want to talk to the press, and then suddenly a few days ago she told our lawyer she wouldn't mind a daytime TV chat with Flora Daly.

"I used to pretend Flora Daly was my friend," Ava tells us over dinner. "I know it's weird. I've always wanted to talk to her about the things that have happened to me. She's, like, a hero."

We get it. She's a frigging screen queen.

"Also," Ava says.

Tonight, for the first time since she came home, she's eating salad. Granted, it's slathered in ranch dressing, but I've grown concerned about her appetite. Pop Tarts and Cup Noodles and other Kmart food. I mean, this is Berkeley, the land of yoga and quinoa and kale. Also, holy hell: My mom—queen of to-go food and restaurant delivery apps—made a salad!

"Also," Dad repeats.

"I want to help people," Ava says. "I've been thinking about it, ever since that lady came up to me and Vera at the park and got all confessional about what happened to her."

We exchange a look. Mom and Dad watch on curiously, clearly unfamiliar with this story.

"I want to go on TV so other girls—girls who are locked up and abused and stuff—they can see that there's hope. Or maybe they're like me and they didn't even really understand it was wrong. 'Cause I was manipulated."

That's a word I've noticed coming up since she started attending therapy—"manipulated." "Sexual assault" are another two. And "consent." And "survivor." She's beginning to understand parts of her own story and all the vocabulary that comes with it.

"Like, I want girls to know it's wrong if men use their power to hurt them," Ava continues, picking out the tomatoes from her salad and pushing everything else to the side. I smile. Some things are the same. When we were kids she used to eat tomatoes whole like apples. "It's not right to be locked up like that, no matter how nice they are to you sometimes or what they tell you about protecting you or whatever. Everyone deserves to be free."

What she says is so plain and yet so passionate—it would be a platitude if she hadn't lived through its opposite. Mom, Dad, and I stop eating and watch her in amazement as she eats her tomatoes.

Our hearts are spilling-over full or our hearts are breaking. I can't tell which. Feels the same.

"Right on, baby girl," Dad says.

Ava stiffens; her color goes ghostly. She puts her fork down and her lip trembles. "Please, don't ever. Don't."

Dad's stunned face is a sight I won't soon forget.

"Ava," Mom says. "Don't *what*, honey?"

"*He* called me that," Ava says, lip quivering.

The room goes so still. I don't think I've ever truly known silence until now. This is bunker silent, deep-space silent. This is end-of-the-world silent.

Ava puts her head in her hands and begins to cry, and when I try to touch her shoulder and say "hey," she shrinks away. "Lemme work through it, okay?"

We sit, our hands folded on our napkin-covered laps as she sniffles into her hands. I am throbbing. I exchange shiny, frozen gazes with my parents as we blink and wait through the excruciating helplessness of this inescapable moment.

The façade of recovery, of healing is so delicate.

Each joy, each horror so fleeting.

37

THERE'S THIS MOMENT every morning when I wake up and upon my first breath I get this sick nail in my stomach that digs in, like maybe it's all been a dream and I'm waking up to the way things were before, there is no Ava again anymore, and then the sweet release as the pain untwists and lifts and I breathe because it wasn't a dream, no, it's real, over and over and over again it's real it's real it's real.

38

THE FIRST DAY I take Ava downtown, we BART together. I expect her to be terrified of the subway and its loud, weird people, like the guy yelling Bible verses and the seated woman reading calmly with a taxidermy squirrel on her lap. But Ava watches it all with wild, wide eyes and doesn't flinch. When we reach the street level, she just says, "Interesting."

We're supposed to go shopping to get her some clothes, something "fresh" for *Flora Daly*. But before we do she goes to therapy—my first time taking her—and I wait for her in an office with a tiny fountain that requires me to get up and pee three times. When she gets out, I expect her to be teary-eyed, but she just gives me a small smile and tells me she's hungry. You'd never look at her and think *trauma queen*.

Ava hesitates as we pass street kids with cardboard signs and cute puppies. She pulls me aside, near a planter.

"Maybe we should help them," she says.

"They just want money."

"Maybe we should give them some," she whispers.

One of them has a sign that says SPARE A NUG?

"I think they'll be okay," I tell her. "They're just crusty kids."

I've learned this blank stare she gives me means, I don't understand you but I'm too timid to say it.

"Travelers," I say.

"But they're homeless," she says. "We have a couch, maybe—"

"Um, Ave, Mom is not going to go for that plan."

The look on her face as she tries to comprehend this is classic.

"It's okay," I tell her. "You can't get sad about it."

I pull her to the crosswalk, amazed that she has space in her
heart for pity for strangers who are spare changing for weed after
all she's been through.

"They have dogs," she says. "How do they feed their dogs?"

"Their dogs are fine," I say.

But she keeps turning to look back at them, the white kids with
Mohawks and battered cardboard signs and spikes on their clothing.
The kind of people I walk by without a stitch of sadness on a regular
basis and rarely even spare a glance at. Am I unkind?

"How come so many dudes in Berkeley look like wizards?" Ava
asks me at a streetlight. A man who does look particularly wizard-
like is handing out flyers in front of a store with copper goddess
statues and sarongs in the window.

"I am a wizard! Tax the one percent," he tells us.

"I've never noticed, but you're right, there are a lot of wizardy
dudes," I agree as I ignore him and keep walking.

We eat pizza and stare through a breath-cloudy window. The
punk moms and their strollered babes, the woman in the jacket
too large for her who is standing on the bench pontificating to no
one in particular about China and Tibet. I see it all like it's new,

too—I've become so accustomed to Berkeley's weirdness. But today I'm like, what would this all look like to someone locked away from the world for twelve years?

We stand in line at a coffee shop and I watch Ava watch everything as I wonder when the police are ever going to catch That Monster and what her days were like in there exactly and what she talked about in therapy, knowing it's not okay for me to ask any of these things and I have to pretend everything is peachy. When I think about it too much I get a lump in my throat and I have to swallow and remind myself I don't know. I don't know the whole story. I just know a few dust-sized clues.

The blankness, the I-don't-knowness, is somehow both a barb and a blanket of comfort these days.

"Can I help you?"

"Two mochas," I tell a barista with a ring in her septum.

"With whip?"

I look at Ava, who shrugs.

"Sure," I tell the barista.

I put cinnamon in my mocha, so Ava puts cinnamon in hers. Her copying my every move is endearing as hell. She sips it and *mmm*s. I ask if she's ever had a mocha and she says nah. As we walk down the street sipping our drinks I rack my brain—was it okay to ask that? Too much? Was I prying by wanting to know about her history concerning sugary caffeinated beverages? I haven't seen her smile today. I forget what her teeth look like. She probably hates me.

We wander into a vintage clothing store and Ava's expression is like a four-year-old at Disneyland. She seems confused about what would or wouldn't look good on her and wants to know my opinion about everything she sees.

"Is this cute?" she asks, pointing to an off-shouldered dress with a frilly skirt.

"It is cute," I say. "You wear a small?"

"Yeah, I mean, I think so."

"Weird that I don't even know what size you are."

"What are you?"

"A medium."

"Wow," she says, like this is impressive.

I smile. "Try it on."

"Would you wear it?" she asks.

"No," I say. "It would make me look like I'm having my quinceañera."

That trademark blank stare. Ava must have forgotten the pictures of Mom at her quinceañera plastered all over our grandma's house. I didn't have a quinceañera. Mom thinks they're sexist now. Plus it would have embarrassed the crap out of me being the center of all that attention. But we used to love looking at the photos of Mom in that giant pink dress when we were kids.

"Birthday party for a fifteen-year-old girl," I say. "It's a Mexican thing."

"Are we Mexican?" she asks, confused.

"Among other things," I say.

A woman holding a pair of leopard-print flats eavesdrops on our odd conversation. Trying not to stare. I have to wonder if she recognizes us from the news. They've left us alone more this past week, but still.

"Mom's half Mexican and half Persian," I say, turning around so the lady can't gape at us. "So we're a quarter."

"I'm a quarter Mexican?" Ava asks in disbelief. "And Persian? I didn't even know there *was* a Persia anymore."

"It's Iran now."

"So, like, our grandparents live in *Iran*?"

"No, our grandpa immigrated. But he died before we were born. RIP."

"What else are we?"

It is such an odd question. It shocks me that she's forgotten all of this about us, about our family, but I know it shouldn't. It's been so long since she was part of us.

"You know, European mutt on Dad's side," I say.

She puts the dress back on the rack, brow furrowed as she thinks about her ethnic background. Our family didn't talk about this stuff much when we were kids. It just was.

"I'm a quarter Mexican," she repeats. "And a quarter Persian."

Yes, we are of mixed race. People have actually asked me "what" I am, as if I'm a different species. It doesn't happen that often, but when it does, it's super annoying. But lucky you, Ava, you got Dad's blond hair, and Mom's olive complexion just looks California-girl on you.

"You don't remember Nana Maria?" I ask.

My mom's mom. She lived in New Mexico and smoked long cigarettes, taught us to make tortillas, was a painter with a house full of color and artwork, used to dance around the kitchen when we were tiny, and had the most insanely decorated house at Christmas.

"I do remember a little bit. She cooked for us, right?"

"Yeah! The tortillas," I say.

"They were gooood," Ava says with a smile, then wanders off to a stack of T-shirts.

She buys a shirt with printed bows on it and some leggings with Mom's credit card. She's all tentative about it even though it's barely twenty bucks. I'm surprised by the quirky things that catch her eye. What is she going to be like, all free to choose?

At a bookstore across the street, I'm stunned again to realize my sister can barely read. I don't know what's stranger—that she can at all, or to see a full-grown girl-woman barely able to sound out simple words. I pull her to the children's section and pick up a book we read as kids—*Ramona Quimby, Age 8*—and she looks at it and says, "Ramen?"

"You don't remember this book?" I ask. "It was our favorite. *Ramona Quimby, Age 8*."

"Maybe," she says vaguely. She touches the cartoon cover. "It's about a girl named Ramona?"

"Yeah. And her sis, Beezus."

"Beezus Christ," she says in a funny voice.

I snort. I actually snort. The more she opens up, the more it's obvious some things don't change. Ava is a goofball.

"That's nice you bought it for me," she tells me as we go outside and step into the sunshine.

"Yeah, thank Mom. It's her credit card." I hand her the Ramona book I just bought for her. "We'll practice reading together."

"I'm supposed to meet with a tutor. That's one of the things on my list—get a GED."

Per Shelly, Ava's been working on a list of things she wants to do with her life. She keeps the crinkled piece of lined notebook paper with her in her pocket at all times. I've caught glimpses of it. It's penned with childish scrawl and says things like "LERN 2 COOK," "HELP PEPLE," and "GO TO FRANTS."

"Totally doable," I say.

"I mean, I'll never be smart like you." She hugs the book to her chest. "I'll probably never go to college. I don't know. I used to want to go to Chablis Online Academy."

What? Oh, right. Scammy for-profit school. Commercials.

"You can do anything you want," I tell her.

"I want to use my powers for good," she says, looking at her shoes, which are actually Mom's running shoes. They're too big for her.

Her powers. Like she's magic. Which she kind of is. Put her in a room and let people know she's Ava Rivers and listen to it get bone-quiet. She casts a spell.

"Ava, you will. You'll go on *Flora Daly*. Tell your story. Inspire other girls. And the more you work with the police, the more chance we have of finding Jonathan and making sure he never hurts anyone again."

She doesn't answer me for a second. She doesn't move. Maybe I made a mistake uttering his name.

"I don't think he'll do that to anyone else," she says so quietly it's as if she's talking to the sidewalk. "I don't want to talk about him anymore today."

A little coal lights up in my chest. "Sorry."

She flips through the book for a moment. Then a wave seems to pass over her. She straightens up.

"But you were right," Ava says. "Like—I can be anything now."

"*Exactly.*"

"Shelly said today that now's all about healing, love, fun, family."

"It is."

"No need to stress. Gotta get with the self-love."

"Where'd you learn to be so wise?"

A guy with no shirt on and a tangled beard comes over to us and asks for change. I turn to ignore him. Ava says, "You hungry, dude? Let me buy you a sandwich or something."

"Ava." I pull Ava's arm and we walk up the street and I can't help laughing. "You can't just say that to him."

"What? Why?"

"I mean . . ."

"He looked all skinny and hungry," she says. "We have a credit card. I don't get it."

Her chin's in the air, and I'm in complete awe of her.

"Ava," I say, looking back at him as he dances barefoot at the bus stop. "When you live in the city, you mostly keep to yourself."

"I spent years doing that," she says.

Her eyes are clear, sober, ringed especially blue around the edges and bleeding muddier in the middles. I can't remember her eyes from when we were children, just that they were blue.

"Being afraid of people," she goes on. "Thinking the world was dangerous and full of thugs and people getting shot left and right. I didn't even try to find out for myself for so long—I believed all the things he said."

Gulp. This conversation seems too deep for daylight, for a smoothie storefront surrounded by college students and business-men shouting into cell phones.

"Now I want to find out for myself," she tells me. "I believe you. But I wanna live and make my own mistakes. You know, most people aren't dangerous. You know that? They've done the math. Way more people are good and safe."

Why is she telling me this and not the other way around?

Tell me, how is she the wiser one?

"Roger that," I say. "Now let's go buy you some shoes."

The sneakers she picks out are in the children's section. I have to go up to the counter to the apathetic woman texting on her phone and ask if they make glittery Converse in a woman's size 7.

"I don't know," the woman says without looking up. "They'd be on the wall if we had 'em."

"Are you, like, so bored of shoes at this point?" Ava asks.

The woman looks up from her phone for a startled second. I'm ready to apologize for Ava's childlike question when the woman shrugs and focuses on her phone again.

"Pretty much," she admits.

Very helpful. We scan the wall but no luck. Ava's sad about it. I tell her we'll make her some with glitter and a pair of white Cons.

"Is it a stupid idea?" she asks me.

"Nah, it's cute," I assure her.

We stop by the drugstore for glitter. I buy her candy but remind her we need to eat dinner with the fam in an hour. I feel like I'm babysitting. Or explaining Berkeley to an alien for the first time. Why that man from Greenpeace is yelling at us with such eager desperation. Who those old ladies dressed in pink are and why they are so pissed about the Middle East. Why there are so many young Asian people with backpacks. And the fact that to get to San

Francisco—I have to explain to her, no one who is actually local calls it "Frisco"—you have to ride underneath the Bay in a giant tube.

"No *way*."

We descend the escalator together. I pull her to the right side.

"People passing go on the left," I tell her. "If you're standing still you stay right."

I let go of her bony shoulder and bask in the fading sting her touch left on my hand. My heartbeat yammers in my chest, *She's real, she's alive, she's real.* An echoing saxophone gets louder, louder, as we enter the yellow light of the bustling BART station. A guy in sunglasses is blowing into the sax at the bottom of the escalator to an eerie, oozy electronic song coming out of a boom box. Ava stops to watch him, dumbfounded, as we reach the floor. I steer her to the ticket machine and buy us tickets and lead the way through the turnstile, where the crowd thickens with people coming up— students with painted faces, middle-aged folks in Cal sweatshirts. We're moving against the crowd of football fans. I get bumped and hang on to my purse and try to ignore the yelling. At the bottom of the stairs, Ava's nowhere to be seen.

I press myself against the slick brick wall, peering past the marquee blinking news that a six-car train is coming in one minute. No reason to panic. My sister is flesh and blood and isn't going to disappear in a heartbeat. She can't get lost the way she *was* lost. I scan the passing faces for a burst of crimped-curled dirty blond and a stricken dust-blue gaze. But no. Football fans. College kids ogling smartphones. Patient old ladies reading paperback books. Ava is nowhere.

Screaming erupts toward the front of the train coming to a stop on the platform. I still don't see Ava. I hurry toward the noise. No doors are opening on the train, and the yellow-lit people inside bang on the window.

A shrill voice cuts through the commotion. "Someone got hit!"

Everyone swarms, and I get swept up in it, sucked toward the tragedy. I'm peeling my eyes left, right, craning my neck to look behind me and above, at the stairs I came down. My blood pressure rises with each step. Where is Ava?

As we get closer to the front of the stuck train, elbows poking me, the hive-buzz of the commotion, the smell of perfume and shampoo and BO all braided together into one indistinguishable aroma begins to wash over me in this sick way and my belly pitches. Panic keeps rising—where the hell is Ava? My ears ring, cold sweat dots my palms.

"A girl jumped in front of a train!" someone yells.

People cry and wail. A man shouts for everyone to stay back.

"A girl jumped in front of a train," a woman reports to those of us behind her.

My mouth dries and knees buckle. *Where is Ava?* Then the horrible possibilities firework in my brain—she's gone again. In less time than it takes to say, *Vera, keep it together*, I push through the crowd in front of me, or try, anyway—it's thick with arms and legs and no one will let me though. I turn around to go backward, back up the stairs where I came from, knocking into people and their purses and skateboards as I make it upstairs, determined to enter the scene from another staircase so I can see who the girl was.

I hold on to the railing, not knowing what to do. Do I call some-one? Do I scream her name? Do I go tell the attendant it could be my sister who fell in front of the train? The saxophone echoes faintly over the electronic music.

"It was a dummy," someone yells.

The crowd hushes with the information, then buzzes with it.

"It was a mannequin," a guy says. "Some punk kid tossed it onto the tracks."

BART cops come to investigate. The crowd disperses.

Sniffing, I glance over the railing near the ticket machines and the escalator and that's when I see Ava, watching the man with sun-glasses blow into the saxophone, boom box at his shiny mismatched shoes. A woman with short hair and bright lipstick stands next to Ava, talking.

"Ava!" I choke.

The relief is a symphony. I sprint through the wide manual turn-stile for bicycles and nearly collide with someone on an electric scooter and several high-looking fortysomething men. When I get to Ava and her talkative companion, I hear the woman's words. *Most Wanted list . . . Amazing, inspiring story . . . Interview you for my blog?"*

"You scared the crap out of me," I say. "Don't ever wander off like that."

"This is my sister," Ava tells the girl.

"Hi. We're going now." I pull Ava's arm, and we walk away from the dumbfounded woman who was getting out her phone to, I don't know, exchange information probably.

"She was a survivor," Ava says.

"So? And that's weird, random people coming up to you and telling you their secrets."

"Why should it be a secret?" Ava asks. She pulls her arm out from my grasp. "Seriously, why shouldn't people just talk about it? Ever watched *Survivors* on TV? You know how many girls are molested or raped? It's not their fault, why do they have to be quiet about it?"

Okay, people are staring. I'm sorry I said anything. Ava is right. She shouldn't be ashamed. But I hate the feeling that strangers know my business—and if they own TVs, which of course they do, everyone here probably knows who we are.

"You don't," I say quietly. Then, louder: "You don't."

"Yeah."

My eyes heat up. I thought she fell in front of a train for a second, I really did.

"Are we still going to ride the subway?" she asks.

"No," I tell her. "We'll just take a Lyft."

I don't tell her I hate the way the man in the plaid shirt squints his eyes like he's trying to place us, or how the two college girls whisper and point. I know we're semifamous. I forgot it for a while, but when I look close enough, they were there all along. The hawkish strangers.

I pull her wrist, which fits easily between my thumb and forefinger. We step back onto the escalator. This time she leans right so people can pass.

"Didn't you buy tickets?" she asks, turning around.

My heartbeat is resuming its normal pace. The way the sun hits her hair, she should be in a painting. Who cares about the mannequin?

"It doesn't matter anymore," I say. "Let's go to the Halloween store."

We buy wigs and weird glasses because why not. We wear costumes while we wait for our Lyft. Ava grins at me, her wig long and ginger-colored, generic nerd glasses. I see myself in her reflection—shoulder-length blond with cat-eye frames. Sisters. Strangers. We burst into laughter together until we have to wipe tears from our eye corners. I want to treasure this moment. And yet I can't help noticing the silver tooth in the back of her mouth when she laughs, and wonder when she got it, what its story was, who paid for it. But I can't ask. I have to bite my words and bide my time.

39

WE FORGET THE horror until a moment we can't. Like the time Mom brings home In-N-Out and the sight of the branded bag sends Ava into a weird headshaking tizzy. "No," she says. "I hate that stuff, I never want to see it again." She gets up from the table and goes into the bathroom, where she audibly gags. (I hear Mom calling Ozzie after Ava retreats upstairs, whispering, "Look into In-N-Out locations, Oz, this could be big.") Or the time she and I are on the couch together and she flips the channel and the Muppets are on and she gets flustered and teary out of nowhere, saying, "This was his favorite and he could do the voices . . ." And then that's it, nothing else. Just me assuring her, "It's okay, it's okay," the only thing I know how to say when in that moment nothing's okay, nothing's okay.

Mom, Dad, and I try to nod and understand and be levelheaded but it's as if the moment the craziness subsides and we slip into routine, into the blissful everyday nothingness of togetherness, some little shard of hurt pierces it out of nowhere and I'm sure, a month after she's been home now, that nothing will ever be anything but an imitation of normal.

40

TO BUST OUT of the anxious sadness that Ava seems to be in, one night we take a walk around the neighborhood and end up in a dark park. I stand in the sand, hands shoved in my pockets, watching as Ava goes down the slide with a grin on her face. I don't let my sadness show—the sadness of seeing a grown girl's joy at a playground because she wasn't allowed to be a true child until now. I smile. I focus on the moon, how bright it is, how lovely Ava looks as she throws her head back and laughs.

"Ava! Vera!" someone sings through the chain-link.

I'd know that singsongy voice anywhere. It's Max. He grins under a streetlamp on the other side of the fence, guitar strapped to his back, clutching a bottle of champagne. I can't hide my shock.

"That was fast!" Ava yells. She turns to me, deadpan. "I invited him. Cool?"

"Cool," I say.

It is cool. It is cool in every way, shape, and form. I think the word "cool" so many times it becomes alien. I just didn't expect him here, interrupting our intimate sister moments. She texts him now and I don't.

Ava and Max drink most of the champagne. I crane my head to take in the blackness littered with cheap star-shrapnel. We sit under the jungle gym, inventing histories. Like what would Ava have been like, had she never been snatched.

"I'd've been smart," Ava says. "Mom and Dad would've sported bumper stickers: MY KID'S AN HONOR ROLL STUDENT."

"In other words, you'd've been a big old nerd," Max says as he plucks his guitar, the sound perfectly improvised and dreamy. "Like Vera," he adds, deadpan.

I show him how beautiful my middle finger is.

"Actually, calling me a nerd gives me too much credit," I say after a moment. "I was invisible."

"You weren't invisible."

What is that flicker in his eyes? I'm confused for a second, but then he looks away and hums some tune and plucks the strings.

"Then by high school I'd've become more, you know, *bad*. Fun," Ava continues. "Punk rock. I could hang with dorks, sure," she says, looking at me.

"Excuse me, I wasn't a dork," I say. "Max was a dork—always bringing his guitar to school trying to look 'artistic.'"

Max stops playing his guitar and winces like I just burned him.

He climbs up on the jungle gym and hangs upside down, somehow still managing to pull off a guitar solo. I watch Ava and Max play tag on the playground, laughing like monkeys. I can't help laughing, too.

Maybe joy is even more potent when you've known the depth of its opposite.

41

GOING BACK TO a job that you already said goodbye to is a serious lemon to suck. It's not Funmakerz' fault. It's not the kids with their sugar-fueled birthday hysteria, or the finicky helicopter parents, or even the Snow White dress that smashes my chest in pancakey ways and—look close—is as stained as a pizzeria tablecloth. It's me. It's traffic and how bored it makes me to drive the same, same, same ways, staring out at the bridges and the skeletal, alien cranes of Oakland as I inch across the freeway. In Portland, I was going to ride my bike everywhere. I was going to wear my raincoat and go on long walks in the woods. Obviously I did the right thing by staying, and Ava is everything. That's my purpose now—to be a sister. I can go to college and join the real world later. I can find another job. Miracles take priority.

Today's party is at Jack London Square, which is at the end of downtown Oakland where the asphalt meets the Bay. Lawns and bike paths and plotted palms and American flags whipping on poles. It's a one-year-old's birthday, and she has no clue it's her birthday or who Snow White is. There's a balloon twister here and a human in a blue dinosaur suit who snubs me when I try to say hello, as if he/she/it thinks blue dinosaurs are on some social level beyond that of imitation princesses. The "Wheels on the Bus" song plays way too many times on the portable stereo. But the cookies are divine.

I have this moment of clarity as I greet the little ones, some of them brave and dashing straight up to touch my skirt, others hesitant, holding on to their mothers' legs and peeping at me shyly. Party children. Right now they're so pure. They don't know hurt beyond skinned knees and not getting the things they want. Even their hair glitters like something special in the sun. And the love—the protective, watchful love of their parents—is their armor in the dark, mean world. For most, that will be enough. Most of the world are lucky ones. Now I'm like them.

After the party, I get in my car and check my phone. Mom texted the word *ELLIOTT!!* The phone drops to the floor, my foot hits the gas, and I burn a little rubber out of the parking garage and almost hit a tourist or two on the way out.

42

MY WHOLE FAMILY hasn't been in one room since I was six years old—since I was a squirt who played with Barbies and had gaps in her smile. And guess what? I missed it. By the time I get home, Mom has left for a fund-raiser and Ava and Dad are on the couch eating popcorn. They mute the crudely drawn cartoon show they're watching and relay the whole thing to me.

Break me in pieces. I *missed* it.

"Mom almost pepper sprayed him," Ava says, covering her mouth like she shouldn't be laughing.

"What?" I say.

"Well, he didn't ring the damn doorbell, he came in through the back and scared her," Dad says. "How he tripped the alarm system I still do not understand. And he looks like a yeti, I mean, he's hardly recognizable."

I sit in a velvet butt-worn armchair. "And?"

"And he was . . . good," Dad says.

The pause is all he needs to insert in order for me to extract the truth—it was hard to tell.

"He brought me this," Ava says.

She beams as she shows me a drugstore makeup kit and a throw pillow with a cat's face silk-screened on it.

"Um, okay," I say.

"No, I like it!" Ava says.

She smiles and hugs the pillow.

Dad shakes his head once, like *whatareyougonnado*.

"But . . . he's gone," I say.

I'm more popped balloon than girl.

"He had some rodeo thing to go to," Dad says.

"Huh?" I ask.

"He's gonna come back next Saturday," Ava says.

No he's not, I want to say. Elliott's Saturday is Scarlett O'Hara's tomorrow. But then again, everything's different now. Elliott might come around and visit now that Ava's alive. It would take a resurrection, wouldn't it?

"Did you remember him?" I ask.

"I mean, yeah, but he looks different now," Ava says.

"Did he hug you? Did he cry?" I ask.

Damn stupid tear ducts. I would like to get them surgically removed. But I am so sorry I missed him, that I missed Elliott and Ava's reunion, I missed the whole family together again.

I hate the feeling that I'm here, I stayed, Ava's alive, Ava's home, and somehow I'm still missing things.

43

I'M TRYING TO catch Ava up. Not just teach her how to use an iPhone, which until weeks ago was a magic she'd only seen on-screen, but fill her in on the secrets of culture and common knowledge that TV never spilled. Like politicians are all liars and most of the world isn't white or skinny. Like the amazing underground music that MTV never told her about. I try to teach her about Berkeley and the Bay Area and its particularities, which is hard, because my hometown shaped me into what I am and it's thus sweetly invisible to me. But we revisit places I've gone a billion times and they take on a new sheen as I watch Ava watching them through her eyes.

The downtown post office, which is occupied with tents and their occupants' hand-painted signs about not being for sale. Ava asks why and I realize I can't tell her. I've never even stopped to read the signs and figure it out, exactly.

Scuzzy, Nag Champa–stinking, record-store-dotted Telegraph Avenue, which dead ends randomly into the stunning university with all its lucky, bright-eyed, eager students. Ava asks me why I don't just go there. Well, it would take an hour to explain the eternal admissions process and the fact that my SATs probably wouldn't be good enough anyway. I tell her I want to take time off to be with family. And, oh yeah, I have to explain what a bong is to her on the way home as we pass the glimmering head shop windows.

San Francisco, with its techies and businessmen and tourists crowding cable cars and pissed-on sidewalks. "Why is that man sleeping in a cardboard box?" she almost screams, and even though I'm sure all of Market Street heard, everyone pretends they didn't, because that's how city life works, kid. And I have to pull her sleeve to get her to stop from leaning down and offering him money. Ava's big heart is a magnet pulling her every which way.

We plan to do touristy things as a fam. Alcatraz, Sausalito, Fisherman's Wharf—the kind of stuff we only do when someone's in town and wants to see it. On our first trip, a wind-whip-you walk on the Golden Gate Bridge, I don't know how to answer her question, "How do you build a bridge? Where do you start?"

"On both ends," Dad says.

Yes, Dad came. It should be blaring on a marquee, breaking news: DAD LEFT THE HOUSE. Dad put on a coat and looks like some surly mountain man or something with his unbrushed hair and unshaved face. I hardly recognize him outdoors, bundled up in clothes so forgotten they're new.

"You start on both ends and meet in the middle," he says.

Mom, I swear, hasn't put her phone down since she got here.

"Just one more picture," she says. "I want a good one to share online."

Ava and I stand next to each other, and she opens her mouth wide and does jazz hands.

"You goofball." Dad laughs.

There's this bittersweet tickle in me as I stand next to her, freezing so cold my teeth chatter even though the sun is high—the knowledge that we're making a memory. We're building something. Ava holds my hand and puts her head on my shoulder for the picture, and I vow never to forget this. It's so meaningful, I'm afraid. I'm afraid of things being this good, all together like this, twinned again, because pain and loss are somewhere below and you can't sit on the apex forever.

44

THE DOORBELL RINGS so much these days, even so many weeks after Ava's return, that I usually ignore it. It's never for me. Often, if I peek through the peephole, it's some stranger anyway who's probably just going to ask if they can write a blog post about us or whatever. I know every damn cop in the city by name. They probably have Ava's number memorized. But one Saturday after a kid's party in the nearby suburb of Pleasant Hill, which was incidentally neither pleasant nor hilly, I peek through the peephole and it's Max Spangler. He shaved. And he looks fresh. He's got a salad bowl in one hand and a skateboard in another.

"Hey," I say, opening the door.

"Um . . . hi?"

His eyes travel up and down and up again. At first, I get a sweet quiver like he's checking me out. It's been a minute since *that* happened. But then I look down and realize I'm dressed like a second-hand princess.

"Yeah, this is how I spend my Saturdays," I say.

"Decent," he says.

Not sure if that's a compliment or an insult or what.

"Ava's off at another lineup or something," I say.

"Oh hells yeah," he says. "You think they've caught the guy?"

"She's done so many at this point, we've stopped getting our hopes up every time."

"Logical." He hands me the salad bowl. "Brought you guys this."

It's greens and a bunch of stuff that looks like squirrel food. I swear there are acorns and pinecones in there.

"No lid?" I ask. "You skated all the way here with a salad bowl with no lid?"

"I maneuvered," he says.

"Sketch."

"I almost dropped it like fifty times," he admits, laughing. Then he stops abruptly and gets serious as a confession. "My mom actually made this salad."

"Thanks, Max's mom."

In the silence, my heartbeat's a thud. As if I have some reason to be nervous around a guy who peed his pants at my house once upon a time.

"How is your mom?" I ask.

"She's quality. She's good. You know."

Max points his brown stare full of feeling at our doormat that says GO AWAY. Which Dad ordered, of course, and Mom hates. She wanted something with poppies on it.

"'Cause you said once she was 'infirm,'" I say.

One part of me wants him to look at me, because it makes me warm and glowy. Another part is aware that I'm sweaty and wearing a not-so-clean Snow White dress.

"Oh yeah, she's still illin'. She's always illin'."

"What's she have?" I ask.

"It's complex. It'd take me, like, several eons to break it down."

"I have several eons if you want to come in," I say.

But I shouldn't have said that. I sounded desperate. I sounded pathetic. I'm gross and he's glorious. He would never.

"Yeah, I should—I should mosey," he says.

"I'll pass the salad along," I say, ignoring my loud disappointment. "Thanks for bringing it by."

"Sure, yeah, it was no thing. No thingy thing. I would like to explain sometime, I just—I got somewhere to be. We should hang again soon. You, me, and Ava."

"Yeah, that'd be fun." I nod and squeeze a smile. But I know it's just Ava he wants. Everyone everywhere seeks Ava. I'm just the bridge to the prize.

When Ava gets home, she takes one bite of the salad and spits it in a napkin. "Hell no," she says.

She gets up and makes popcorn and eats that for dinner instead, melting cheese on top of it in the microwave. Ava's dinners are semihorrific sometimes. And I was right, she was at another lineup.

"Any luck?" I ask.

"They're never going to catch him," she says.

Her expression goes dead and she turns on the TV—a commercial for face wash with a blissed-out chick splashing her cheeks with milk is on. If the remote were in my hand, I'd change the channel, but Ava always watches ads.

It's like a chill blew through the room. We're silent. The TV is loud. I don't ask any more questions.

45

AVA REDECORATES THE guest room, because it's not a guest room anymore—it's hers. Now it's hot pink with stenciled white unicorns running along the trim and glittery handprints Ava added randomly in the middle of it. Her new bed is a princess bed with a purple canopy. It looks like a child's bedroom. The pugs sleep with her in her new bed. She's crazy about dogs. She still wonders out loud about Madonna and talks about how she misses her and how she used to paint her toenails pink. Ava talks more about Madonna than That Monster. Mom tells me it's because it's a positive memory. Mom's all about positivity these days—KEEP IT POSITIVE! screams the permanent Post-it note on her steering wheel. It's hard though, in the middle of such uncertainty. "Positive" has more than one definition, you know.

46

WHO KNEW CRIME victims needed publicists? I've learned all sorts of fun facts since Ava came home. One of them is that apparently victims of complicated, high-profile cases need an entourage. Ava is a sick kind of star. Being a victim of an unsolved case is basically a full-time job with nonstop appointments. Publicist, lawyer, tutor, FBI agents, advocates, therapists, and of course the ubiquitous police officers and good old Ozzie, who stinks like the cologne section in a drugstore every time he steps his motorcycle boots into our foyer. Now we've got a new member of the entourage, this media specialist who was recommended by another specialist of some sort.

The media specialist is a woman with the world's brightest eyeshadow who is a total fifty-foot-fake-out for a twenty-year-old but who is, up close, my mom's age. Maybe it's the peroxide-pixie hairdo. In the living room, the media specialist coaches Ava on posture and eye contact and video cameras. Our day-trip luggage is in a neat pile. Dad and I stand off in the foyer cramming breakfast bars in our mouths. Dad's dressed in a suit jacket and he trimmed his hair himself and is it weird to say he looks handsome? Mom, pure *Martha Stewart Living* meets *Glamour*, takes notes on her phone as the media specialist explains about the better side of the face and how to talk to the camera.

Two months, almost, since Ava got home, and this is the first and only interview that she's doing. If it were me I'd have gone for NPR. You don't have to worry about pretty on radio. But Ava's doing *Flora Daly* and I'm a little afraid the ticking time bomb of fame is going to blow back in our faces after this one. All hope of fading into the proverbial wallpaper is smoke once Ava's visited with the superstar of daytime TV.

Thankfully, all I have to do is sit in the front row with Mom and Dad. I don't have to say a word. I'm basically an extra. But just in case, I did have to pick an outfit that would look good on camera. Gray button-up dress. Gulp.

We're accidental celebrities, us Riverses, living someone else's life. We ride in a shiny Lincoln Town Car with a uniformed driver. We have first-class tickets and are boarded first on the airplane. Ava and I sit next to each other in our own little row. She's glowing. Reflective as the moon; so am I. Since she came home, she's put on a few pounds and rosied up, and she's in a pink party dress that flares out in an explosive tutu with fishnets and her glittery Converse, her hair ever-wild. People stare at her everywhere we go. And it's not just because they recognize her from the TV pictures and the 'loids. She looks so much more alive than the paparazzi snapshots of her with her bandaged head or hiding her face while ducking into our house in sweats. She's an eyeball magnet. She puts a staring-problem spell on everyone around her.

"I got bad butterflies in my tummy right now," she says,

white-knuckling the cushy divider between us. "I've never been up in the sky before."

"You have," I say. "We flew to New Mexico to see Nana Maria when we were five."

"Nana Maria," she repeats.

I look across the aisle to see if Mom's ears perked up. I expect the usual flinch she gives when I mention her mother's name, who up and died within three years of Ava's disappearance and whose quick and mean exit absolutely devastated Mom at a time when she was already absolutely devastated. But Mom's got her headphones on and eyes closed already while Dad mutters words like "ridiculous" and "capitalism" as he flips through a SkyMall catalog.

"How'd she die?" Ava asks.

"Cancer."

"Oh no! Was it brain cancer, like Priscilla DuMont?"

"I have no idea who that is."

"She was on *An Extravagant Universe*."

"Ah," I say.

Daytime soap. Cheeseball central.

"It wasn't brain cancer," I say. "I forget what kind of cancer it was, to be honest. Mom doesn't really like talking about it."

I whisper the last part.

Ava drops her voice, too. "I'm sorry."

"No, it's okay. It's not you—Mom's not a fan of feelings."

Ava rests her head back and turns to look at Mom, who must be listening to some audio-meditation or something because she appears to be in some Buddha-like state as she smiles and closes her eyes.

"I'm glad she can be happy now," Ava says.

"Me too."

"And you're happy, too, right?"

I smile. "No, I'm totally miserable."

She squeezes my hand. A stewardess gives us a patronizing smile, like we're adorable kids, and I suspect she recognizes us.

I need to stop.

It shouldn't matter anymore what strangers think they know.

47

LA IS EXACTLY what I expected, sparkly city-sprawl screaming with billboards. Clogged freeways, smoggy palm-peppered horizons, and people who look as if they spent way too much cashola on faces. The studio is past a few kiosks and gates. It's a big, unmagical cement building. Inside, the set is cheerfully lit, the chairs lined up in rows and waiting for asses. I can tell Ava is in heaven, though, her eyes as bright and wide as studio lights before she's whisked away to "makeup and prep." Mom accompanies her, protectively, touching up her lipstick as they walk away down the hall toward the doors with the stars and the word GUESTS on them. Dad and I take our seats in the front row of the audience that says RESERVED. Several tech show employees come and introduce themselves to us as we sit here, raving about how totally honored they are to have Ava Rivers on the show and how *amazing* our story is and how they seriously broke *records* with requests for studio audience tickets and it's just so *awesome* and such a *miracle* and an *inspiration* to not just *America* but women *everywhere*.

I don't mean to be cynical, but you can see it in their eyes; this is their job, they say things like this, they eat family tragedies up like mimosas and pancakes. Blah dee blah. I am so proud of Ava and I'm sure she'll be magnificent, but I stare up at the blinding lights and beg the universe to please just let this pass quickly and don't make us any more famous. I exchange glances with the off cameras and plead, Please don't point yourself at me.

Some doors in the back open, a crew member directs people to their rows, and crowds of excited strangers take their seats before the lit but empty stage. Dad and I are still mannequins, staring forward, and I'm sure he's just as uncomfortable as I am, avoiding eye contact with everyone. In fact, his knee is jiggling like he's jonesing. This probably sucks a thousand times more for him because he's peoplephobic—or just plain misanthropic, I don't know anymore. Finally, ten minutes after shooting was supposed to begin according to the tween-looking PA who brought us water when we were seated, I lean into Dad and ask how he's doing and he says, "Christ on a pair of water skis, I need a cigarette." I nod to a set of doors to the right, past the half-pulled curtain and the tables filled with crappy food spreads, and he gives me a hard look for a second before getting up and making a beeline for the door. I follow him. We prop the door open outside with a nearby brick and head around the corner.

We hover near the Dumpsters, facing another studio lined with trailers. He lights a cigarette and inhales it like it's oxygen.

"This place," he says. "It's a mecca of self-important assholes."

"Not a Flora Daly fan, I see."

"I mean, I want Ava to be happy, she is a strong, amazing human being to share her story with the world, and I know she's had a decade-long love affair with television, but . . . I'm on Mars, here."

"Me too," I tell him. "Can I have a drag?"

He sighs, like he doesn't want me to, but hands it to me anyway.

"A hundred bucks says your mom ends up onstage tonight," he says.

"Psssh, watch, she'll get her own *show*."

"I always knew she'd be a star." Dad leans on the Dumpster. I notice his shoes for the first time today—scuzzy Converse giving him away beneath his fancy slacks and sports jacket. "Just didn't think it'd be for this."

"Who—Mom, or Ava?"

He pauses. "Both, actually."

Just then, we hear a thud. A guy with slicked hair, a weak teen 'stache, and a headset pops his head out.

"Vera Rivers?" he asks.

I put my hands behind my back and hide the cigarette, wondering if I'm in some kind of trouble.

"Ava wants you onstage with her," he says. "She doesn't want to do it without you. Can you come back to makeup? We have five till airtime."

I swallow, heat from panic and embarrassment spreading over my cheeks. I want to scream "no" and run behind the Dumpster. Me? On TV? For a brief moment, I contemplate if death would be better than this. But Ava's in there awaiting her debut. She needs me. There's no way out of this except back through the door that says QUIET—TAPING IN PROGRESS.

"You're a good sister," Dad says, squeezing my arm.

I follow Teen 'Stache back through the doors, a long back hallway with scuffed cement floors, long black curtains, murmuring people with clipboards and headsets. I try to ask him what I'm supposed to do up there onstage, but he mutters indistinguishable words into his headset. When I get to makeup, a woman beats my face with a thick beige powder and when I say, my voice climbing, that I have no idea what I'm supposed to do, she says, "You'll be great." Then she sends me through another passageway where I go behind a stage and three women with headsets on hurry me onto the stage platform and into an empty chair next to Ava. My mother sits on the other side, unperturbed as a professional. But for me, it's a nightmare realized—audience a stranger-sea, blinding lights, cameras on dollies gliding across the floor, and some voice from nowhere counting down. Ava turns to me, eyes twinkling, and squeezes my hand.

"Thank you," she whispers.

"Of course," I say.

A deep silence fills the room as the announcer introduces Flora and she struts out, sporting a glittery jumpsuit that catches the lights like a disco ball. Then the audience unleashes a tsunami of applause. Flora does an intro into her mic as she sits next to us. She's so dead serious, with the inflection of a news anchor, that I'm sure she means it, but it seems fake. Ava and Mom stare at her as if they're watching a goddess incarnate. I paste a smile on my face and tell myself soon this will all be over.

"This is," Flora tells the audience, waiting a beat for extra drama, "the *first* interview ever to be done with Ava Rivers. Joining her we have her sister and her mother. Thank you *so* much for coming on the show today. I—like the rest of America—have been following this story since you went missing at the age of six and am simply *elated* that it has such a happy ending. Welcome home. Ava, may I ask—what is it like being back after so long?"

Ava is so poised and well-spoken. "It's like—it's like having your wildest, craziest dreams come true. Every day I wake up and expect to go back to where I was. But I'm here. I have my family. It's unbelievable."

"And the question undoubtedly on everyone's mind—where *were* you, exactly?" Flora asks, resting her elbow on her glittery pant leg, leaning forward to offer Ava the mic.

My throat constricts. This seems so garish, so invasive, having this overdressed, overpowdered stranger asking the most intimate questions about our familial tragedy.

But Ava nods and leans in to answer. "I was in a man's attic. I still don't know where, exactly."

Flora nods slowly.

"She was kept indoors for years," my mom explains. "Details are still getting worked out. The police have their best on the case and, undoubtedly, we will have answers soon."

"Over a *decade* in a man's attic," she says. "Your kidnapper. And no one can even say what region you were in."

"Not yet," Ava says.

"Have you tried hypnosis?" Flora asks.

"No," Ava says.

"It is on the table," Mom says.

"But I don't want to," Ava says, with an ever-so-slight whine that makes me wonder if this is a conversation that has happened at least once between them before.

"Why not?" Flora asks. "Wouldn't you be willing to try anything to find your kidnapper?"

After a moment, Ava replies. "Yes, but then there are some things I don't want to remember."

"Ava, what about the other women who could be his victims?" Flora asks, in the softest, most concerned voice ever. Still, it raises my blood pressure. "Shouldn't you be trying everything?"

It isn't until my voice leaps out of my throat that I realize I've been sitting here in complete silence. "You have no idea what she went through," I blurt. I willfully still the shake in my voice, the sweat breaking out under my makeup. The cameras swivel their heads my way. "Or how hard she works, every day, to be good and strong in the face of the swarms of reporters and cops and all you story-hungry people with your prickly questions. Trying to adjust to this life that is both her old life and her new one at the same time. She's doing her best and then some. She's a hero."

"See, that's why I wanted my sister on with me today," Ava says, grinning at me.

The audience laughs.

"Your sister is right, though," Flora says. "Ava, you are a hero. That's why you're such a star."

Ava's joy now seems even bubblier than childhood joy. Look at the grins of the audience members as they feverishly applaud, Ava's eyes shining as she raises her hands up and enjoys the sunshine of their standing ovation.

My sister is better than alive.

She is resurrected.

48

ON THE FLIGHT home, Ava puts in her earbuds and gets quiet and she watches her reflection in the dark window of the airplane with a shiny stare like she's a beautiful stranger.

I'm in awe of her strength, her cheerfulness through the trip home, and the pizza we eat together on the couch as she flips through the channels and chatters about shallow aspects of today's filming—the lunch spread, the smell of the face powder, the microphone they taped to her chest. She's exuberant, and I am truly amazed at her unstoppable positivity, the way she keeps circling back to the hope that her story will help people.

After the lights go out, and we've all retired to our bedrooms, I hear her crying two doors away. I get up and go to her door, knock until she stops.

"Ava?"

"I'm fine," she says in a clearly not-fine voice.

"Can I come in?"

She opens the door, puffy red eyes, mascara rivering down her cheeks. "I'm sorry but please . . . just leave me alone, okay?"

It's more commanding than I've ever heard her, and though it hurts to be pushed, I'm proud of her for being firm.

"I'm here if you need me," I say.

"You don't even know me," she whispers.

I reach for her, but she flinches.

"I just—I just—maybe this is all wrong," she goes on. "I don't deserve this. Why'd I go on TV? What was I thinking?"

"It's for the girls," I say, pretending to be steady when I want to mirror her and turn into a puddle.

"I don't even understand anything, how I got here, what is going on," she says. "Nothing is right, I'm not myself."

"Ava."

"I'm not."

Finally, she lets me hug her, but only for a second. Then she pulls away and wipes her eyes, black splotches on her sweatshirt sleeves.

"You went on TV today," I say. "Because once upon a time, you were a girl and you were locked up and the guy who did that to you is still out there and he needs to be found."

She makes a face, like she's heard this a thousand times.

"And think about the other girls out there, locked up, who you wanted to tell your story for. To give them hope."

"How I felt when I saw that Lifetime movie *Girl in the Bunker*," she murmurs.

Relief spreads. Her tears are gone. The daze has settled in. She yawns.

"Sorry," she says. "It was a crazy day."

"It was."

I retreat to my room and hear nothing but her blaring TV. In bed, I put my hand over my thumping heartbeat, reliving the conversation, thinking, *She's not unbreakable after all.*

49

AVA'S OUT WITH Mom at an auction to raise money for some missing children's org one night when Max comes over unexpectedly. I answer the door and see him there dressed all spiffy thrift-store couture with a dark chocolate bar in his hand.

"Yo," he says.

"She's out," I tell him.

"Actually, I'm—I was just swinging by to see how it's crankin'."

"Well, I can give her the message."

"I mean, with you."

"Oh," I say, taken aback. I look down at my pajamas and the paperback book in my hand. "I'm clearly having a very exciting evening."

"Have you seen the moon?" he asks, breezing over my self-deprecating comment as though he doesn't even notice what I'm wearing. "You should really come out and look at it."

"Um, sure, okay," I say.

I grab my coat off the wall, put my book down, and go outside with him. We sit on my porch steps next to each other, me on my guard because . . . well, because two minutes ago I was on the weathered moors between Thrushcross Grange and Wuthering Heights and now I'm sitting outside pondering the fat, shiny eyeball of the moon with Max Spangler. Alone. With him, I mean.

"Here." He hands me a chunk of chocolate, bites the bar, and makes ecstatic noises.

"Thanks."

"So my mom's infirm," he says, as if picking up in the middle of a conversation. "But it's not like she's bona-fide sick, you know what I'm saying? She's a sufferer of psychosomatic illness."

"Explain?"

"It's like, mind and body work in tandem, so she thinks she's sick and then she convinces herself and it manifests in her body, so she actually *is* sick at this point. Her fake Lyme disease has totally crippled her for real."

He directs his monologue at the moon. I'm not sure if I'm a companion or a one-girl audience right now.

"I'm sorry," I say.

He shrugs and munches his chocolate.

"Why are you telling me this now?" I ask after a long pause.

"You asked."

"Yeah, like, weeks ago. It seemed like you didn't want to tell me about it."

"It's wearing on me," he goes on, as if he didn't hear what I said. "Not to be all woe-is-me. I mean, the situation with you Riverses is way more intense. I just—" Finally, he looks at me so sincerely I almost want to laugh, because there's chocolate on his mouth. "I thought you'd understand. Like, sometimes I want to jet. Kills me every time I think of NYU. If not college, I want to get to be a selfish deadbeat and go be a busker with a backpack and a Eurail pass or whatever. I have a friend who went to Peru on vacation and never came home, he dug it so much, he fell in love with some Peruvian goddess and works at a hostel. . . ."

"You think I understand that staying and doing the right thing sucks," I say. "Yeah, I do, and in one way, it does."

He nods. When he keeps on pointing his stare at me, it slows my blood in my veins so divinely. The chocolate on his lips looks delicious. I get a pang, letting myself think, not for the first time, that Max and I could be really sweet together. But then I dismiss my thoughts as schmaltzy moon-induced idiocy, or hormones. I could never let a boy or anything else in the mean blue world come between Ava and me. He was her friend first. It would be too confusing. The last thing she needs is confusing.

"Remember when they tore up the football field?" Max asks.

I breathe in, the memory a knife. "Oh, yes."

"I remember watching you stop and stare at it through the fence," he says. "Utter blankness in that stare. Nobody home."

Max barely acknowledged me in high school, hallway passings, diverted gazes, and faraway, dreamy stares I was sure my sister's ghost lived in. I'm so shocked to hear he saw me, the incredible invisible girl.

"I was like, she's got to be feeling *universes*," he goes on. "I thought, imagine life being the twin of a kid who got snatched up and dot-dot-dot. Who everyone's always pining after. I mean, worse than death."

The same blankness he speaks of clouds my expression now. It happens automatically, the way a snail might recoil into its shell. It hurt so bad, the sight of that upturned soil, the tractor arms slashing violently as everyone in school watched, eager, hoping for a body. Sometimes the hurt itself became so intense that it morphed into a kind of painkiller.

"It was worse than knowing the worst," I say. "Until she showed up alive. Then it was all worth it."

I think he detects my suffering, because he changes the subject and starts rambling about how he got a job going door-to-door and selling knives. They're really swanky knives, he tells me, standing up and shoving the chocolate wrapper in his pocket. He should bring them by and show them to me sometime. "Sure," I say. "Come show me your knives." We say goodbye. I don't mention the chocolate on his lips. As I close the door behind me, though, I find myself running my tongue over the same place on my upper lip, the ghost of the taste in my mouth.

50

TURNS OUT I couldn't defer my enrollment in school. In a couple months it will be application season and I have no motivation to do it all over again. My parents tell me I can take a few semesters off, princess, be Sister of the Year, figure out "next steps."

October sneaks up on us; Halloween candy and cheap plastic-packaged costumes appear in drugstore aisles and pumpkins pop up on porches. Still no rain. The weather didn't get the memo yet that fall's here. Typical California. One Saturday morning at the buttcrack of dawn I get a call from my supervisor. He's nearly hysterical. Cinderella's got "food poisoning" again (aka her weekly hangover). We have a rich-girl birthday party in three hours. Where the hell is he going to find another Cinderella at this point? But then I get an idea, *dingdingding*. I ask him, did you know I have a twin sister? And an old Cinderella outfit?

"Do I know you have a twin sister?" he jokes. "Have I ever seen the news? Are you telling me *Ava Rivers* is available for children's parties?"

"Don't even," I say. "Seriously. If it's going to be all weird celebrity-styles, then forget I mentioned it. I don't want anyone knowing who she is."

"Get me a Cinderella and I ask no questions and phone no paparazzi."

"You do, I'll sue," I half joke.

I mean, we do have a lawyer now.

I get up and throw my Snow White outfit on the bed and go rap on Ava's door. When I relay the news, her dazed just-woke-up expression doesn't change.

"Do you really think I can do it?" she asks doubtfully.

"Put on a blue dress and fool a bunch of four-year-olds? Um, yes. It's really not hard."

Her puzzlement melts and she smiles. "So . . . I have a job?"

"Congrats," I tell her, tossing her the dress.

It's a little big on her. It needs safety pins. I pull her hair into a Disney-style topknot and we watch some YouTube videos of Cinderella songs. We practice singing for a half hour or so while I put on her makeup. Her voice is low and throaty and beautiful. We have to transpose the song down a few steps so she can hit the notes. But she has pitch. And, I realize as I powder her up close, flawless skin.

"It's all that never-leaving-the-attic," she tells me. "Best sunscreen in the world."

I pull back from my cheek-powdering to look her in the eyes.

"It's a joke," she says. "Ha ha."

"I can't believe you're cracking jokes about that."

"Why not?" she asks. "Shelly says humor is healing."

"You are definitely my sister," I say, putting the powder puff away.

Ava's phone rings. She gets up and glances at it. "How about no." She rejects the call and the ringing stops.

"Unknown caller?" I ask.

"Ozzie. Won't leave me alone. It's like, I have a life, dude. Chill."

"Probably just has some questions to ask you."

She rolls her eyes. "Yeah, doesn't everyone." She checks her teeth in the mirror. "I'm a princess now. I don't need to talk to detectives."

Dad snaps a pic of us with his phone as we try to leave the house. He makes us pose against the banister.

"This is too cute," he says. "My princesses."

Ave rolls her eyes. "Daddy."

He gets the picture, kisses us both on the forehead with a big *mua*, and we're off.

The party is a big one. It's a joint birthday celebration for two little girls. There's a balloon twister and a Raggedy Ann–ish clown, a two-tiered cake and an overenthusiastic DJ playing music out of ridiculously large speakers.

Ava makes a hell of a Cinderella. I'm not just impressed by her singing—she remembered every lyric to the songs we practiced— but her social skills. She charms the parents and delights the little birthday crowd.

I wait for the dark shadow that sometimes follows her to appear, but it doesn't. Not today.

She's full and real and strong and courageous. I watch her flit around the back lawn with a gaggle of cake-smeared little girl faces following her every move—out here, in the screaming sunshine under the bluest cloud-free sky, she's Cinderella.

51

OUR LOCAL GROCERY story is Berkeley Bowl, an overcrowded cornucopia of health food and organic produce. I'm not talking your ordinary apples and pears, I'm talking sunchokes, Mexican star fruits, and pineapple guavas. Ava and I walk over there sometimes and hit Max up, who lives on the way, and the three of us pick up lunch and eat it in a lawn-filled stretch in the middle of Adeline Street or a nearby park. Ava and I grabbed packaged sushi today, and Max is inside at the burrito bar. The sun shines like it has no idea it's fall, and Ava and I sit on a cement bench out front next to bins of pumpkins and wait for Max.

Ava pets a dog tied to a nearby pole. He's wearing a scarf. "You are adorable, dude. And so fashionable. No, you can't have my sushi." She sits next to me. We ignore a couple who stop to make out in front of us like they can't help themselves before continuing on with their groceries. "Is it wrong that I find public displays of affection disgusting?"

"No. Agreed. You love each other, great, keep it to yourselves."

"Right. Like, I don't need to see your tongue. Ever."

"I'm not even down with holding hands," I say. "Like, why? Just so the whole world knows?"

Ava's quiet, looking away, and I wonder what she's wondering.

"Did you ever date someone?" she asks.

I think of Madeline for the first time in a while.

"Yeah. It didn't work out," I say. I don't want to elaborate and she doesn't press me to.

"It's weird to think of you with someone," she says.

"It's been so long it's weird for *me* to think of me with someone."

"Is it wrong, I mean, I want you to find someone you like but . . . but then . . ."

"Then they'd be my everything," I tell her.

"Exactly."

"Is it weird I feel the same way about you? Don't get me wrong, I'll be so happy when you're at the point when you're ready to date. But . . ."

"Always with the *but*s," Ava says in a creepy old man voice.

I laugh.

"But seriously, I wouldn't—I mean, I wouldn't just blindsight you," she says.

I never correct her Ava-isms. They're too adorable.

"I'd never just, like, meet someone and be all 'toodles,'" she goes on.

"I certainly hope you'd never say 'toodles.'"

"Seriously. And I hope you wouldn't ditch me either."

"I wouldn't. But, Ava—I mean, when you find someone, when you're at that stage, I will be happy for you. You don't have to worry about how that would make me feel. I'll be okay."

"Look, Veer," Ava says, shoving a spicy tuna chunk in her mouth. She used to say raw fish sounded nasty, but after I made her try mine a few weeks back, it's all she ever wants for lunch. "I'ma spell it out. You know where I came from and what happened."

Barely, not really, I don't say.

"I hate talking about it, even with Shelly," she goes on. "But I'm all . . . jacked up. I don't know what I want. All the jacked-upness, like, covers everything. You know? It's part of me."

A guy with a clipboard and no shoes on comes up and interrupts to ask us if we're registered voters—it's part of the Berkeley Bowl experience, the people who try to get you to sign about a thousand petitions—and Ava listens politely and signs everything he has. He says, "Have a blessed day," and leaves.

"Go on," I tell her.

"I just . . . I don't know who I am yet."

She stares at her glittery sneakers, which could use a touch-up job.

"Maybe I'm into chicks." Ava devours more sushi, not even ashamed to talk with it in her mouth. "Who knows? Maybe I'm asexual. I'm just saying, the idea of, like—like, having a boyfriend, like, 'Oh, hold my hand and talk about babies and—'" She shudders and almost gags. "*Chills*. Not good ones."

"Understandable."

"But if you found someone, I mean, it might be hard, but I'd be hella happy," she says. "It's gonna happen eventually."

Hella. Ha. She's officially an East Bayer now.

"Unless we're spinsters," I tell her.

"Spinster sisters," she says with a grin. Then Ava finishes chewing and closes the sushi box. It's empty.

"You ate it already?" I ask, unopened box still in my hand. "Max isn't even out here yet."

"I know. I was just so hungry. And it was *soooo good*."

When Max comes out with his foil-covered burrito, the way he glances at me as he pushes back his mirrored sunglasses, how he stops in the rush of silver shopping carts as if he forgot himself for a moment, his wide, goofy, crooked smile, makes me wish things were simpler. But he's too close to Ava now. I can't complicate things.

We walk through the neighborhood, the three of us in stride, Ava in the middle. We pass a pot club painted with fish and a dog collar shop with a marquee that says YES WE JUST SELL DOG COLLARS. It isn't until we linger at a stoplight and Max pushes the walk button to make some kind of beat and sings, "Let's go, light, let's change sometime tonight," over it that I notice the acorn squash in Ava's hand.

"Um," I say. "Did you take that?"

"I did," she says, looking down at it, surprised, a little guilty, as if she doesn't quite understand why it's there.

"Why?" I ask.

"I really don't know. You want it?"

"No."

The light turns green and we walk. A grandpa with a green mustache rides by on a bike.

Ava turns to me. She puts her hand on my elbow. "I know what you're thinking," she whispers. "I won't do it again. I want to be good. I don't know why I did that."

"It's okay."

I'm just surprised. I've never seen Ava do anything even close to shady before now.

When a bearded man with a face tattoo asks if we can spare any change, Ava hands him the acorn squash. He ponders it deeply as we walk away. Once we get to the park, Max and I eat our lunches in silence as we watch Ava chasing birds. His knee almost touches mine. For a moment, I let myself pretend he's my boyfriend. We're sitting here together, picnicking, me and my super arty cute boyfriend. Then I don't even let myself pretend. I'm a bad sister. He's my sister's best friend. The only one she has besides me.

52

ONE AFTERNOON, AVA and I get back to the house from thrift-shopping and Elliott's there. At the dining room table. Grinning and standing up to bear-hug us.

He looks older. Dark facial scruff and wavy brown hair that could use a trim. His grin, though, is the same—lopsided, contagious. And his muddy green eyes are clearer than last time I saw him. I judge the diameter of our hug. He's not too skinny, he's not too fat. He might be all right.

Here we are, together, the five of us, listening to Elliott's insane story about riding ATVs in Mexico and getting held up at gunpoint by Mexican police. Laughing at his description of his latest girlfriend, Desrea-Jean, who is a "pawnshop owner with a heart of thirteen-karat gold." Ava watches him with slack-jawed wonder—yes, girl, our brother is a comedic train wreck. He's a one-man show. How long has it been since I've seen him? Was I still in junior high? He seems clean. He's talking fast, though. My parents don't look suspicious. I shouldn't be so cynical. Of course he's clean.

Dad at the head of the table opposite Mom. Ava and I on one side, Elliott on the other. No yelling. No tears. No holes. We're whole.

53

MOM TAKES ME out to breakfast one morning. Me. Alone. By myself. Where are the reporters when you need them? Mom's life is a never-ending train of obligations that surround Ava now. They lunch, shop, mani-pedi, attend meetings about the scholarship fund in her name, Mom chauffeurs her to Ozzie and the police station, etc. But Mom doesn't have time for one-on-ones with me. I swear it's been since that movie we saw before The Resurrection occurred. Seated across the table from her at a nose-in-the-air café that's some French word I can't and don't care to pronounce, I expect a bombshell of some sort. But all she says is "I'm so glad you're around for Ava. She really looks up to you."

"Seriously?" I ask.

I hide my flattery momentarily behind a napkin.

"She talks about you *constantly*," Mom says. "She's your biggest fan."

"Well, once she gets out in the world a little more she'll realize how lame I am."

Mexico and Canada are tied to a nearby parking meter we can see from the window. They watch Mom and me eat pancakes—excuse me, *crepes*. Such desperation on those little pug faces. I have to laugh.

"I'm still . . . having a hard time talking to her about what happened to her," Mom says. "Making any sort of sense out of the details. It keeps me up at night—the scenarios."

"Me too."

"I mean, I ask her anything, she's quick to change the subject, you know? Is it like that with you?"

"I don't ask her details," I say. "I figure she'll share them when she's ready."

"I have a hard time resisting. I want the case solved so badly. I drive around all the time, every man I see—is that him? Is that him?"

"She wasn't in Berkeley."

"She was somewhere within driving distance, Ozzie thinks."

"Is that what everyone else thinks?"

"They're still entertaining ideas as far away as Canada."

"There's no use," I say. "Driving yourself out of your skull trying to solve the mystery. I mean, there are people working full-time on it so we don't have to."

Mom, poised goddess—I so often misinterpret your clenched anxiety for strength.

"I hope she makes friends," Mom says. "Has a normal life."

"She will."

"How can we put this behind us when he's still alive and free? How?"

"We don't. We put it aside, and we focus on everything that's going right. Like Elliott."

"Ugh," Mom says, in a good way, clutching her heart with a fork still in her hand. "Isn't it wonderful?"

"I was like, pinch me."

"He has never called me since the Turkey Incident," Mom confides. "I still to this day don't understand what I did wrong."

"You didn't. He was high."

"He said he was 'whacked-out on espresso drinks.' I don't know what to believe," Mom says.

Um, not that, Mom. Not that.

Mom's eyes zero in on a man a few tables over with a camera up, taking a picture. We both freeze, but then realize he's just taking a picture of the restaurant name in the window. We relax and go back to our jelly-bellied crepes.

"Did you see that rancid story in *Us Weekly*?" she murmurs.

"Yeah. I can't believe they included that picture of Dad in that bathrobe—"

She shakes her head painfully. "This is why I hired that publicist. And still, all these awful stories from 'sources.' I can't trust anyone. I asked your father—did *you* tell *Us Weekly* about our dinner with Elliott? Of course he denies it."

Ava may be home, and we spend a lot of time together as a family, but that doesn't seem to have moved my parents any closer. They still sleep one story apart and dress like they come from different income brackets. They still snipe at each other in quiet moments in the kitchen in ways that begin playful and end in resentment. Since Ava came home, it's a shattering surprise to learn that not everything is destined to change.

"What drives me most crazy is I don't know. I don't really know what happened to her. She was gone twelve years, I could fill you in on twelve minutes of it, maybe. I hate how much I don't know."

"We *don't* know."

"Yet everyone wonders," Mom says. "I mean, everyone's minds goes to those sick places. I mean, how bad? Her details are so scant and everything's so foggy from the drugs he gave her. I don't want to know. But I have to know. You know?"

"Your mind goes to those sick places, Mom, because . . ." My throat hurts and I have to drink a sip of ice water to finish my sentence. "Because that's what happened to her."

We're quiet for a moment—long enough that the waitress comes and asks if we're okay. We're okay. We're okay. She goes away.

"I love you, Mom."

She pats my hand. "You're growing up to be such an impressive, strong young woman. And I'm a selfish mother, Vera, because I'm so glad you stayed in Berkeley. We need to have more 'us' time, don't you think?"

The way she focuses on me, really focuses—it's like she sees me for the first time in years.

I think about that breakfast all week. I live off that breakfast and those compliments and that hand pat. Is it disgusting that, at eighteen, I love and need my mom so badly? That the love and need aches because trying to hold on to her attention is like trying to harness the wind? In the drugstore, where Mom stops for mouthwash, we wait in line and pretend we don't notice the cover story in the newsstand with Ava's smiling face on it and the words MONTHS LATER, MADMAN STILL LOOSE—THE SHOCKING TRUTH ABOUT AVA RIVERS.

I find myself staring at the picture like I don't know her, wondering, what is the shocking truth about Ava Rivers? What is it? If only it were as simple as a five-dollar purchase to know.

54

LATER IN THE week, after a princessing gig, I come home late to a dark house that still smells like dinner. I pass through the kitchen and stop at the cracked door to the basement, where I can hear Dad strumming his guitar. Major chords. He's singing something about a-rockin' and a-rollin'. It's the cheesiest. I laugh into my hand. I pause in the dark living room, eyeing the slit of light beneath my mother's door, and freeze there for a moment. She's supposed to be at some charity thing. I saw it on her jam-packed calendar. But her reading light is on, so I push the door open a sliver.

"You're home?"

"I'm taking a hiatus from some of the events," she tells me.

Shock dumbs me. Mom is so loyal to her charities and so busytown that the last time I can remember her skipping out on anything, she had the stomach flu. Volunteering is a way of life for her.

"What? Don't look at me like that. I'm cutting back on obligations to put more energy into Ava's case. And spend time with family."

"Groovy."

I don't know why I said "groovy" just now. I guess everything is so not itself that even my vocabulary is alien. My house is full of contented people in their rooms.

I head upstairs and stop at Ava's closed door. Some kind of game show applause blasts from the TV. Remember when, not so long ago at all, a twist up the staircase meant a hushed, dark loneliness I shared with no one?

God, I love the comforting muffled noise of an occupied home.

I'm about to head to my room when the door cracks open, the blue TV light shining through the crack. Ava peeks at me.

"Thought I heard you," she whispers. "Wanna come in?"

I step inside her room, which is messier than mine—and that is a feat. Her sheets and covers are even on the floor. I wonder about the psychology of it and then let it go. We sit on the bed together. She hugs her legs. She's swimming in Mom's silk pajamas.

"It's hard to sleep sometimes," she tells me. "As you know from my dumb outbursts, right?"

"Not dumb."

She turns back to the TV. A world stirs behind her eyes. I want her to tell me everything. I place my hand on hers, our matching mood rings clicking as they touch.

"Sometimes I wake up in the middle of the night and I still don't know where I'm at. I think, 'This is a mistake, this is a mistake.'"

I nod. "It's going to take some time to sink in."

"And I get scared . . . 'cause I feel so lucky." Her eyes shine. "Like, I don't deserve this."

"But you do."

"I'm never going back there," she says quietly.

"Of course not."

Where is *there*?

"You won't," I repeat.

She watches her hot-pink toenails. "I don't want him to find me. Not that I think he'd look. But what if he did?"

I can't help the words. They leap from my mouth. "Where is 'he'?"

"He's probably sitting in his house right now," she whispers. "If it'd been a while ago, he'd be playing video games. But now I'm sure he's just reading his Bible. Or who knows—maybe he's turned on the news and he knows what deep trouble he's in. Maybe he doesn't even care—turned his worries over to God—or maybe he got chicken and ran off. Thing is, he's not the type to run."

Ava grasps her hands so hard her nails dig into her knuckles. They make marks. I put my hand on hers again and say, "Stop, stop." She looks down with this robotic expression, like her fingers don't even belong to her and she doesn't know why they're doing what they're doing.

"I just want it to be over," she tells me. "But it's never going to be."

I wait and breathe.

She watches the TV, a muted deodorant commercial.

"You can tell me anything," I say. "I'll just listen."

She breaks her gaze with the commercial. Dry.

"You know, sometimes it wasn't so bad. It was mostly boring being there. I was alone most of the time, upstairs, in my own room. The attic. I watched a lot of TV."

I nod, thirsty for every drop, every crumb of story. I'm quivering here on the edge of the bed.

"I looked out the window. There were paintings in my room, of flowers. Sometimes he let me downstairs and I sewed up his pants or swept or whatever. It wasn't that bad, except for those things, it wasn't that bad."

So she does remember. It throbs. Everything I already knew in my deep, dark ocean comes floating to the horrible surface. She was raped. She was kept. This is real now, not a dry news briefing.

"Have you told anyone else what you're telling me?" I ask. "The paintings, the flowers . . . these are all clues."

She nods, shrugs. "I tell."

"Can I ask you something?" I say. "Did you ever see yourself on TV?"

"Couple times."

"Didn't that give you hope, to know we were looking like crazy?"

"By the time I saw stuff, I was older. I wasn't even sure if it was me. Jonathan didn't call me Ava. He said I didn't have a family. Nobody wanted me. Nobody'd bother looking for me and they'd never find me." For the first time since she began talking, her eyes flash with emotion. "Don't look so sad. I'm here now."

Instantly, with no warning, I'm blubbering into my hands. Damn me.

"You crying only makes it worse," she tells me, her voice rising, breaking.

"I know."

We turn and face opposite walls, and then I hear her sniffing. We both turn back to each other, teary-eyed and fighting a losing battle with the weepies.

"I'm dealing with it. There's a lot to be thankful for. We should be here now," she says in a high-pitched voice.

"I know, this is so great," I agree, voice a squeak.

"So lucky."

"So damn lucky."

Our expressions are both about to disintegrate when one of us smiles—I'm not sure who, it seems to happen so quickly and multiply. The grins grow. The tears are laughed out and wiped away. She squeezes my arm. I yell jokingly into my hands. And the conversation shatters into a joyful jargon that is kind of hard to explain. We talk about crazy Elliott, and Ava throws the kitten pillow at me. We talk about Max and his silly scats. We hear Dad's singing through the radiator and imitate him and burst into giggles.

We lie side by side and say nothing.

Before I leave her room, after a silent hour of TV watching on her bed, I notice the Ramona book splayed open on her floor. I'm about to say something when Ava grabs her phone and takes a selfie of us.

"Looklooklook," she says.

In the picture, our eyes are different colors but identically glowing. My short jet-black doll haircut and her wild blond curls. I want this picture. I want this moment. I want forever to be real and I want it now.

55

LATE ONE NIGHT later that week Ava comes to my room and says she's got a craving for chicken wings. Or "chicken wangs," as Ava likes to call them in a weird nasally voice. Probably from some commercial. I drive us to a diner decorated wall-to-wall with Barbies and with punk music blasting. Ava and I never go out at night like this. We order milkshakes. I feel our age exactly, in the most refreshing way.

"I love Mom," Ava says. "But sometimes I wish she'd, like, take a break from me and my case. You know?"

I chomp a celery stick, surprised. It's the first not-100-percent-positive thing I've heard Ava utter about our parents. "Her full attention can be rather overwhelming."

She gnaws a dainty chicken bone. "She took me out to lunch a few days ago . . . she was all therapisty with me. At one point, we were looking at the menu and I was like, 'I don't like tuna.' She was all, 'Does it trigger a painful memory?'"

I roll my eyes, and both of us giggle.

"*Tuna*," she says.

"She's just trying to help in her own weird way."

"I wish people would just treat me normal," Ava says. "Like you do."

I point to my mouth. "You have sauce right here."

"Exactly," she says.

She wipes it off with a napkin.

"Can I ask you something? What's the deal with Mom and Dad?" she asks. "Are they okay?"

"What do you mean?"

"He's downstairs, she's upstairs." She pushes the plate of bones away. "I've never seen them touch."

"It's temporary," I say.

My throat's constricted. I gulp water.

"We seem like a happy family," she says, searching my eyes for an answer. "We're happy, right?"

"We are now."

After I get up and pay the bill and use the stickered, graffitied bathroom, I go outside and see Ava's seated on the hood of my car, her glittery Converse moving back and forth in a little dance. I see what I think is foggy, cold-night-air breath exiting her mouth—and then my eyes move down her arm and hey, whoa, she's smoking a cigarette.

"Where did you *get* that?" I ask, shocked.

"A guy."

"A guy?"

"He was outside smoking. I think he worked here. He just went back inside."

"I didn't know you smoked."

"I haven't in a minute," she says.

Her eyes look sad-shiny under the moon. I want to know it all—when was the last time you smoked? Where have you been and who *were* you? But I can't bring myself to press her. Her trust is this delicate, tamed thing. She talks to me and laughs with me and she's not the way she is with my parents. I don't want to jeopardize that with careless curiosity.

I can't bring myself to sit on the hood of my car, POS that it is. I lean against it, next to Ava, and we both watch steam pour from a vent coming out of the dark wall of the diner.

"Let me have a drag," I say.

She hands me the cigarette, and I take a puff before handing it back.

"He bought me smokes and peanut butter cups on Mondays," she says almost too softly to hear it.

My mouth purses up with a question.

"Like some reward," she continues.

I watch her profile as the smoke billows out. *I don't know you,* I think, *even though you feel so familiar. I don't really know you at all.*

"I never want to eat a fucking peanut butter cup again," she says.

I ask before I can stop myself. I just kind of exhale the one-word question. "Who?"

"Him. Jonathan."

"But Jonathan *who?*"

The front door to the diner opens, yellow light illuminating the blue-with-dark street, and a couple comes out, arguing about something. Their conversation disappears as they climb into the car and close the doors. Ava's dead-to-the-world eyes are fixed on a streetlamp.

"Why does it matter what his last name is?" she finally asks. "Why does everyone keep bothering me about it?"

"Everyone's . . . bothering you?"

"Ozzie's the worst. Sitting there asking me the same questions over and *over*. Like he's trying to trap me." She exhales the cigarette through her nose like a pro. Ava. A smoker. "I mean, say I knew—which I don't—but pretend I did. What then? Who cares? What's done is done." She hops off the hood of the car. No dent. "Nobody's getting those years back and the best thing is to not keep *focusing* on all this bad that happened—just . . . let's move on, people."

"Right."

Wrong. He needs to be in jail. Electric chair? I won't pretend I haven't joyfully entertained the idea.

Ava bought a fake fur coat two sizes too big for her at a thrift shop recently, and this is her first time wearing it. It engulfs her. It's ridiculous. I love it.

She puts a fake fur arm around my shoulders. It's like getting hugged by a yeti, but I don't care.

"I wanna make the world a better place," she says. "I can't undo the ugly that happened. But I can spin it, you know, into something better."

"You remember more than you act like you remember, don't you?" I ask. And the second I feel her arm drop—the cold night nipping my neck again—I regret it.

"There's still a lot of blurs," she says. She takes another drag of the cigarette. "You think I'm a liar."

"I didn't say you were—"

"I'm trying my hardest," she says in a shaky voice. "I can't remember it all at once. Pieces. Shelly says puzzle pieces. Don't tell me I 'act like.'"

"That was stupid. I—I didn't mean that at all. I said it weird."

"This was my puzzle piece today," she says, holding up the glowing butt of the cigarette and then inhaling. "Cigarettes and peanut butter cups."

She throws the butt on the ground in the parking lot, and I instinctually step to it and put it out with my boot. I don't know why. I'd rather be the kind to let it burn.

In the car, we're quiet. Ava settles the radio on a college radio station playing Ethiopian music. "Listen to *these* jams," she says. "Now this I've never heard before."

I bite my lip as I drive. Stoplights. Crosswalks. Bikers. Pedestrians.

Ava asks, "Why do you grab the steering wheel like that?"

"Like what?"

"Like—I don't know—you're choking it."

I look down at my hands. Jesus. They *are* choking it. Is this how I always grab the steering wheel? Is this how tense I am? I release my hands and hold it again, looser.

"I hate driving," I tell her. "I just got my license senior year. I'd been avoiding it."

"Why? I can't *wait* to drive."

"I'm just . . . I don't know. It's scary. Tons of steel maneuvering around other tons of steel at so many miles per hour—I don't want to hurt anyone."

She rolls down the window as we pass the bright lights of stores. "Once my TV got stuck on the shopping network for a month."

I try to imagine Ava in That Monster's attic, with her flower pictures and her TV, her cigarettes and peanut butter cups, eyes glued to the shopping network.

"For a *month*," she repeats, smiling.

"Jesus."

"It's funny," she says, laughing. "Not everything is tragic."

"Do I look tragic?"

"Yes. Anyway, there was a commercial for this program—this I-know-everything guy. Inspirational, you know. It was about building your own reality. I probably watched that commercial, I don't know, a hundred times. And it was about how you think negative things, well, negativity comes. You think about car crashes, you'll get in a car crash. Veer, you've gotta build your own reality like that stupid I-know-everything guy."

"I've always wished I was a stupid I-know-everything guy," I joke.

I want to believe it's that easy. But wishes and will have never seemed to steer my life anywhere useful. And the best stuff in life— Madeline (in the beginning), getting into college in Portland, and Ava's sudden return—they were all uninvited surprises.

"Don't kill me," Ava says. "But I'm going to ask you to stop for cigarettes. I got a taste for them again."

"Mom's going to *hate* it if you smoke."

"Not in the house," Ava says. "I promise. Or basement with Daddy only."

I sigh and pull into a 7-Eleven parking lot. Ava goes inside and I track her through the fluorescent-lit window. Some ripped dude in a muscle shirt is in front of her in line, and he turns to talk to her. A surge of protectiveness electrocutes me and I fight the urge to run inside and tell him to leave her alone. But she just laughs at something he says. I realize she's an adult. And she's not delicate and broken. She's strong as hell. Love bursts, paralyzing me for a second, it's so potent. I grin and turn up the Ethiopian music as I watch her jog back to the car, back toward me, and I think, *This is reality*.

She climbs in and sticks two cigarettes in her mouth. She lights both of them and hands me one. I roll down the window and blow clouds out into the fresh night air. I ask her if she wants to go home, and Ava's face goes blank and she seems to stop breathing. She gets too still to even blink.

"Ave?" I ask softly.

She looks like a still picture, eyes wide at some unseeable thing, mouth hanging slightly open.

"Shhh," she says. "Just let it pass."

She reaches out and turns off the radio. We sit in silence and she finishes her cigarette with that glazed expression. My mind becomes horribly blank.

"I'm okay now," she says as she throws her cigarette butt out the window. She turns the radio back on. "Thank you."

She smells the tips of her hair, and I drive into the night, still quiet, still in the dark.

56

THE DAY *FLORA DALY* airs, Max comes by to watch it. He sits between Ava and me on the couch. I can't help noticing he smells like he's been chomping mints and has the top two buttons of his polyester shirt unbuttoned. Who is he trying to impress? Because it's working. Elliott joins the party, too, about twelve and a half seconds before it's due to air, of course. He drove a sad-looking Vespa here this time and says he and Desrea-Jean called it quits.

"She gave me lice," he says. "Don't worry! I shampooed it out before coming."

"Jesus, Elliott," Dad says. "If you bring parasites into this house again—"

"Shhh," Mom says, turning up the TV. "It's starting."

Dad turns the lights off like we're in a theater, and the room quiets. I steal a glance at Ava's face as she watches the screen. Max is there between us, gaping at me with shiny puppy eyes.

"What?" I mouth.

I actually touch my face, thinking I have a booger on me or something.

He shrugs and goes back to watching. But when the *Flora Daly* logo flashes and the applause rushes in full stereo, I feel his hand beside my hand, warm, soft, his fingers ever so slowly creeping up mine.

Hello, goose bumps, my old friend.

I can't even concentrate on the TV. For one eternal second, I contemplate how sweet his mouth must taste, how perfectly my arms would probably fit around him, how much I would enjoy ripping his shirt open. I pull my hand away, slowly. When I turn my head again, he's watching the screen as if nothing happened. It takes way too long to get my heart rate back to normal—like, a whole commercial break.

Elliott jokes so much through it about the stupid faces Flora is making—I mean, he's right, it does look like different nuances of fartface—that Dad has to keep *shhh*ing him and Ava giggles her ass off and I pretty much miss everything. I actually don't look bad on TV. I look like someone else.

Later, in the privacy of my room, I pull it up on my computer and watch again. It's a half hour long and a lot is added in besides the interview, mostly vague background on her abduction I've heard before, although some details in the voice-overed intro are new— how he told her the neighborhood was full of criminals so he was protecting her when he kept her locked inside. How he kept the radio blasting techno in the bathroom so no one could ever hear her call for help out the one tiny window if she ever tried to.

Ninja star in my heart.

How she never tried to scream or escape, not even the one time he left the upstairs door to the attic unlocked, because she was afraid of murderers and thieves and the big bad world he told her about. How eventually, after years of this, she started realizing it was lies and asked for her freedom. How she also barely remembered where she came from at that point and was simultaneously terrified of him ever granting her wish.

And then a lot of it is Flora talking as if she knows so much about the epidemic of girls kept in attics.

At the end of the half hour, after Mom's unspun several monologues about how awful it was all those years searching for Ava's body and thinking Ava was a lost cause, Flora asks Ava, "If you could see Jonathan right now, what would you tell him?"

Ava looks up nervously.

"Look at the camera. Say it to the camera, in case he's watching," Flora urges her.

"I'd say . . . I'd say . . . ." Ava blinks rapidly as she stares into the camera, into me, and into everyone watching. "I'd say, why did you do that to me? Why did you hurt me like that and just dump me in a parking lot after all those years?"

I don't know what it is, exactly—the evident pain in her expression like human prey, the confusion, the way she looks away at the end and doesn't seem to care when *Flora Daly* flashes the forensic sketch of That Monster again—but I'm sure of something deep and dark and strange at this moment that never even crossed my mind when I was there in the studio watching this in real time.

"You don't *want* him to get caught," I whisper.

57

THE WEBSITE FINDAVARIVERS.COM just has a static message now, courtesy of Dad, who has never quite learned the knack of subtle punctuation.

AVA CAME HOME AUGUST 4TH!!! ALIVE AND SAFE!! THANK YOU FOR YOUR SUPPORT AND YOUR INTEREST!!! WE ARE NOT DOING NEWS INTERVIEWS!!! AVA IS HAPPY AND ADJUSTING TO LIFE BACK HOME NOW!!!

The photo of Ava is the princess picture, with me cropped out.

58

HALLOWEEN IS DEAD to me. Bad memories. Plus we're too old for that crap. The last time I trick-or-treated I wasn't even in a training bra. The only thing going on is a "no costumes" party at Max's house that Ava and I are invited to. I'd rather stay at home rereading my Poe anthology, but Ava's insistent.

"A *party*," she says, inking her lips with neon-pink lipstick. "We *have* to."

"Since when do you care about parties?"

"I like Max. Don't you?"

"Not as much as you."

She gives me a blank look. "We have to," she repeats.

I guess we're going to a party.

Max still lives with his mother, an "infirm" neurotic who sells tie-dye on Telegraph Avenue. She has locked herself in her room apparently and left their small south Berkeley cottage to the partiers. Max's house is filled with all sorts of weird bronze statues of ladies with a thousand arms and men with elephant heads. They have beanbags instead of couches in the living room.

"Yo," Max yells over the drumming going on in the kitchen. He waves at us from the doorway to the back porch. His shirt is hot pink and says, THIS IS WHAT A FEMINIST LOOKS LIKE. The room smells hotboxy. Between Max and us girls, a dude is banging on a conga drum while a girl in sandals dances. "Hey, kids, this is my buddy Ava and her sister, Vera."

Ava and I wave with our unopened beer cans. The silence is long and awkward. I start inching backward, toward the safe, cozy, empty living room, but Ava inches the other way, toward the people on the back porch and the smell of clove smoke. I double back and follow her forward. Um, when did she become the leader?

I had friends in high school, mostly class friends who buddied up with me for assignments and drifted away once our schedules forked in opposite directions. I had Madeline, for a minute. Since then, I've had a hard time letting myself get super close to anyone. Though I want it so bad. I'm like a magnet, repellent. Or was, before Ava came home, I mean.

It's been some time since I felt I had someone.

She holds my arm and pulls me with her to the porch. We stand next to Max, who's telling a story about a man so wise he doesn't need to eat.

"He's called a *breatharian* because he just needs, like, *air* to live."

"That's fresh," some dude with a goatee and a bottle of whiskey says.

"Incredible," breathes a girl with a dolphin tattoo.

BS, I think.

"What a liar," Ava says.

She lights two cigarettes and hands one to me.

Max laughs softly. "That's what he *claims*, anyway."

Everyone goes quiet, the spotlight of the moth-buzzing porch light on Ava and Max.

He puts his arm around her and pulls her closer to him, and I flinch a little as she moves away from me. Is he allowed to grab her like that? Is she okay with that kind of touch? But she doesn't even seem to notice. "My girl was missing for *twelve years*."

His girl? Those two words cut so many ways.

Ava drinks her beer as the people in the shadows murmur in response.

"Like, you ran away?" Dolphin Tattoo girl asks.

"I didn't run," Ava says. "I was stolen."

The sound of my hand on the beer can makes everyone turn around to look at me.

"They still haven't caught him," I say.

"That's *crazy*," a guy says. "I just realized I saw you on TV. I mean, *man*."

"But, like, what do you mean? Where were you?" a girl asks. "I don't get it."

"Bella, this is Ava *Rivers*," the dude tells her.

"No *way*," the girl says.

Ava swallows the rest of her beer—how she drank it that fast is beyond me—and drops the can on the porch steps with a *plunk-plunk-plunk*. Everyone is quiet, watching her. "Mind if I have another?"

"Go for it," Max says.

I follow her inside. She swings open the fridge and stares into the yellow light.

"Don't you think you should, like . . . not just start talking about this with strangers?" I whisper.

"What, why?" She closes the fridge and holds up her beer. "It's what happened."

"But it's kind of private."

"Is it? I mean, the freaking *Enquirer* knows."

"You're right. I guess I was just thinking, you know, it's an open investigation . . . I don't know what we can say and can't without clearing it with our experts these days."

She pops the can open and sips. "They're never going to find him, Veer."

My own voice echoes in my head from the other night—*You don't want him to get caught.* Am I being paranoid? Why on earth wouldn't she?

The deadness that has storm-clouded her expression is chilling. She doesn't move for a second and honestly, I'm a little scared.

"Ave."

"Shhh," she says. "Just shhhhh."

Ava doesn't move. She closes her eyes. I freeze, too, respecting the silence. After a moment she breathes in and is back again. She blinks and drinks another sip and looks at me.

"Sometimes I need a little moment. And then I'm good. Hey, question."

"What?"

"I don't get what's up with Max's shirt. What's a feminist, exactly? Is he making a joke?"

"Knowing Max, he's probably dead serious," I say with a pang, because is there anything dreamier than a boy proud to wear a pink shirt proclaiming he's a feminist? "A feminist just means you recognize the world's unequal—that we exist in a system of patriarchy where men enjoy privileges women don't. And you want it to get better. You think women deserve to be treated well. You think they're worth fighting for. You think the system of oppression and inequality has to end."

I don't think I've chosen words so carefully since my college admissions essay. I feel the fire in my throat.

Ava nods. "Are you one?"

"Loud and proud."

I squeeze her arm and she smiles at me. Max comes in, cracking his knuckles and singing a loud, soulful *whooooa*. He's too adorable. Make him stop. The bathroom calls, and when I return to the kitchen, Ava is slouched against the wall with a dreamy expression as Max leans into her and talks lowly. For a second, I am the invisible woman. The alarm I feel must be jealousy. I don't recognize it.

He brought me chocolate. He tried to hold my hand when he was over, and I didn't let him, but maybe I should have. Or maybe he's like that with everyone. They pull apart and notice me.

"Hey," Max says.

Ava's got a simper on her lips, like the two of them share a secret now. I can't believe that Ava is home and we're attending parties and she's flirting with boys. If someone had told me six months ago that this would happen I would have called that someone a mean-ass liar. I'm happy for her. But if I'm so happy, what is this hole in me? What is this heart-smashed wish blooming into self-pity? What is this fear she's going to slip away?

Max's mesmerizing brown gaze settles on my bangs. "We were just rapping 'bout . . . well, basically, the awesomeness of you. Rocking your Snow White dress. With your book smarts."

I smile like the sun is shining on me.

Everyone hushes when the three of us step outside, back into the stinging cool air. Finally, after an eternal pause, the girl with the dolphin tattoo asks Ava, "So . . . what's it like being back?"

"It's like . . ." Ava says.

All eyes are on her. No one out here is even daring to breathe.

"It's like Marty McFly, walking out of a time machine . . . or, no. Wrong movie." Ava swirls her beer in the can and gulps the rest, crushing it with her boot on a porch step. "I'm Dorothy back in Kansas, and I am finally *awake*."

Everyone laughs and someone says, "Right on."

I beam next to her. She's fierce and unafraid. She can hush a group of people with her story. I wandered around the world for twelve years, half a person. I didn't even really understand this until I stumbled into my other half.

59

AVA COMES AND knocks on my bedroom door one morning as I browse crappy-looking jobs on Craigslist. It's cold outside, November now, bust-out-a-scarf weather. Ava's in her fur coat and pajama pants. She looks wide-eyed with worry.

"Didn't sleep well last night," she says. "These *dreams*."

I give her a hug. The fur is soft on my cheek, and she smells like cigarette smoke. She goes limp in my arms.

"Want to go get coffee?" she asks when we pull apart. "I need something or I'm gonna go crazy."

"Sure," I say. "Maybe you want to call Shelly first?"

Besides her near-daily check-ins with various PD peeps and Ozzie, Ava sees Shelly at her office twice a week and calls her sometimes between to "process."

"I don't want to talk about it, Veer, I want to just . . . I want to get coffee."

"Okay."

She goes back to her room to get dressed and I do the same. When she comes back, knocking on my door, she's still wearing her fur coat. She's also wearing that wig we bought at the Halloween store on our first hangout date.

"Um," I say.

"Let's wear wigs."

"Why?"

She shrugs.

I stall for a second, not sure what to say. Then I ask myself, *Vera, what are you afraid of? Looking stupid? You're not the person anymore who's afraid to be looked at. You're twinned to the damn sun.*

Funny how you don't notice the changes in you until they've come and gone. Dead stars and starlight.

"That's a great idea," I say.

I fish through my knee-high closet mess and dig the blond wig out, give it a brush, and put it on over my short black hair.

The ride down the hill is quiet. It's early. People are walking their dogs or babies and otherwise, the world is fast asleep. Ava puts a cigarette in her mouth and leaves it there, doesn't light it. She's wearing a huge pair of Jackie O sunglasses.

"Some days . . ." she says to the side mirror. "Some days the bad things just—they take up all the headspace."

"I'm sorry."

I let those words sit there stupid and useless for a moment.

"You can tell me anything," I say.

"I know I can. You're the only one. I could tell you anything— but some things I don't want to."

We pass a gospel music store and two Indian restaurants and rows of mismatched, multicolored houses. I get nauseated, a combo of no food and the sickening thoughts of Ava in that attic.

Will Ava and I ever be two sisters without a ghost between us?

"I have bad days, too," I say. "Before you came home, most days were bad days."

"That's so sad," she says, taking the cigarette out of her mouth.

"It was sad. Everyone was sad. Sad was, like, the default. Sad was this inescapable reality."

"But the pictures in the albums, after I was gone. You guys still looked happy. I mean, you'd've made it. Right?"

"We survived," I say. "But we didn't exactly live."

"I survived, too."

"You really did. I don't know how."

"I never stopped hoping," she says.

I did, sister. I lost hope pretty early on, and I'm ashamed.

"Always hoped I'd get out. Or, I don't know . . . make it all better the way it was somehow, make it all okay." She tucks the cigarette behind her ear and braids her fake red hair. "I fantasized about everything. I went all over the world when I watched the Travel Channel, you know? Amazonian swamps and Turkish mosques and crap. I went *all* those places. I watched the History Channel and visited the *moon*."

"Reality's overrated," I say.

"*Hella* overrated."

We pull in front of a coffee shop, a place with a fancy French name for "rooster" that we just call The Cock. It's open early, it's open late, there's always seating.

"But I don't get why you'd be unhappy." She flips down the dash mirror and applies her red lipstick in the shape of a heart. "I mean, our family's the best. Mom's, like . . . this queen. You know? Always dressed to kill, always busy." She smacks her lips and flips the dash mirror back up.

"Yeah, but busy means she used to never spend a day at home,"

I say, holding out my palm. Ava drops the lipstick in it and I flip my dash down and redden my own lips. I look like a funny drugstore Marilyn in my cheap blond wig. "She was a beautiful stranger."

"Mom is beautiful," Ava says. "And Dad's hilarious."

I just keep going. I give it to her.

"I love Dad," I say. "And now that he's not super depressed, yes, he's hilarious."

"He was depressed?"

"He didn't leave the basement for a long time. He quit his job, he started your website . . . he was just . . ." I shake my head. "You don't have any idea, Ave. Everyone's different now that you're home."

The silence is long, long, long.

"That's good, right?" she says in a little voice.

"The *best.*"

She leans over and kisses my cheek. In the rearview, I see she left a little red blob. My fingers instinctually fly up to rub it away.

"Don't!" Ava says, swatting my hand. "Just leave it."

"But—"

"Who cares? It's cute."

"Easy for you to say," I say. "You don't have one."

Ava points to her cheek. "Sock it to me."

I lean over and kiss her cheek and leave an identical kiss mark.

"There," she says. "Now we're even."

We get out of the car and as we walk toward the glass coffee shop doors, there we are in the reflection—in our wigs, with our big jackets and kiss-marked cheeks—and despite her nightmares last night and our depressing conversation, we're grinning.

Then Ava's face goes slack. Behind us, Ozzie's getting out of his Prius at the curb.

"Girls," he booms.

"I don't want to talk to you," Ava says without turning around. "I don't answer my phone when you call for a reason."

She pulls my arm so hard it hurts.

"Come on," she whispers.

We go inside the coffee shop. My blood tingles in my veins.

I glance behind us at the glass doors, where Ozzie watches us with a stunned expression for a moment and then disappears. "What just happened?"

"I don't like him."

"He's working your case. For free."

"Whose side are you on?" Ava says in a hiss of a whisper. "I don't want to talk to him. He follows me. Did you know that?"

"I didn't."

"He gives me the creeps, okay?"

Here's the thing: Ozzie's kind of derpy and aesthetically challenged. He wears too much cologne. He's got puppy-dog eyes for Mom. But I've never been creeped out by him. Not even once.

Still, I don't say anything.

We both know whose side I'm on. Always.

60

IT'S BEEN A few centuries since we bothered with the family dinner thing. Nobody cooked in my house after Ava disappeared; we reheated. But soon as Ava came back Mom and Dad re-created this dinner tradition, and it's funny how we all settle back into that oak table and gravitate to our old places. Dad finds his old HOT STUFF apron with the muscled man's chest on it and cooks elaborate dinners on the weekend. I don't tell Ava that we ate store-bought frozen meals in our rooms for years, that this family-gathering thing is Rivers 2.0. Wouldn't that reflect badly? I want her to think we're this version of us, always have been. Ava's not the only one who gets the privilege of forgetting.

We Riverses do outings. We ogle paintings in museums. We are a party of four and sometimes five at restaurants. We get steamed drinks from trendy coffee shops and cruise bookstores. We go on walks to the police station to check for new news. We take the dogs to the park and throw a Frisbee. We go to a really bad play about GMOs spoken in rhyme because Mom wants us to. We go see an aging rocker forget the lyrics to his own songs at a club because Dad thinks it will be fun. We wait in a long line and get our pictures taken with drag queens from TV who Ava says are her heroes. One strange celebratory afternoon, we stand in a field and watch the sky and wait. Elliott has jumped from a plane, and the speck of his parachute gets closer, closer, until finally he lands in the grass with a look of bewildered horror on his face. There's dirt on his mouth and he's shaking, but he says he'd do it again right now. His instructor informs us as we pick up his keys and wallet from the Skydiving Adventures building that Elliott is no longer welcome there. None of us ask any questions. We sit in silence for good chunks of time. We are family.

61

WHEN AVA'S OUT getting tutored for the GED test she's taking next month, Mom and Dad come to talk to me. They bring Greek takeout and we sit at the dining room table munching on soggy pita. They tell me that Ava announced to them this morning that she no longer wants to talk to Ozzie, the cops, the FBI, the sex trafficking nonprofit people, or Shelly.

I know she's anti-Ozzie, but I'm shocked at the news about the rest of her entourage, because I was just hanging out with Ava yesterday and she mentioned nothing about this.

"Ozzie's suspicious of Ava," Mom says.

"Um . . . *what*?" I ask.

"He thinks she knows more than she's letting on. More about Jonathan, more about where she was," she continues.

"Bunch of BS," Dad mutters with a mouth full of pita. "I don't trust that hack with the—"

"With the *what*?" Mom asks, cutting a falafel ball into a dozen tiny pieces. "What are you even saying?"

Ah. I forgot how prickly the air used to be in here. Missed it, I didn't.

"What does that even mean?" I ask. "Come on. She was drugged for years, never let outside, confused by stupid TV shows. Of course the details are going to be a mess."

Mom says, "Ozzie asked her to take a polygraph—"

The anger is automatic, pure heat, a bullet fired from my mouth. "Mom, Ozzie can go to hell. Did you know he's been following Ava? She says he gives her the creeps."

"Following her?" Dad says.

Mom looks as if I stabbed her with my spork. "I had no idea."

"I'll bet it's Ozzie's fault Ava wants a break from the whole investigation," Dad says. "It happened right after he showed up at the house this morning. She was very upset."

I was gone all morning partying, which, when you're a paid princess, is much less fun than it sounds. So this happened while I was out.

"Ozzie's also been chasing ridiculous leads," Dad says. "Ignoring all the new evidence we have and focusing on hunches and clues he had back before we even found Ava."

"Then boot Ozzie off the case," I tell them.

Mom shakes her head. "I thought we could trust him."

Dad crumples his wrapper violently. "Vera's right. Ozzie's off the case. *Off.*"

"I'll tell him at our meeting tomorrow," Mom says.

"Good," Dad says. "Right now we just want Ava to be getting healthier, stronger. The cops can wait."

I pick the grape leaf off my dolma, trying to imagine what it would be like to be ridiculed and victim-blamed and asked to take tests like some kind of perpetrator when you've been locked in a man's attic for years and your head is barely screwed on straight. "Yeah, let's let her have a break. I mean, she's been doing this investigation full-time every day since she got home. She's making progress."

The details are coming back, albeit slowly. Just from tiny little discoveries about fast food she ate, there are now sketches of That Monster at every In-N-Out and every Domino's within five hundred miles. Tips are rolling in every day to the feds and the police. We're all getting impatient. I'm surprised my parents are even open to letting Ava take time off.

"It took twelve years to find her. Maybe it's going to take a while to understand the whole story," Mom says. "But, Vera, tell her she can talk to us and that she has to talk to Shelly. And if she tells you anything, you *have* to tell us."

Man, when she makes eye contact she *makes eye contact*. I have to will myself to not look away from her, getting flooded with guilt even though I've done nothing wrong.

Right?

I think of the puzzle pieces Ava has shared with me. The attic, the cigarettes and peanut butter cups, the pictures of flowers.

Do I know things no one else knows?

Do Mom and Dad not know the same details? I press my tongue, hard, to the roof of my mouth. Awkward silence, except for Mexico and Canada whimpering beneath the table. My parents' eyes are on me like they're trying to see inside my head.

"Does she share things with you?" Mom asks.

The desperation in her voice is unfamiliar.

"You two seem so close," Dad says. "Do you . . . know things?"

"Dad," I say, a guilty smile fluttering my lips. "Dad, I know what you guys know."

I know more, a nanny-nanny-boo-boo voice in my head says.

Shut up, I tell the nanny-nanny-boo-boo voice. *It's not about knowing more or being closer to her. Stop being childish.*

Isn't it funny how we're multitudes?

I love Ava. I love that I'm her favorite. It shouldn't be a victory. I could tell my parents the few scant details Ava's shared with me. I could get them to lean in and listen to me and look at me and give glorious attention in ways they haven't in years. But I would never risk Ava's trust. And come on—the facts that she smoked cigarettes or ate a certain candy bar aren't exactly game-changers anyway.

"I know what you know," I say.

"She hasn't been skipping her meds, has she?" Mom asks me, her brown eyes wide.

"I have no idea. I'm her sister, not her pharmacist," I say.

Suddenly, both my parents seem to realize they're leaning in like bloodthirsty dogs, and they relax in their chairs and go back to eating their food for a minute.

"How's . . . everything?" Mom asks.

"Great," I say.

"Great," she repeats.

"Ladybug, you're a good sister, you know that? Getting her that job, hanging out with her all the time, going on walks, helping her get clothes—"

"You crack me up in those wigs," Mom says. "I haven't even seen a paparazzo in weeks."

"It's getting better, isn't it?" Dad asks, surprised.

"You guys have so much fun," Mom says. "She really loves you."

I beam.

The sun pours through the sliding glass door. Our backyard is a magenta ooze of bougainvillea and dew-licked knee-high grass. Summertime, all of us used to spend days back there together. When the grass was still short, when the garden was lush, when the patio furniture wasn't peppered with rust. I see us all rise up like vaporous ghosts—Mom planting flowers, Dad snapping pictures, Elliott practicing swinging bats at softballs, Ava doing somersaults, me lying on the grass with a book.

When dinner was ready, we'd all sit here, at this table, the five of us, and talk—talk so much there were no silences. Talk over one another until Dad had to quip, "Hey, hey, what is this, a pub? One at a time." We had so much to say. It was so loud.

Then it was the opposite.

"After you talk to her," Mom says. "Do one more thing for me."

Mom's intent. She's a whirlwind, but when she finally gives you attention, it's a hot spotlight. "Tell her to stop smoking."

So Mom knows about the cigarettes. Of course she does. Maybe Ava and I share no secrets after all.

But I nod. I thank them for lunch. Mom gets up and grabs her purse. She has a meeting with Ava's publicist. Dad says he's going to go on a walk.

"Excuse me?" I ask.

This is a man, please understand, who had to eat vitamin D supplements for years because he didn't get enough sunshine.

He puts on a scarf and hat that do not match. May I also point out it is sixty-five degrees outside? "I've been walking."

"I'm trying to convince him to quit cigarettes," Mom says.

"The walking helps," Dad says with a shrug.

Mom's been home a lot more. She's cut back on the charity stuff and is basically a professional mom now. Organizing Ava's life with her and relaxing at home is her career. Tutoring appointments, police meetings, therapy, manicures, field trips to museums, endless window-shopping. Not to mention the hours Mom spends online searching for clues to help Ava's case. Her dedication can be intense. Maybe I'm understanding why Dad's all into walks now. I wave goodbye to them. I watch them go together, through the window, then part to go their own separate ways—she to the car, he to the sidewalk. I feel a swell of love for them.

In the backyard, I sit in a lawn chair, watching the ghosts. I marvel at the trees, the worlds unknown to me that occupy their branches. It seems amazing an entire universe was back here the whole time, alive, quietly writhing, and I'd ignored it.

62

IT'S MID-NOVEMBER AND college applications are due in a couple months. A few months back I told myself I'd reapply to the University of Portland for next year, but Ava's return still feels so fresh, and That Monster is still out there somewhere with a hefty reward from the FBI over his head, and we have no answers. I can't will myself to move forward in my own direction—away—until something happens. So I'm here. And that's fine. It's where I want to be. Ava seems to be growing up at an exponential rate thanks to tutors and special programs, finding normal again. I'm so proud of her. But sometimes I feel like her shadow, lurking nearby her with no shape of my own.

Elliott stops by one gloomy morning in a rusted Camaro that's missing its hood. I'm the only one upstairs, still in my pajamas at 11:00 a.m., and he tells me to get dressed and we'll go "hustle up some trouble somewhere." He's cracking his knuckles and grinning and I have to wonder, I do, but he *looks* clearheaded, so I go get dressed, happy to hang out with my big brother again, just the two of us. It's been years. Honestly, I'm giddy.

I get in the car with him. There are smashed French fries and dirty socks on the floor beneath my feet.

"Nasty, Elliott," I tell him.

"You think this beater is mine?" he asks. "My car's getting caps right now. A Benz."

"Whose car is this?"

"Eh, this guy I work for, Chucky."

"Work for doing what?"

"Upholstering furniture, stuff like that."

"I didn't know you upholstered furniture. Also, I thought you didn't have your license?"

"Got it back. What is this, the Spanish Inquisition?"

"Um—"

"Nobody expects the Spanish Inquisition!" he yells in a British accent. He peels out of our driveway and down the street at a speed that turns several heads.

"How's life?" I ask him.

"Oh, it's the best, dahling, it's simply the best," he tells me in a raspy, fancy old-lady voice. Then he drops it. "This is nice, me and you just hangin' out like old times. Right?"

"It's been a short forever," I tell him. "I miss you, Elliott."

The words leave my mouth and linger in the air, the pang of them settling in and realizing themselves. I do. I miss him. He's been coming around more than ever, and when he does, nobody yells and everybody smiles and we live in the moment of this unexpected togetherness. And yet, I miss him so badly.

He drives to Lake Merritt, the silvery city pond nobody's allowed to touch or swim in. We park and grab Mexican food and eat on the grass as other people dog walk and Frisbee. I've been here before, of course, but right now it's fresh. The apartment boxes jutting up. The mirror-shine of the water, the friendly trees. Like if you plopped me here I might not know where I am for a minute. I don't get out enough. I miss strangeness. I daydream about hopping planes sometimes, starting a life.

I chew my burrito and consider whether I may be a selfish jerk.

"I've been stuck," Elliott begins, and I try to place his accent. He finishes his taco and balls up the foil wrapper. "Chugging my engine, never getting ahead. Is that life? I don't know."

Oh. It's him. Took me a moment to recognize him—no character, no bravado, no affectation. My brother.

"I guess we all go through dark times," he keeps going, tossing the foil ball into the nearby can with NBA aplomb. "I was angry and into all kinds of garbage. Since Ava came back, I lifted my head out, was like—huh? Really? Twenty-four, this is what I'm doing? I don't know if you know, but—but I've kinda got caught up in some bad stuff."

I perk up, stunned he would ever say such a thing out loud. "No, really?" I ask sarcastically.

"Yeah," he says. "Been strung out over and over again. I keep screwing up, same ways, different days. I do good and then nothing seems to stick, you know?"

"I know," I say.

"Been thinking about hitting up a meeting or something. Finding a support group."

"A twelve-step?"

This is not my life. My brother at my side, my captivating, random brother—whom I sometimes give up on or live in fear for, who lies so much you begin to believe nothing and everything he says, who has never once owned up to or even answered a question about anything resembling a *problem*, who accepts help from no one and famously sabotages any familial support that comes his way—now breezing by "meetings" in casual conversation. This is not my life.

"Something," he says.

He gets to his feet, and we walk through the stomped-on grass to the path. Runners pass us with headphones, middle-aged women power walk in intimate conversation, friends sip coffees on park benches.

"I admire you," he says. At least that's what I think he says. He's walking so fast I have to hurry to keep up, and I do.

"What?" I ask, catching up.

"Staying home, giving it all up to be with the family," he says. "'Cause you know it's easy to run away, or maybe you don't know."

"I don't," I say, hoping my jealousy doesn't shine.

"You're a better person than me."

"No," I say automatically.

Although I am. I know I am. But guess what? It doesn't necessarily make mine the better choice.

"So what?" I correct myself. "I've always been a pleaser. Does it make a difference?"

He slows down and lights a cigarette and watches me for the first time as if he just truly noticed I'm here.

"Sometimes I feel like furniture," I tell him.

"What's that mean?" he asks after a moment of staring.

What's that mean, brother? Take a look at your life versus mine. How free you are. How you've had the chance to actually screw everything up to find yourself just because. You got to escape the ever-sad reality of the Rivers family weepie. Good for you, buddy. Must be nice.

I bite my tongue so hard I taste metal.

"Nothing," I say.

We stroll again.

"I feel like if I was really going to do it I'd have to come home," he says with utmost seriousness, his eyes so bright they are Dad to the everythingth degree. "Like, start again."

Oh, crap. He's crying. My brother is flicking away tears. The last time I saw him cry he hadn't even started shaving yet. I look around us, as if any oblivious stranger might also go, Oh my God—Elliott Rivers, dry-eyed ghost, he's here and he's *crying*. But no one looks at us. We're nobodies, like everybody else. Lately, I've been shocked by our nobodyness—the photographers and reporters have fast become rarities.

"I felt guilty is the truth," he says. "I mean, still do, but it's different."

"You couldn't have done anything."

"Halloween—"

"You were twelve," I say, louder.

I've said it many times before. Just not in person, and not when he's probably sober.

"I was a kid," he agrees, as if he's defending someone else, which in a way he is.

We're all strangers to our little past selves.

"It wasn't all my fault," he says.

I'm shocked. I've never heard him say those five words before.

"I think I'm letting go of some mean demons inside me," he says.

"We've all been," I say.

I give him a side hug, and he wipes his eyes.

"You ever feel like you're living in a Lifetime movie?" he asks.

"Every damn day."

We laugh and watch the ducks in the oil-slicked water. I spy chip bags and bottle caps in their sludge and wonder how they make it, how they quack so cheerfully and swim so eagerly.

We both continue walking and pretend he never cried and all is sunshiney. He jokes about my job and tells me that they should hire his just-thought-up alter ego, Mr. Cactus Man. I tell a story about the time a kid bit my ankle and I had to go get a shot at a hospital. I make him laugh. I don't care that I'm technically an adult. I still fill up with pride when I'm able to make my big brother laugh.

It's times like this that I'm sure everything's right and staying home is the best thing—not just for them, but for me. I'm getting to know my brother again, whom I only knew via intoxicated random phone calls. He's talking about meetings and coming home. We're opening up and saying things we've never admitted out loud.

"I was never really happy until right now," he tells me in the car.

"Right now? Right this second?"

"No, not then. Right . . . now," he tells me.

"Like, that second that just passed?"

"No . . . nnnnnow," he jokes, clasping the air, as if happiness is a thing we could catch like a fly.

63

I LINGER IN Ava's doorway one night when she lies on her bed watching sitcom reruns.

"Come in if you want," she says with the inflection of a robot.

Her mess is alarming, and I joke that she's going to be on one of those hoarder shows as I sit on the edge of the bed. Her light is off and she appears completely zoned out as she lies hugging a pillow, eyes glued to the flickering rectangle on the wall, laugh track filling the silence.

"So how long are you going to do this stubborn not-talking-to-anybody thing?"

"Not you, too," she says, annoyed.

Mom and Dad have been relentless about her returning calls and getting back into the swing of interviews and therapy. Mom's also been harping on this book deal thing—she thinks Ava should take up a publishing house on a book deal. It's a lot of money for college.

"College?" Ava had asked, incredulous. "I'm technically not even in third grade right now, Mom. And how exactly do they expect me to write a book when I can barely even read?"

"Someone would ghostwrite it," Mom explained.

We had to explain the term to Ava, of course.

Ava laughed nervously. "But first there has to be an end, right? I mean, there's no end to this. They haven't found him."

Of course, then Mom started back in about cooperating with the police and how important it is. But the way Ava's eyes had flashed . . . I swear she looked afraid or saddened at the prospect of it—the end. I wondered why, because in my ending, in my head, that villain, That Monster, is orange-clad and stuck in a cell forever. And the thought of it explodes me with joy. It should her, too.

Now, in Ava's dark room, I don't follow up with my question about police. I also skip over asking if she's been taking her meds and seeing Shelly because I don't want to be another voice in the nagging family choir. I listen to her talk about how Max took her to Albany Bulb, a stretch of nature built on a landfill, pocked with murals and sculptures and homeless people.

"All this art," she says as she watches the screen. "Made out of trash."

She changes channels restlessly. Frantic cooking shows, NASCAR, black-and-white movies, an outdated action flick, finally settling on Nickelodeon.

The cartoons reflect in her shiny eyes. She's got her blankets pulled up to her chin. Her skin's dry around her nose, like she's been washing it too much, and she has some acne that's been picked at.

"Are you okay?" I ask softly.

"Fine," she says. "And dandy. Spectacularizimo." She wipes her eyes, and I put my hand on her shoulder. "I feel like I'm stuck here, stuck in time, like a kid in a grown-up's body—I don't know. I'm scared it's all gonna go away. It's like, I was so special for a minute, now what?"

"How can you think you're not special, seriously?"

"Like—I don't know—I haven't gotten an email in three days," she says. "From anyone! No one asking me for interviews or anything."

"You always turn them down anyway."

"And Mom said that one book publisher said never mind and took their offer away."

"But—you want to write a book now?"

"No," she says. "But I also—I don't know. I'm like, I'm scared." She sits up and looks at me, pained, honest. "Who am I? What am I going to do with my life if I'm not Ava Rivers anymore?"

"You'll always be Ava Rivers, even without the dumb-ass cameramen chasing you down."

"I want a normal life," she says. "But I can't figure it out."

"Can't figure what out?"

"What is a normal life?" she asks me.

It's not rhetorical. She's leaning forward, desperate for an answer.

"I really have no idea," I tell her. "I've been trying to find one since I was six years old."

I put my hand on hers. Our mood rings shine, side by side, both turquoise.

"Look," she says. "We're the same."

She gives me her hairbrush and asks me to brush her hair. I sit behind her and start at the bottoms, teasing out the tangles and snags with painstaking painlessness, then run the brush up higher, higher, until it goes from scalp to tip.

64

IT HAPPENS SUDDENLY, the way the nights turn cold. Ava withdraws, takes multiple showers a day, brushes her hair compulsively, and when I crack jokes she seems preoccupied. This is more than down day after down day. This is another *d* word I'm all too familiar with.

Everyone notices. Dad pulls me into the basement one day and confides that he's worried about her. She's erratic. She's skipping out on her appointments. When Ozzie tried to call from a blocked number the other day, she threw her phone so hard on the floor it shattered.

"It's not her fault," I say. "He won't leave her alone."

"This behavior's not like her," Dad says.

But it *is* like her. I've seen this side of her—they haven't.

Still, I promise Dad I really will talk to her, make sure she stops skipping therapy appointments and is taking her meds. I know it's weird and selfish, but I love the way my dad looks at me with pleading eyes and speaks in that low, confidential tone, like he needs me. For a bitter second, I think of all the years he never did until now.

When Max calls, Ava will pick up and leave the room. I hear their voices through the wall sometimes when he comes over and they lie on her bed watching TV. The hairs stand up on my arms, and I wait for gross make-out noises or something but never hear them. Don't be jealous, Vera. You're her favorite, you're her twin, nothing can take that away.

One night she comes to my room, ghost white, rapping on my door. She's hugging her comforter and a pillow.

"Can I sleep in here tonight?" she asks. "My brain's being ugly."

"Of course," I say.

"I want to sleep where my bed used to be," she says. "Beneath the window."

She spreads the comforter on the floor and lies there.

"I want to be a little girl," she tells the ceiling. "Nothing bad happens to me. I live in this house. I have a family. My name is Ava Rivers."

"Ava?"

"My name is Ava Rivers and everything's okay." She closes her eyes and takes a deep breath in.

My heart. The truth rumbles deep, an imminent earthquake. It's been so easy to ignore—those unthinkable, undescribed things that happened to her. But they're there. Forever. Inescapable. Scars.

"Ava." I try to come and hug her. But she turns away, on her side, and faces the window.

"I'll be fine," she says. "Just shhh—let it pass."

The night is crickets and airplanes. I chew the inside of my cheek. There are new asterisks on her arms, scabby constellations that bring tears to my eyes like they are my burns, that is my skin. I know Shelly is working with Ava on not hurting herself. But all the help in the world doesn't seem to work fast enough sometimes.

65

I SPEND THE next day trying to convince Ava to call Shelly. Call someone. Nope. She bites her fingernails, picks at her scalp. I find an excuse to stay by her side all day. Try to cheer her up with dumb suggestions: Let's wear wigs. Let's go thrifting. We do, but she's joyless and spaced out. She doesn't buy anything and doesn't seem to care her wig's crooked. I crack jokes, I'm met with silence. As we drive around and the college radio station plays weird experimental electronic music—which she switches off, saying, "I hate this crap"—I have to remind myself to breathe. She's not going to do anything crazy. I won't lose her. Because, man, the thoughts that happen, the quick montage of tragic possibilities, they terrify me.

I have to cheer her up and get her smiling. I have to spit shine the world.

As twilight bruises the sky, she runs into a liquor store for cigarettes. In the running car, my worried eyes in the rearview, I get an idea. She hops back into the car, and I drive to my—our— elementary school.

"What's this, a field trip?" she asks flatly as we park across the street from the cement buildings and the chain-link fence protecting a playground.

"Yeah," I tell her, unbuckling my seat belt. "We're hopping in a time machine."

She doesn't say anything as I get out. She follows me with her hands in her fur coat's pockets, cigarette dangling from her lips. We open a gate in the chain-link fence, and I lead her across the blacktop, toeing over Four Square chalkings and passing handball courts and tether poles with no tetherballs. There's a mosaic mural with children playing ball. As we head toward the swing set, she bends her neck up to catch an eyeful of the night-kissed air and its dull shine—a handful of stars like glitter from yesterday's party. She kicks the sand in the sandbox we trudge through.

"School," she says.

"Remember?" I ask her as we get to the swings.

We sit side by side, hands clutching the chains, not swinging in our black rubber seats. Sitting and hanging. She still hasn't lit the cigarette between her lips. A part of me wants to ask her for one so we can smoke them together like sharing secrets. But a bigger part of me wants her to stop, to take care of herself, to never ever burn herself again. To make my mom proud.

"Kindergarten," I say, pointing up to the flat red building in front of us.

She squints at the door up there, a small, dark mouth. There, inside, once we sat in the same classroom.

"Who was our teacher again?" she asks after a short forever.

"Ms. Rosario," I tell her.

"Ms. Ros*ah*rio," she repeats in a theatrical voice.

"She was mean and too tan. She looked like a raisin. Silver hair to her butt. She hated me because I was always a problem during nap time."

"And me?"

"You got in trouble for talking," I tell her. "You and Max."

"Max."

She pulls her phone out and starts texting. I wait for her to come back, I wait for her to have that aha moment where the past comes roaring back and engulfs everything and we sit and get lost in it together. Instead, the light of the phone shines her face pale blue in the darkness.

"Hey," I say. "Hello?"

She drops the phone back into her pocket. "Sorry."

"*Do* you remember?" I ask.

"Moments," she says. "Little . . . Yeah, I mean, that raisin, Ms. Rosario. The classroom, tiny desks, nap time." She shakes her head, surveying the empty school, everything miniature. Once this place was a world. Now it's a dollhouse. "Nothing before I came back here is real. It's all just some weird déjà vu. I'm sorry I can't sit back with popcorn and watch the memories with you."

Ava's voice cracks on that word, "you," and she pulls out her lighter. She flicks it and flicks it. A flame never comes.

"Shite," she says, and tucks the smoke behind her ear.

I could take this silent moment to tell her smoking is dangerous, that the starry burns on her arms sting me, too. But I've got a concrete tongue.

"I could imagine growing up here," Ava says, her voice getting hoarse with emotion. "It would've been nice, you know, elementary school. Lunch boxes and recess and little backpacks. That wasn't my life."

"It was for a brief—"

"Right, but it *wasn't*." She wipes her nose. "It was this other place. I come here—it's like seeing a stranger's school, or some set in a movie I saw once or something. It's not real."

Her cool dismissal of the past breaks me. I've never felt more alone, on this still swing next to my sister, in a dark, empty playground of my elementary school. Squint my eyes and I can see our little ghosts flitting around with jump ropes. Then mine, alone, bewildered, always scanning the playground for a sister who wasn't there. Afraid of the bus driver. Afraid of my friends' dads when they came to pick them up. Afraid of every man I didn't know—potential kidnappers.

"Sometimes I wake up and it takes me a minute to remember I'm Ava." Her eyes, her voice, are full. "Because I wasn't Ava before, you realize. I had a different name."

"Yeah."

It's like she's ripped from me all over again.

"It's important to keep talking about all this," I finally say, the words hurting as they vacate my throat. "You need to keep on with the police. Who knows who might remember you from somewhere."

Her voice climbs. "No one knew I was there. No one cared. They're never going to find him."

"Yes they are."

"He's smarter than all of them," she says. "And I've just been the flavor of the week. TV stations aren't even airing it anymore. Ava Rivers, one-hit wonder."

I can't tell if she's joking. Nothing about it is funny.

"No," she says. "Nobody's ever going to find him. Guess what? I don't even know if I'd want them to."

There it is.

Yep.

I've wondered, I don't say. Wondered so quietly within myself I barely heard my own wondering.

She gulps and then goes on, her words coming out slowly. "It's complicated. I'm so mad at him. And then also—don't tell anyone I said this, okay?"

"Of course."

"I actually love him. I actually *miss* him sometimes." The tears fall from her eyes, but her face is not crying. "He wasn't all bad. Sometimes he just watched TV with me. He bought me coloring books and stuffed animals. Once, I had an allergic reaction when a bee got in somehow through a cracked window and stung me. My whole head swelled up like some crazy cartoon. He got me medicine. He saved my life."

I had no idea she was allergic to bees. And the idea that That Monster actually both stole and saved her life at one point makes me hate him more—his power, his ugly power.

"I know what you're thinking when you look at me—you're thinking, she was raped. She was abused." To hear those words roll out so unflinchingly always takes the wind from me. "You're thinking, that's the worst thing in the world, the worst thing that could ever happen—besides me being dead. But you're wrong." She holds her head back and sucks a huge breath through her nose, lets it out again. "The worst thing isn't that part. The worst was being abandoned, forgotten about. Like when he didn't come upstairs after work. He forgot about me for days and would just come by and give me cold pizza or read me the Bible. I was so hungry at the end. I needed him. He didn't even want to look at me anymore. Then I was a ghost. I was a ghost girl."

I taste my tears before I realize they're there. Ava's are dropping onto her coat and not changing her expression in any way.

"Sometimes it's like I hate him most because he didn't love me anymore," she says.

"Have you told anyone this? I mean, every detail? About what he did?"

"Most of it. I've never told anyone I love him—you don't understand, it's—it's gross."

I hide my disgust. Not at her, of course. At him. At the situation. "But *you're* not gross. It's totally natural to have feelings for your captor. You lived with him for years."

"I know it is, Shelly's told me that. But I hate talking about it." She wipes her nose on the sleeve of her coat. "Please, Veer, don't tell nobody."

"You need to tell the police everything you know."

"I don't *need* to do anything."

I sigh. "It hurts me so much that this person did this to you and he's still out there."

"And I hate that it hurts you." She sniffs and stands up. "I really do. But you can't tell, okay? You've got to *swear*."

"I swear," I say reluctantly.

"On our sisterhood."

"I *do*."

God, I wish I could talk to someone about this. I think of telling Max sometimes—I'd love to hear what he thinks, and I trust him completely. But I can't break a swear on sisterhood.

We get in the car, the expansive nighttime city quiet transforming into the contained car quiet.

"You mad at me?" she asks.

"Not mad."

She lights a cigarette.

"You should quit smoking," I blurt as we turn past the mural and its empty lot and onto our street. "It's bad for you." I glance at her arms, her poor scarred arms. "You need to take care of yourself."

"Okay," she says. "Sure, whatever."

She says it so dismissively, but after a second she throws her cigarette out the window just the same.

"Love you, Veer," she whispers.

"Love you, too."

We head inside and go to our rooms. If you could bulldoze the walls, there we'd be, the two of us, just twelve or so feet apart. In bed, in the dark, I'm a fiery swirl that begins in my chest and swirls outward. Love throbs fierce and mean.

Ava comes knocking an hour later and sleeps on my floor again that night. I can't sleep anyway. I keep thinking about That Monster, that demon my brain won't stop painting pictures of out of the Most Wanted sketches—a Pillsbury Doughman with serial killer eyes. My imagination runs with the scant details, giving him a mouthful of bad teeth, a sick laugh. *He-he-he*. Vomitous. I've never hated someone I've never met so much in my life. Ava starts sleep-talking in the dark and I sit up, listening sharply for clues. But she just mumbles phrases like "Them legs though" and "I couldn't eat all those pizza bagels" and "A few minutes can save you a few hundred in car insurance."

66

I GET UP Thanksgiving morning and am greeted by an explosion of pumpkins, gourds, and spicy-smelling fat candles all over our house. A homemade banner that says TANKFUL hangs over the fireplace, one sheet of printing paper per letter. I point the typo out and Mom says, "Then please fix it. It was your father's *one* job." She's in the middle of making a Thanksgiving playlist on iTunes. Her earrings are gold maple leaves that match the centerpiece.

I go back to my room to hide with Ava, a little freaked out by the scene downstairs. Ava's been happier—rays of sun peeking through the clouds. We sit on the bed in comfortable silence. She gets up and faces the window overlooking the backyard—the Rivers jungle. I scoot off the bed and go to my closet, pick a cranberry dress, and change behind the closet door. Since Ava sort of moved into my room with me, we have our unspoken agreement in regard to privacy. Though when it's her changing behind the door and I pretend to be busy with my phone or making my bed or whatever, I can't help wondering how her body is different from mine. I shudder to imagine more scars.

I step out, dressed but shoeless, and fluff my hair in the mirror.

"You're so purty," Ava says in a yokel voice that is very Elliott.

"Thankee."

"And smart."

I roll my eyes, secretly flattered.

"That book you're reading is, like, a thousand pages long," she says. "Confession—I tried to read a page and I felt like I didn't know half the words."

"It's a Freud reader. He has his own lingo. It was for a class I was supposed to take."

"You were supposed to go to school."

I shrug. "You were supposed to never be kidnapped."

"I made you stay."

"No."

"Can't you just, like, go to Cal Berkeley?"

I don't tell her the deadline is in less than a week and there's no way that's going to happen.

"Or how about you and I move to Portland? You help me write my memoir. Wouldn't that be cool?" she asks, excitement striking her face for a moment.

"You've never even been to Portland."

"I'm sure if you love it, I will, too."

I shake my head. Sometimes her admiration is so pure I feel I don't deserve it. And although I've had my own fantasies of leaving town and starting over and taking her with me, there is no way I could do that to my parents. I mean, she can't live with them forever. But at least longer than a few months. They've missed out on so many years with her.

"Why you all sad-faced?" she asks.

I smile at that way she's adopted my phrases.

"I don't know," I lie, staring at my stockinged toes, black against the white carpet.

I'm an anvil. Paralyzed. A stone in the stomach of this big house, Ava. I'm filled with an anger for the person who hurt you that is transformative. It's hard to explain.

She comes next to me in the mirror and puts her head on my shoulder. When we were girls, we never slowed down for such gestures. We were busy as bees. We bickered and hollered and thumped our sneakers up and down the stairs. Our eyes are different colors now—different from each other, different from how they used to be, hers paled, mine darkened. We are women. Not just our shapes and our features. Our expressions. The shadows. I snake my arm around the furry back of her coat and squeeze.

"I'm must be PMSing," I say.

"Tampino—the 'ladylike' tampon," Ava says in a commercial-lady voice.

We crack up for a minute and then head downstairs.

"Whoa," Ava says when she sees the decorations and the actual silver platters Mom has assembled. Mom stops her neurotic search for napkin rings and is still for a moment, gripping the counter with her fingers. Her nostrils flare and she smiles and shakes her head.

"Yes, yes, this is really happening," she says.

Louis Armstrong sings about skies of blue and clouds of white in the silence.

"Is Elliott coming?" Ava asks.

Louis sings about the bright blessed day and dark sacred night in the silence.

"He's bringing *pie*," Mom says with the same amazement someone might say, *He has risen from the dead*.

Mom comes over to us, and we hug. The rush is potent, druglike, and—for one blissful moment—it erases the tension I've been carrying with me.

67

THE HOUSE IS full of music and noise. Dad slicked his hair back and is wearing a suit jacket from his marketing days. On the bottom, worn pajama pants and slippers. The conversations overlap. Dad splashes wine in his favorite elephant-head mug and tells Elliott about some random book he read about feces. Elliott, who, by the way, shaved and looks boyishly handsome as he sips (doesn't guzzle!) wine, too, coaxes Dad on with an overeager tone and poo puns— "Book sounds like the shit"—that Dad either totally misinterprets as genuine interest or chooses to ignore. Meanwhile, Ava relays the plot of some reality show to Mom. See, okay, it's about a gang of bikers who pick up people's litter, track down the litterers, and throw the litter back at them or disgrace their yard with it or whatever. My mom's like, and you think these people are making the world a better place? Ava says, well, yeah, why not?

Take a picture, brain. Now. Right now.

I can't remember the last Thanksgiving Mom and Dad spent together. It's usually been just Dad and me and some frozen meals or maybe takeout and a movie, Mom off at a soup kitchen. Ever since the Turkey Incident, Elliott's had excuses to get out of any holiday. Or, more recently, he hasn't even phoned to bother to coin an excuse. Last year Dad and I were at Denny's and we didn't seem to be thankful for anything. If I remember correctly, the word "sorry" was exchanged multiple times over sliced pie. Ava has no idea. She thinks this Whole Foods spread and the bone china and cinnamon candles are our tradition. We're fancy and classy and conversational. This is us. We hold hands and thank the migrant workers for the vegetables, the free-range organic birds that gave their lives, the Chinese workers who assembled the table we're eating on and the clothes on our backs. We're less than half joking. Dad, whose lips are wine-kissed, whose plate is a mountain of turkey with a small mustache of gravied potatoes, has these wrinkles around his eyes— sun wrinkles, smile wrinkles—and he looks so unstoppably happy. Like right now his smile actually means something, it's not just a flash that says *I'm okay*. Look around the table. We're all smiling that way. Ava, to my right, is smiling biggest of all.

Mom is thankful for Ava. It's the obvious answer. Elliott, of course, grins and says he's thankful he was born a man and not a turkey. Then he gets more serious and says he's thankful for second chances.

What am I thankful for? "I'm thankful for this," I say in a whisper.

Ava squeezes my hand and says she's thankful she's home and she's thankful for me.

"My best friend," she says. "My soul sistah."

My cheeks bloom warm and I say, "Awww."

But I tell you, add up all the sunlight I ever stood under and it still wouldn't feel as good as those six words.

Dad raises his elephant mug. "I'm thankful," he says, tearing up. Oh, geez. I have to look at the mangled foothill of turkey on his plate or else I'm going to cry. "I'm thankful that we finally found Ava after all these years, that all those hours and heartache looking for her were worth it."

"Cheers," we all say, raising our glasses.

Thank you, hope, for not making chumps of us.

68

AVA AND I sit near the window, Ava up on the bed, me cross-legged on the floor near her. We both wear my pajamas. Outside the window, the ash tree swishes. In the moonlight, it appears midnight blue against the paler backdrop of evening.

"I don't mean to sound like a cheeseball or nothing, but do you realize how lucky we are?" Ava asks. "I mean, a lot of people out there don't have this. They don't have turkey and silver dishes and they don't even have family."

"I do know."

"And, like, *Berkeley*, man. Everyone seems like they're in a good mood everywhere I walk. You got houses painted with rainbows and old ladies riding their bikes and random strangers with their drum circle at the flea market on Sundays."

"It's not all like that."

"It is to me." Ava exhales out her nose. "There was this little hole in one of the window boards, marble-sized. I used to just stare out the window through that hole sometimes, just stare at the weeds and the house across the street and the kids shooting each other with Nerf guns in the yard. Running through sprinklers. The way the sun hit their mom's silver car, how she washed it on Sundays and the dad pulled out the trash bins to the curb cursing and grunting on Mondays. The highway behind—I'd count cars—how many red, how many blue, how many white cars."

I'm startled. Everything she said is a clue. There has to be more to this, some reason she wants to keep this to herself, but I can't figure it out. I bite my tongue. I want her to keep talking.

"I'd think, it looks so pretty out there, I want to be there. I want to go home, I want to have a home like the ones I see on TV. But it was so confusing because he said where we lived was so dangerous. Thing about danger is, you can't see it. First he said there were murderers and kidnappers out there."

Her kidnapper scared her with threats of kidnappers. I mean . . .

"Then after some years I gradually started catching on, seeing out the window, all the quiet houses and nothing ever happening except maybe a dog chasing the mail lady or whatever. I was like, it's not dangerous out there. Then he went through trying to tell me there was radiation poisoning, like from a nuclear something or whatever, and I was like, well, then why isn't anyone in those hazmat suits like the movie I saw about nuclear winter? He was mad I'd been looking out the window again and he boarded them up even better after that, but he couldn't really argue and so I knew then, I knew he was a liar. Then one day everything got different, everything changed. He became suddenly religious. He told me I was the evidence of his sin. He didn't hit me or lock me up anymore. He said he was sorry, he cried and asked me to forgive him. But it was confusing to know he'd been lying to me."

I'm trying to memorize the clues in her ramble. Why? Why? Why is she saying these things now? Why to me and only me?

"He said he had lied because he was afraid of losing me, that he was weak," she says. "I did believe that. I mean, he got real sad sometimes. I felt bad for him."

"Don't you dare pity him."

"I can't help it. He was all I had. You know his mom used to burn his arm on the stove when he was a kid? He had scars all up and down his arms. His dad was a drunk, split his skull with a wine bottle."

"I'm sorry, but I don't have room in my heart to excuse anything he did based on his childhood. A lot of people have bad childhoods and they don't steal little girls from the street."

"Never mind, I hate it when I start talking like this. It doesn't solve anything. Just shut me up." She clamps her hand over her mouth for a minute, closes her eyes. My mind races for the proper response. The details have piled up so quickly they're overwhelming.

"Don't shut up" is all I can say, even though the thought of her continuing to talk makes my gut twist.

Ava releases her hand from her mouth. "I just—I just was trying to say I wanted this all along. Staring out that window. Or at the TV. I mean, this is even better than my hopes. A mansion with gourmet food and a twin who's, like, the best friend I could ask for and a big brother who could be a model. I mean, we're *rich*."

I shake my head.

"I guess rich just depends on where you been," she says.

"I love you," I tell her. "I hope you know."

And I don't just love at that moment, I am one step inside love, I experience love in 360. She puts her hand on my head for a moment and we giggle tiredly.

We end up watching dumb reality TV in her room. Ava's

transfixed by the screen, talking to it like it can hear her. "Girl, no. Don't even act like you're that stupid, you really think you've been dating a dude online who's a famous rapper but *doesn't own any cameras*?" I laugh along with her, but the sickness in my belly is more than holiday overindulgence. It's the details swirling around my head. The sad window that looks out onto the lawn of a family she watched. The fact That Monster was once a kid whose mother held his arm to the stovetop's fire. And I have to sit here and take it, and not bring it up or ask questions for fear of pushing too hard, take what Ava offers me calmly and never urge her to tell anyone else.

I get up to go to bed, so silently sick, like I will never be anything but sick, like being well is the passing feeling and sick is the permanent state.

69

"IT'S BLACK FRIDAY," Ava keeps saying. And then a random vampire laugh. "Mwha ha ha ha!"

We're both still in our PJs, eating leftover pie and watching TV in the living room. Commercials currently on mute.

"I love how evil you make it sound," I say.

"It is evil. Didn't you see on the news how that lady got trampled to death outside a mall?"

"Humanity is gross."

"Agreed," she says. "Hey, we should dress all goth and go visit a cemetery or something. For Black Friday."

I laugh. "Um, sure."

"I'm serious. Let's, like, make our own holiday."

I savor the pumpkiny heaven in my mouth for a generous moment before realizing Ava's not joking.

She's so infectiously, awesomely weird.

I shrug. "Sure."

We finish our pie and head upstairs to pick out black outfits, each changing behind the closet door. Me: miniskirt, fishnet leggings, leather jacket. Her: black jeans, black shirt, black eyeliner on her lips. Even the eyeliner is mine.

We look ridiculous, and I couldn't love it more.

Mountain View Cemetery in Oakland is more than a cemetery—it was designed by the same dude behind Central Park. It's more than dead people. It's green slopes and colorful trees and picnicking lovers and dog walkers and wine-drinking hipsters. Max waits for us by the fountain at the entrance, playing his guitar, wearing shades on a cloudy day. Pure album-cover material. Max is so lovely and his voice is such honey that the sight of him almost hurts. I park and we get out.

"You ladies look hip," Max says.

"Happy Black Friday," Ava says dramatically.

Max's laugh is infectious and hilarious in itself. It hasn't changed since grade school.

We hoof it up a hill, passing contemporary headstones etched in Chinese and featuring pictures of smiling people, freshly flowered graves. Max drops a few details of his Thanksgiving, alone with his mother, with a burnt Tofurky and a fight about wailing.

"Excuse me—did you say *wailing*?" I spell it out for him.

"No, like Save the Whales. *Whaling*."

"You don't want to save the flipping *whales*?" asks Ava.

"I do!" he shouts. "We *both* want to save the whales. I don't even know how we were *fighting* about it. That's how it is with my mom."

"God, I'm so glad we don't fight with Mom like that," Ava says to me.

"Yeah, Mom's not a fighter," I say.

We stop in front of a bunch of dead Bakers and Smiths and Doolittles who never saw the twenty-first century. Mothers, daughters, sisters, men.

"Nobody fights in our house," Ava tells Max. "It's like—it's like a sitcom without the annoying laugh track. Everybody's always in a good mood."

I smile, no teeth. It's cute that's all she knows.

I don't know why people say "naïve" like it's a bad thing.

"We have a good family," I say. It isn't a lie.

"Your family's cake," Max says. "I have this memory, your mom painting with watercolors while your dad was on guitar, board games stacked in the living room—all that noise and music."

It floods back to me as he describes the scene, the buried years before everything changed.

"Your mom's transformed," Max goes on. "I mean, don't get me wrong, she's fierce either way. It's just . . . she used to be different."

I'm surprised he noticed. This boy, who only stopped by to send a balloon heavenward on the missing girl's birthday.

"How?" asks Ava.

"You don't remember?" I ask.

I don't know why I keep expecting her to remember. She was so young.

Mom used to be like a mom, is all I can think to say. She spent her hours at home, gardening, cooking, making art, reading books with us. She tucked us in at night. Then it all stopped. She was out. Her calendar inked and full, her car never in the driveway. She became cold, coiffed, a queen. How to explain it? Like even when she was studying you she wasn't really listening? Like there was no space inside her left for anyone, like there wasn't a spare moment?

"She was really busy for a long time," I say.

"*Hella* busy," Ava chimes in, as if I'm not explaining this for her benefit. "You know how many lives that woman's probably saved?"

This is true. I've been so selfishly zeroed in on the holes that I forgot that somewhere, she's an angel to many faceless someones— filler of soup bowls, soothing voice on a crisis line, sage advice-giver.

We pass a green pond with a graffitied cement bank. The sun blankets the oaks and graves in gold. Ava takes Max's arm. We make it to the rich people's monuments up top, the ones that could be stone houses with steps and etched angels and marble rooms. We climb over Merritt's and Crocker's mansion-graves and descend a long set of stairs and a few paths to pass Gwin's pyramid. I leave Ava and Max on the steps of a steepled mausoleum and step inside a cool tomb where my own blood stops in my ears.

My very breath seems to echo off the walls.

"I am in the heart of something," I whisper silently.

Right here in this cemetery, remains are quiet, spread out beneath the hillsides, armies of skeletons, all once people. Real people. With families and sadnesses and epiphanies and moments where they felt so not alone it seemed eternity was possible. Ava's voice drifts from outside. What if I lost her again? What if we had lost her? Inevitably I'm going to lose it all someday, and boy does that thought sting.

Kiss me, nothing.

But Jesus jazz-handsing Christ, they're laughing so loudly in the graveyard. It squashes the seriousness. I step into the sunshine. They're chasing a balloon down the road, a balloon slowly sinking in the air. Max leaps and finally reaches it and they shout hoorays.

"We got it!" Ava screams at me.

And it seems so significant, I have to wait a second before joining them, make sure the burning in my corneas will not lead to an emotional display. I'm cool. It's all good. I join them and guess what, the balloon says HAPPY BIRTHDAY.

70

WE TREK UP to the apex, to a point that overlooks everything. Oakland, the Bay, the bridges, the hills of San Francisco. Reminds me of when Max and I climbed up to Indian Rock that short forever ago.

"You"—Max stands, holding the balloon—"got, like, a worlds-deep stare." As if he's one to talk, with his molasses slay-you-pretty eyes.

Ava's pissing in the bushes.

"So?" I ask.

"You're like a *forest* of girls."

"You're a forest of weirdos."

He laughs wildly, and I can't help joining him. Then we get serious in unison, and the quiet is so loud.

"I don't know what's going on between you," I whisper, hurried. "Not my business. But please be careful with her, Max. She's so delicate."

"What? No, we're not— She's like a *child*. I mean, not— I don't mean that as an insult, it's just—"

"Exactly," I agree. "She is."

And for a brief moment, the clouds pass, the sun shines. Maybe the dynamic among us three is different than I thought. It isn't him and her and then me standing outside their flirtatious bond; it's him and me, the adults, and her, forever-child stunted by stolen years.

Ava comes around the corner, wiping her hands on her fur coat, the moment broken.

"I think I splash-pissed on Priscilla Diller's grave," she stage-whispers. "Am I haunted?"

"Well, it is Black Friday," Max tells her.

We wander, studying gravestone after gravestone, until it's almost dark. Ava insists we find a grave with today's date as the birthday to leave the balloon at. The confidence with which Ava leads us up and down knolls as we all squint at tombstone dates makes it easy to forget what we're doing is as silly as dressing like a goth on Black Friday.

"There!" shouts Max finally.

We sit at the grave of Heidi Little, with a dirty white lamb etched on her stone. Max plucks his guitar strings. That zing I get listening to my dad or Elliott play—the hairs-on-end deliciousness of sound—it comes back as we sing her the happy birthday song.

71

WE GET HOME past dinner. My phone is dead. Apparently so is Ava's, which is why our parents stand outside, greeting us with murderous glares as Ava and I get out of my car after I park on the street.

"Why are you home so late?" Dad asks.

"It's not even eight," I say.

"And you don't answer your phones?" Mom hisses.

Ava shoots me a what-the-hell glance. "They both died."

"You don't *charge* them?"

"Sorry," I say, hands in the air. "Everything's fine."

"Well, we're not tele*pathic*," Dad says.

Wouldn't that suck, I think loudly.

I'd rather run up the street and hide in a neighbor's bushes, but we go inside the house.

I can feel how uncomfortable the anger makes Ava as we put our purses away in the foyer. Mom stands there, Dad behind her, the hall light behind them making them both dark figures. As Mom steps closer to us, I can tell she's been crying. Her mascara's a mess, which Mom does *not* let happen.

"Mom?" I ask, alarmed.

"Let me look at you," Mom says to Ava. "Come here. Come here right now."

"Mommy," Ava says in a small voice, stepping back into the coat rack.

"Come here right now and let me look at you," Mom demands.

"Michelle," Dad says.

Ava comes forward, wide-eyed and almost cowering. Mom steps up to her and takes Ava's chin in her hand, as if she's surveying Ava's face to make sure she has no scratches or is indeed sober or something.

"Mom, what are you doing?" I ask.

Mom lets go and steps back. "See?"

"See *what*?" I ask.

"Mommy?" Ava asks again.

Ava and I exchange a look.

"Everything's fine," Mom tells us as she stands with crossed arms. "Sorry. Charge your phones next time."

"Um," I say.

"I'm going to bed now," Mom tells us.

"Michelle," Dad says to her back as she leaves the room and closes her bedroom door.

I swear everyone can hear my raging heartbeat in the thick silence. Dad's sorry blue stare meets mine. "We had a rough night. If you see Ozzie, let us know. Your mother wants a restraining order."

"Why?" Ava asks, clearly scared.

"I don't want to go into it," Dad says. "I just—if you see him—if he tries to call you, Ava, tell us."

"Dad, what did Ozzie *do*?" I ask.

I can't imagine what must have happened while we were out. All sorts of bizarre, frightening possibilities play out in my mind.

"Nothing for you to be concerned about," Dad says.

"Is it about Jonathan?" Ava asks.

Every time she utters his name, it threatens my stomach contents.

"Don't worry," Dad says. "You're safe. It's really nothing to do with you."

We say our good nights, and Ava and I go upstairs to whisper about what happened.

"Mom's never like that," I say. "Something must have gone down."

"I'm hella creeped out right now," Ava says. "Like, why won't they tell me? It must have something to do with the case, so why wouldn't they—"

"I don't think it has anything to do with your case. I think it had something to do with . . ."

The stupid love triangle, I almost say. You know, Ozzie loves Mom, Dad resents it, Mom pretends to not notice. But Ava doesn't know anything about that.

". . . with?"

"I don't know, actually," I say. "But you know Mom. If it was anything sketchy, she'd have the feds send someone to watch us."

She bites the inside of her cheek. "True."

We settle on my bed and pass a bottle of nail polish back and forth. We blow on our fingertips and watch music videos on my computer. A commercial for diamonds comes on, a stupid commercial telling men that what we women really want are sparkling stones that kids halfway around the globe died for. I've never liked diamonds. Now I truly despise them, because that was *his* name for her.

"I don't know if I ever want to get married," Ava says.

"Me neither. I mean, I want to fall in love. And live with someone. Maybe adopt a kid or something. But I don't care about getting married."

"I'm glad I didn't really get married when I was away."

Away, like she was off at summer camp.

"I kind of tried to kiss Max last week when he took me to Barney's," Ava says. "I didn't know he was gay."

"I didn't know he was gay either," I say, shocked.

Shocked because he's totally flirted with me. Shocked because we went to high school together and I can think of three different girls he dated, arty types with heavy eyeliner. Shocked because my sister tried to kiss him, shocked at the jealous sting in me.

He can't be . . .

"It's probably better anyway," Ava says. "I just thought it would make me happy to kiss him. For a second, I thought it'd make me happy. But I don't know what I want. I don't even know if I like him like that."

"He's just a good friend," I say. "He's a really good guy."

I mean it, too. Maybe I'm right now realizing the full strength of his goodness—no ulterior motives, no weird crushes, he's just a damn good person.

"I do wish I could cuddle sometimes. You know, be held," Ava says.

I wrap my arms around her. The scent of my fake coconut shampoo has never smelled so delicious as it does in her crimp-wavy hair.

She relaxes as I hold her. She doesn't make a peep. And I'm aware, in the warm, perfect here, that nothing lasts. Love is an excruciating delicacy. Maybe that is its force.

72

IN THE COMING days, I try many different tactics to extract the truth of what happened with Ozzie the other night. I approach Dad in the basement all casual-like. "Not going to talk about it with you, Ladybug." I beg Mom as she powders her face in front of her vanity. "Vera Rose, it's not your business!" I corner them both early in the morning at the breakfast table and swear myself to secrecy over my own dead body, which makes no sense to me really but hopefully conveys just how serious I am.

"It's over," Mom says. "Doesn't matter."

"Where are you going?" I ask her.

I assume she's about to say, to the station. Which is where she's usually heading off to—something police-slash-Ava-related, where she brings her briefcase filled with notes—or off to meet Ozzie, although obviously not that anymore.

"I'm taking a class," she says.

"*Really?*"

"An improv class."

"Whoa. Way to go, Mom."

"I just . . . I need to do something. For me."

"Words I never thought I'd hear out of your mouth."

"Yeah, well, took me long enough," she says.

The self-awareness, the sudden subtle shift in her—I find myself staring at her like I hardly know her, like she is full of surprises.

Dad's on the floor, doing his pre-jog stretches. "Maybe it's time for you to find some new hobbies, too," he tells me. He says it gently, but man, it stings.

I go upstairs, swallowing, thinking, *I could be a visitor like Elliott. But I stayed because I wanted to do the right thing.* I go back into my room and confront the sight of my boxes, those stupid boxes I can't bring myself to unpack filled with items that apparently don't matter that much. Ava's still sleeping. I soften, seeing her hair and the way the sun catches it. I grab a book. I sit in the corner. My eyes fall on the page, and I disappear into the ink.

73

AVA AND I buy a shimmery pink Christmas tree for our room and drape rainbow lights around our bed, and by the first week of December, Ava has learned to pluck every bad earworm carol on my ukulele. She bought a terrible sweater with a homemade felt elf on it that has googly eyes and wears it daily. Usually I hate the holiday season, all drugstore hype and fake family cheeseball bullcrap and the same movies on TV and people stringing lights up on their Berkeley Victorian houses that they won't take down until February, but this year it's like it used to be—Dad fixed the fireplace, Mom bought hot chocolate K-Cups for the Keurig machine, and we decorated the banister with tinsel that clings to our hair and clothes for days. When we put the leftover decorations back in the garage, I show Ava her boxes—dust-kissed and Sharpied with her name. I open the top one up and pull out a tiny turtleneck with ice cream cones on it.

"We saved all your stuff," I tell her, proud.

The weather in my sister visibly changes from sunshine to a chance of rain. She won't reach out or step closer or touch the fabric in my hands.

"Remember?" I ask.

"Don't." She turns to the wall and shakes her head. "God, that makes me sad for little Ava."

I keep holding the turtleneck for a moment. But she doesn't turn back around to look at me until I've put it away, closed the cardboard on it again, and tucked it back in the dark corner it's been in for ten years, where it will probably be for ten more.

74

THE MEDIA HAS a toddler-level attention span. Reporters and photographers never seem to come around anymore, and the ones who do aren't big shots with fancy digital cameras and release forms, they're local bloggers. Ava agrees to meet with the feds and the police again, although not as much as she did in the beginning. And obviously she doesn't see Ozzie anymore. I drive her to appointments at the station sometimes and watch her sit at a desk and look at pictures and say, "No, not him. Not him. Not him." The police are always super apologetic about how long it's taking and promise they're going to find him.

"Not unless they knock on every door a thousand miles in every direction," Ava tells me privately as we sit in the car in the police parking lot. "And at this point, if he saw the price on his head, he'd be running now anyway."

"Not even a tiny part of you wants to see him behind bars?" I ask. "Suffering the way you suffered?"

Ava thinks about it. She doesn't move, and I wonder if I pushed her into one of her stuck trances.

"I think it would be better if I never saw him again," she says finally. "A part of me wants to, though. Part of me wants an explanation. An apology."

I don't know how to respond.

"I really hate it that I even want those things, but it's my truth," she says.

It takes me a moment to gather my thoughts, weigh them on my tongue, form them into words.

"You're brave to say it," I say. "And you're an incredible person to not want revenge."

"You're an incredible person to just let me be myself. And love me even though I'm all messed up."

"You know you could tell Mom and Dad and they'd still love you, too, right?"

"Nobody loves me like you," she says.

Her eyes shine. I reach out and squeeze her cold hand, start the car, and drive into the cold night.

75

AVA AND I have our own little Christmas Eve, after dinner, after Dad and Mom go on their nightly walk. Ava and I trade a few gifts upstairs near our tiny pink tree. She got me strange things: a tie-dye shirt that says BEZERKELEY, knit mittens, and a Snow White diary with a lock on it, gifts I swear a nine-year-old girl would give. I love them and tell her I love them, wearing the mittens. They smell like Nag Champa. She bought them at the street fair where Max's mom works.

"I found the journal in a free box," she says. "Reuse, recycle."

"Nice."

I pull out my gift for her. It's a photo album, shiny black leather and Bible-thick, filled with color-copied pictures I picked from every photo album in our house. It begins when we're babies, side by side, identically shut-eyed and wrinkled in pink beanies and blankets. Flip the pages and we're toddlers, in matching strawberry dresses, my hair already a shade darker, hers golden and wild. Us bigger, on a carousel, or blowing out candles in a half-and-half cake. At the beach, digging girl-sized holes. Next to Dad at a baseball game, Dad's arm around each of us back before he became a vampire afraid of the sun. Elliott, me, and Ava on Christmas morning, bed-headed and greedy-eyed. I didn't know whether I should put the picture there at the end, of Halloween. For starters, there are shadows everywhere and the quality could have been better. It was our last photo. Two angels, six years old. I included it.

She seems stunned by the gift—stunned good, stunned bad, I'm not sure yet.

"This was my life," Ava says.

She traces our shapes in the Halloween picture.

"This is how it was," she goes on.

"Yeah."

"Then I was gone."

The room is so still. Even with the window open and the sound of salsa music and hooting coming from a party nearby, the nothingness is big.

"This is . . . the nicest present, Veer."

"I wish there were more pictures. I mean, I wish we weren't cheated out of so many years."

"What if I wasn't locked up at all," she says. "What if I was here. What if this was my life." She points to the Christmas Day picture. "Like, what if we'd shared all these Christmases together, and this was just, like, another."

The Christmas lights on our pink tree go blink, blink, blink.

We agree to go on a walk. Ava heads downstairs to grab her coat. As I put on my boots and a pair of leopard-print earmuffs, I stop and flip to a random page in the photo album. I know I put this picture in there, but it's unfamiliar to me for a second. The table—glitter-flecked Formica—I don't know it. My mother, in pigtails, frown lines on her face and bags under her eyes. There's a broom behind her, and my father is asleep in the background, on the couch. He has a mustache, and his plaid pajamas don't match. I can't place the time. Judging by the domestic gloom that seems to shade the picture, the palpable exhaustion, I must have copied a photo from after Ava's disappearance and placed it in there by mistake. But then I see the babies in diapers in the corner on the floor. The babies that are actually us. This picture is old, eras before disappearance, back when everything was supposed to be different. In one way, everything was. I close the book.

"Ready?" asks Ava when I meet her downstairs.

The dogs think they're going on a walk and race around the enormous tree in the living room.

"All right, you little slobberpuffs," Ava tells them, grabbing their leashes.

We walk out into the midnight blue, the smoky smells of chimneys and maybe even barbecues, the twinkling promise of red-green lights strung lazily on porches. We walk so long we pass Ashby and head down California, wordlessly heading back into the neighborhood where we once lost her.

"Merry Christmas, my friends!" a probably drunk man with a cane calls out to us as we step into the street with the gasping, scampering pugs. "Christ our Savior is born!"

"Also Santa!" yells Ava.

As we walk, I remind her about how she broke the news that Santa wasn't real to me when we were six, because she'd asked Elliott and, of course, he'd told her the truth. She nods and smiles, but I can tell she doesn't remember.

We stop in front of a possibly abandoned hoarder house that's been there as long as I can remember. A bunch of laminated paperwork hangs on the chain-link about the development coming in here soon and the permits it requires. An eerie hush floods me. Far away, a group of off-key voices are caroling, "It came upon a midnight clear," and my eyes hurt in a way that burrows down, deep down, into a place in me even I can't touch.

"Vera," Ava says in a quiet voice. "I'm glad it happened just like this."

"Me too," I say.

She squeezes my mitten and for a brief, unclenched, blissful second, there are no questions.

76

ELLIOTT CALLS US on New Year's Eve afternoon, and the three of us—Ava, Elliott, and me—talk on speakerphone. Ava and I sit up at a lookout point at the graveyard. You can see the bridges reaching silver across the Bay, the puddle of Lake Merritt in the middle of Oakland buildings, Angel Island far out in the water, oil tankers like alien robots along the lip where Oakland meets the Bay. We sit on the marble steps of a dead rich man's tomb and have a telephone conversation. Jokes and funny voices, cheerful catch-up about our holidays. Elliott's got a "new pad that is *killer*," he assures us. We need to see it. In fact, get in the car and party New Year's with him and see his new "killer pad" and he's just doing so well, he's so proud, he's made all this money landscaping, he's gotten really into landscaping and he would drive to visit us but his car is being painted right now so why don't us girls come down and spend New Year's with him?

The invitation, out of nowhere, stuns me especially because in all these months and years we've spoken on the phone, he's never once asked me to hop in my car to see him. But I know. I know I'm special now that I'm Ava's twin sister again. Obviously I understand why. Everyone loves a ghost. I am not bitter.

"Sure," Ava says.

We exchange looks. A nearby grave is etched with a name, DEWITT. I snicker and say okay.

A while later, it's seventy-something mph, we're munching gas station snacks, mariachi music blasting, robot-lady smartphone GPS leading us to see Elliott. The I-5 freeway is ugly, treeless, brown, slaughterhouse-stinky, and superstore-dotted, but at night, tonight especially—with the thunder of the car's movement and the lights beating by in a flicker-flicker-flicker, the dull stars' secrets overhead, it's a New Year, there's speed and momentum in it already—it is beautiful and we are lucky.

We play twenty questions. Turns out Ava is thinking of a woman who was the assistant on a game show I've never even heard of. Once we're more than halfway there Ava gets contemplative and doesn't talk for a long time, even when I say her name. She watches out the window, night bleeding everything blue.

"I feel sick." Ava throws her fur coat in the backseat and fans herself with a map. She rolls down the window even though it's capital letters FREEZING.

"You going to throw up?" I ask.

Her eyes are closed, fingers to temples. "Wish I could."

I watch her out of the corner of my eye.

"Vera," she says. "Vera, you can't tell anybody, but this is where I was."

I have to remind myself to do very simple things—keep my foot on the gas, hold the steering wheel, inhale and exhale.

"Two freeway exits ago, that's where I lived with Jonathan."

Two exits ago—in the forgettable nothing-burb of Satterfield, California. Here, really? *Here?*

"You're kidding me," I say.

"No, no, I'm not, and I didn't even think I was going to tell you, but there it was, I did."

"Why are you telling me now?"

"Because here we are," she says hoarsely. "I've been dying to tell you. It sucks that you trust me so much and then I haven't told you the whole story. But here we are. I can't drive by it and not tell you." A bead of sweat drips down her forehead. "Turn around. I'll show you." She covers her mouth with her hand. "I can't believe this."

I get off on the freeway exit and turn back onto the same freeway, going the other direction.

"So—what do you mean?" I ask. "You *know* where you *were?*"

"Don't hate me. He took me out on drives a couple times. Kept me locked in the van. I recognize this. It's something I never told anybody. It's like I didn't fully remember it until now, till I saw the signs."

Maintain, Vera. Keep the tone down and don't flip. "I don't—I just—I thought you had no idea."

"I knew a little more than I said I did."

She weeps, shriek-like, and I swear to God I'm about to crash the car into the median right now. She muffles her face in her hands and then recovers as we approach the exit.

"You were in Satterfield, and you knew this all along?" I ask.

"I knew I shouldn't've told you—"

"No, it's okay, Ave, it's good. You realize how good this is?" I ask, unable to stop my voice from shaking. "Now they can get him."

"No, no, *no*. That's what I didn't want—I didn't want them—never mind. I'm not going to show you."

"But it's this exit? Hopper Street? This is where you were?"

"Please. Don't ever tell anyone."

"Ava, I've never broken your trust. I will never tell anyone anything. Is it Hopper?"

Hopper is a hundred feet away, and we're speeding toward it. I keep turning to look at her for a reaction. Frozen, staring ahead, finally she nods and I exhale, letting off the gas so the car slows to a halt on the exit ramp. We sit at a stop sign on a lampless street.

"Are you okay?" I ask.

"I'm fine."

"You were here."

"I was here."

"That's—that's amazing—amazing that you—you remember."

"Yes."

"I—I—I don't even. I don't know what to say."

A car honks behind us.

"Right," she tells me.

I drive down a long road flanked by dry fields and windmills. In the distance is the garish glow of big-box stores.

"When I saw those signs, I was like, no, no, no. I closed my eyes. I thought I could make it disappear," Ava says.

"Why didn't you say something to the police?"

"Because I don't want anybody knowing where I was."

"Why not?"

"It's complicated," she mumbles.

We pass the big-box stores. Now we drive into the dark, seemingly approaching nothing.

"If we knew where you'd been we could help you," I say.

"That's exactly what I don't want—help."

Her fingers absentmindedly trace the shapes of the scars on her arms.

"Oh no," she moans. "It's coming, I think."

"What?" I ask, bracing myself.

"Turn left here," she says lowly. "Willow Point. Promise, Veer, *promise*, like, on every mom's grave ever that you won't tell nobody."

"I promise."

We turn left into an oasis of tract housing marked by a wooden sign that says WILLOW POINT. She tells me to slow down as we pass conjoined twin town houses. She's disoriented at first, we make a wrong turn, but then she sees a playground with its plastic gym shining and knows where we are. She doesn't know most street names, but knows landmarks—the swimming pool, the bench, a big oak, and then a row of houses all the same. A cul-de-sac. The end of a cul-de-sac. I park and turn off the lights. We can hear the freeway, airplanes, and I swear I hear my own blood cells speeding through my body.

"There," she says, nodding toward a brown cookie-cutter house like all the others, except with an ugly rock lawn. The lights are off.

"That's where you were."

I appear calm, but I am a fireworks factory of questions.

"I don't want to stay." She chews her lip. "I'm afraid."

"We have to call someone."

"No, no, we have to just *go*."

"If you won't then I have to go to the police, Ave." I try a stern big-sister voice on for the first time. "I have to. I can't keep this secret."

"I thought I could trust you," Ava almost screams, her voice wet, animal, terrified. "*Please*. Please don't. I thought I could trust you."

I have never heard this desperate version of my sister. It's scary.

"Don't betray me," she begs. "I shouldn't have shown you. I'm so dumb."

"You can trust me," I say, breaking.

"Don't betray me, Vera. Please."

I am broken.

"I won't," I whisper.

I sit for a moment longer. I imagine that I have a stick of dynamite I can put on the doorstep and *KABOOM*, and I picture a swarm of police and uniformed heroes storming the house, a flood breaking the windows and smashing the doors and swallowing it all up. The end.

But I have to drive away. Ignition. Lights. Gas.

"Okay," I say as I turn out of the cul-de-sac and the hellish town houses disappear in my rearview.

Tears run down Ava's face. Normally I would catch them like the virus they are, but instead I go cold. I am a girl made of metal. I grip my steering wheel and grit my teeth.

"It's so complicated," she says, wiping her face on her arm. "I can't even talk right. It's just—it's an ocean, all this. And every time

I start talking about it I think it'll feel good but then—then I feel like I'm drowning."

"Hey, me too. I feel like I'm drowning, too."

"Oh, man," she moans. "That's why I hate the truth, look at your face, look at what it does to you."

The mirror reflection of pain and knowing is the worst.

"I like knowing this," I correct myself, in a tone that nears sarcasm. "I feel honored you showed his house to me."

"Can you believe that there are times I even *miss* it?" she asks.

I don't answer.

"Shelly says it's normal," Ava says softly. "That's some freaky kind of normal."

"It's okay," I tell her.

The silence is long and somber. The silence is filled with sighs and bumps beneath the tires. My brain keeps circling back to that cul-de-sac. Once again, I relive the shock of the freeway exit, the town house one of many in a row. She was there all along. There, upstairs, my sister.

We get home to a dark house and get ready for bed upstairs. We don't talk about what happened. Ava fell asleep in the car and her eyes are only half-open now as she brushes her teeth and gets into her pajamas. We sit on the bed, and she says hoarsely, "Thanks for driving."

I hug her, hard. She hugs me back. I pull away and touch a scar on her arm.

"Don't ever miss that man," I say. "He hurt you. And all of us."

"Those?" she asks, looking down at her arm. "But I did that."

"I know," I say after a moment. And I do. So I'm not sure why hearing her say it sends a shock through me. "It doesn't matter."

"No," she agrees.

We get in bed and turn off the light. She reaches out and touches my hair.

"Happy New Year," she says.

"Happy New Year," I echo.

77

IT'S A BIZARRE-heat-wave-in-the-middle-of-winter kind of Saturday, and Elliott comes over for some "fam-damily fun time."

"Look at this," Elliott says. "Now, this's some Corona-and-limes kinda weather right here."

"Climate change," Dad says sadly at the gorgeous sunshine.

The whole fam pitches in to clean up the backyard. Ava and I complain at first, but once we're out there weeding the clover and sour grass, trimming back the bougainvillea, sweeping the porch, wiping down the chairs, and busting out the barbecue, cracking jokes and weird voices, it's an almost perfect afternoon.

I think everything's going to be all right. I really do. I can feign forgetting. Jonathan who? Satterfield where? We eat veggie shish kebabs. Mom tells a story about when us kids threw rocks at a beehive in the ash tree back here and got stung. Elliott turns it to the most hyperbolic tall tale of all time—"They stung my eyeballs and my spleen"; "The bees were like three inches long, some kinda superbees"—and we all laugh, especially when Dad jumps into the story and talks about how he came running out in a panic hoping to save us, swatting the hive with a broom. Of course, he got stung worst of all. His face was swollen up. He looked like a cartoon.

I haven't thought about that in so long. I don't remember it happening—just the cleanup afterward, the shock of ice on my forearms. Seems strange that Ava didn't react to the bee stings then. She said she was allergic. That Monster saved her life. Must have developed over time, the way my asthma did.

Elliott's charm is cranked to ten today. He grins and chews gum, and his knee dances. I study his actions throughout the evening but eventually come to the conclusion that maybe this is just him. He tells my parents he's been house-sitting for his boss, who owns a dozen iguanas that roam free around the house with him. He wishes, he tells me with a bit of a side-eye, that we'd come to see it.

I catch him alone at the end of the night. He lingers in the kitchen, staring at the open refrigerator.

"I don't need another beer," he says, and closes it.

"Hey, sorry we bailed on New Year's."

"No big."

"Ava got really sick—"

"I know. Chill, sis. Why you got your face all scrunched up like that?"

"It's not scrunched up."

"You look like this." He flexes every muscle in his face inward. It's amazing a person so attractive can, in one second flat, turn so unrecognizably hideous.

"I do not," I say, in a voice that's a throwback to ten years ago.

Outside, Dad's picked up his guitar and plays a song about a woman named Lola with a dark brown voice. I start toward the door.

Elliott pulls my sleeve kind of hard, and I stop in place.

"Ow," I say, even though it didn't hurt. I snatch my arm back.

He half hugs me. "I love you."

"I love you, too, you big weirdo."

"I am a pretty big weirdo, huh?" he asks almost proudly as we walk back outside.

The yard looks so trimmed and prettied. I put the shovels and hoe away while Elliott takes the guitar and starts playing a song about a zombie possum that I'm pretty sure he's making up as he's going along.

Still, though, I can't stop thinking about Jonathan's house. How he lives there. In disguise. A monster in human skin.

I have a secret.

I have a big, burning secret.

And I don't know how much longer I can live with it.

78

MAX SWINGS BY to visit with me on nights when Ava's out with her tutor. I haven't told Ava that he's done this now multiple times. I don't want her to feel like I'm stealing her closest friend, although I'm sure she wouldn't mind. That first time Max stopped by, we hung out on the porch with the moon and the chocolate. The second time we sat on the couch in the living room and I put the TV on mute and we shared some Thai food he brought over and talked about books and art and lucid dreaming and music and traveling. Tonight, though, I'm ready for him, his visit isn't a surprise, and I brushed my teeth and put on a dress and tights before the doorbell rang. He's got vegan taquitos and guacamole and we spread it all out like a little picnic on the floor of my room. The way his eyes linger on my stockinged legs makes me positive he likes girls. Or, at least, he likes me.

I want to enjoy him; I was so looking forward to his visit tonight, and my pulse shot up when I heard his skateboard coming up the sidewalk. But I've been so dark lately, my thoughts have been so black and preoccupied and sick with the knowing since Ava showed me Jonathan's house last week, that it's hard to pretend to be happy right now. Also, vegan Mexican food? Enough said.

"Some crazy weather," he says. "Right? The weekend was freaking tropical, and now it's arctic out there."

I shrug.

"You all right?" he asks.

"Yeah."

"You're all melancholy."

"I'm just tired."

"Is it Ava?" he asks. "Something happening with the case?"

"Nothing's ever happening with the case."

"Look at you, all downhearted."

"Have you ever heard of a high-profile case like hers taking this long?"

He shrugs and holds a taquito like a cigar between his fingers. "I'm not some expert on the subject or anything."

I swirl my taquito around in the guacamole. I can never tell him the truth about anything. Not the big truths, like the fact Ava knows where Jonathan lives and is protecting him for some sick reason and I'm a crazy person who has had cinematic fantasies of blowing his brains out. Not the medium truths, like the fact that I have a growing crush on Max and I can tell he reciprocates but that there is no way we could ever be a thing because Ava. Not the itty-bitty truths either, like vegan Mexican food is gross and shouldn't exist.

My stupid eyes well up.

"Um . . . spicy?" he asks.

"Yeah," I say, spilling over and crying. "It's spicy."

"No it's not." He watches my face with wide-eyed panic. "It's mild. I asked for mild. What's wrong?"

I shake my head and weep into a napkin. It feels cathartic to cry, it feels horrible to cry. I wish I could suck back all the tears and seize the heaving, but it's taken me over now and I have no control.

"Okay," he says. "Um—clearly there is something really *up* right now."

His hand's on my back, hesitant, as he rubs a circle light enough that I might not even notice it's there.

I'm stuck in the terrible falling-apart for a moment and then it lifts, and then I take another napkin and wipe my tears and blow my nose. I can't look him in the eye even though he's staring at me with hard concern. I pretend to be interested in eating and reach for my food.

"Can you maybe elaborate a little on why you're having a mental breakdown?"

"I'm not having a mental breakdown," I say, annoyed.

"Why you're freaking out and sobbing all over the place?"

"Thanks for being so sensitive."

"I'm just joking. I'm sorry. Hey, I just—I don't know what to say right now. I've never seen you cry."

"Allergies."

"Um, yeah, okay."

"A lot of dust in the room right now," I joke, cracking a smile.

There is so much sweetness in his gaze, so much inquiring sweetness, that I have to look away again.

"You can talk to me," he says softly. "What we have here . . . it's not like I'm going to run telling Ava anything you say."

"Ava doesn't even know you and I have been seeing each other," I say. "I mean, not 'seeing' seeing each other. Just—you know, she doesn't know you come over and we hang out."

"I haven't said anything either. You think she'd get heated about it?"

"I don't know. I don't know how she'd react."

He nods. "Yeah."

"I know she tried to kiss you. And she thinks you're gay."

I look at his face for an answer, but he just nods.

"Are you?" I ask.

"I mean, she asked me if I was into guys, I told her yeah . . . she assumed it meant I was straight-up gay. Seemed simpler to just let her run with that."

"You're bi."

"That a problem?"

"No. So am I."

He shrugs. "I think everyone is, really."

"But you didn't kiss her back."

"Nah, I don't . . . feel that way about her. I love her, don't get me wrong. But I don't—you know—not that way."

He squeezes my hand, and I squeeze it back. His hand is so soft. It's been so long since anyone touched me besides Ava. How electric even something as simple as a palm in mine feels.

It makes me sad.

"Sometimes, I can't tell you why, it's really hard being her sister," I tell him, looking at our hands.

"I know it is. I know."

"It's been rough. Which is why I had that little allergy-related accident a few minutes ago."

"You know, I realize you're not superhuman. You're allowed to cry."

"Thanks."

"You going to eat the rest of your food?"

I can't pretend to enjoy it anymore. "I'm over it."

"You were over it on the first bite, admit."

"I was."

"Doesn't matter what you say and don't say, Vera," he says. "Your face has always told me everything."

What a delightful, terrifying prospect.

He eats my food. This boy, I tell you, is string-skinny, and he eats like a human garbage disposal. Then we slip out of the house and go on a walk, shivering in our coats, and hop a chain-link fence into a closed playground. He pushes me for a while on a swing. Then he comes around the front and holds the chains to make the swing stop. He leans down and gives me a warm kiss, gently touching the hair falling around my face with one hand. His lips are just as amazing as I always thought they'd be. I don't stop kissing him for a long time, because I know as soon as I do, I'm going to have to tell him that we can't ever do this again.

79

I'M GETTING MY oil changed. I wait outside in a plastic chair, squinting at my Scrabble game on my phone, when a pair of boots appears on the asphalt in front of me. I recognize those black cowboy boots. More specifically, I recognize that precise stomp of them. I look up and see a dark, burly shadow against the bright sun. Ozzie. Oz. Ozzfest. He's wearing aviators and, behind his giant mustache, he smiles.

"What the hell?" I ask.

"Hi, Vera."

"You getting your oil changed, too?"

"Yyyeah."

"You're not getting your oil changed."

"Can we talk?"

I sit up straighter, put my phone away. "About what?"

"I've tried to talk to your parents," he says. "They . . . won't listen to reason."

"They want a restraining order." I get increasingly uncomfortable, taking my purse onto my lap. "You know, they wouldn't like this—us schmoozing like this."

"Can we talk?" he repeats.

He sits into the plastic chair beside me, screeching it along the pavement.

"How you doing?" he asks.

"Um . . . fine."

"How's . . . school?"

I roll my eyes. Cut to the chase, man. No one in life was ever in desperate need of some small talk.

"I'm not in school," I say.

"I figured you'd be at Berkeley!"

"Well, I'm not."

"You know, my ex-wife is head of admissions," he says. "I could introduce you. I don't mind."

It's been years since Ozzie sat down and had some kind of conversation with me that had nothing to do with my missing sister. I know he's a kindhearted person, hence the whole years-long obsession with Ava's case for free, but I also suspect him right now of buttering me up. This doesn't feel right. He gives Ava the creeps and my parents cut him off so suddenly—who knows what went down. I cross my arms in front of my chest.

"I'll be quick here," he says, as if he can detect my distrust. "It's about Ava. I highly suspect she's not telling you quite a chunk of change."

He words it in this weird way, like he's trying to intrigue me. But really I just think he's an idiot. Of course she's not telling the truth. She's trying to protect her captor, who lives in Satterfield. How's that for the truth, sucker? Slap a badge on me and call me a detective.

"Yeah, I don't want to talk about this with you." I stand up and sling my purse onto my shoulder. "You're not on her case anymore, dude. Let it go."

He has to pry the plastic chair from his ass as he stands up, too.

"Just hear me out, then I'll go. I studied this case for years. Her story—there are holes, there are parts that don't match up. She's not—"

As he speaks, something in me boils over. Deep anger. It happens in one second—snap.

"*This man is harassing me!*" I shout to the world.

His mouth hangs open, startled.

People snap to attention, birds fly away.

He has a kind face. Fierce, bright eyes that you know have studied violence and beauty. I've seen the way that he watches my mother—with a gentleness surprising for his loud, stomping frame. This man is lonely. This man cares deeply, perhaps too deeply, for my sister's case. I don't wish him ill, but I want him to stop talking, I don't want to get in the middle of some fight he had with my parents, I don't want to know his theories.

I lower my voice. Almost a growl. "Please," I say. "Just go away."

"Sorry," he says.

He backs up, his boots clicking on the sidewalk.

"If you ever need anything, you know where I am," he says in this gruff, official way.

I turn away and walk up toward the lot where my car is. It's ready. As I drive away, Ozzie's nowhere to be seen, like I dreamt him up. Poor Ozzie. He probably feels like he sunk his goddamn soul into this case and now he's cut off. He's probably driven himself insane trying to find That Monster. I shouldn't've screamed. It was so unlike me, really.

I look into the rearview, alarmed at the stranger there in my familiar face.

80

I DON'T KNOW how long it takes—days, weeks, some mix of both—but I slither into aimlessness. Sleep in late, later. Stop checking my email as often, let my phone die for hours on end, forgo leaving the house except to go pick up takeout at nearby restaurants, eyeing the sun with contempt. California can't even manage to have a freaking winter. When Max texts me asking if he can come over, I fake sick so many times he tells me I'm starting to sound like his mother. I hang out with Ava when she's around and try my best to be cheerful, watch god-awful reality shows and laugh at them with her, answer appropriately when my mom or dad comes through and asks questions of me, always about Ava anyway: *Where's Ava?* if she's out. *How's Ava doing?* if they haven't spoken in a day or so. Ava's great, actually. Ava's got three weeks before she takes the GED and she's doing driving lessons and getting pretty damn good at the ukulele. It's me who's losing my mind, not that anybody notices, not that they should, because I feel I'm covering it up well. But my secret is eating me from the inside out.

"Let's go for a walk," Ava says. "Come on. You need cheering up."

"Walking outside when it's witch-tit cold is not going to cheer me up."

"We'll wear big coats. And wigs! Let's wear wigs like we used to."

"I don't want to wear—"

Of course we wear them anyway, because Ava always gets what she wants.

We walk through the neighborhood, saying hi to dogs and their walkers, stopping to pet a calico cat on a porch. Ava comments on the DRUG-FREE ZONE sign on a street corner as if she's never seen it before.

"Berkeley, I love you. Why do they put that there?" she asks in astonishment. "You think some druggie really looks up at that and thinks, 'Ah, actually, I won't do drugs now'?"

I smile weakly.

The ash trees hiss with wind. The streetlamps are worlds brighter than the moon or stars.

"Something snapped in you."

"I don't know," I tell her.

"I hope it wasn't 'cause of me."

Her fake hair is blown back by the breeze, and I see her real hair, puffy and trying to burst out beneath it.

"I hope what I told you—and showing you that house—didn't drive you off the deep end or whatever," she goes on.

"It's not your fault."

We walk for a bit, holding hands. We head down Ashby and turn on California, and I wonder who is leading whom. A few blocks up there are police lights and fire engines parked. The chain-link fence appears to be blocked off by yellow tape, and cops are barricading the streets around it.

"Shoot," Ava says, adjusting her wig. "I guess we're not going that way."

We head back. Even though the short walk and sharp wind and quick chat with Ava reenergized me, the second I saw the police cars and fire engines and the street blocked off like bad news, like a movie crime scene, it clicked inside me that what I need to do is very simple.

It doesn't matter what Ava wants. If she doesn't want the cops to know where he is, fine.

But tomorrow I am going to drive to Satterfield, California, and I'm going to see Jonathan.

81

NEXT DAY AT noon I'm about to sneak out the door as Ava comes in, running around to show everybody her printed page that says PASS for the GED. Mom is bathing her dogs in the backyard, but I hear her cheer. Dad comes up from the basement and calls Ava a genius.

"That's amazing," I yell from the foyer, car keys in hand. I push memories of my own high school graduation out of my head, how Mom showed up just for my name to be called and left before I was able to hug her goodbye and how Dad made an excuse that day about being sick, or maybe he was sick, I don't know.

"Amazing," I yell again, hoping Ava will hear me, but she's shut the back sliding glass door to talk to Mom.

"Ghost girl," I tell the empty room. "I am a ghost girl."

I turn to leave right as the doorbell rings. When I open the door, Max is there on our porch with this zeroed-in stare, this razor gaze that sears through everything to make me feel so exposed even though I'm in the world's most engulfing peacoat.

"Hey," he says. "How you been farin'?"

"Fine," I say. "Busy."

"So that's why you've been avoiding me."

"I haven't been— Look, I'm sorry, right now's not a good time. Can you come back later?"

"I'm actually not here for you, I'm here 'cause Ava texted and said she wanted to pop some bubbly to celebrate her GED."

"Ah."

I'll admit, it stings a little.

"Max!" Ava sings, dancing into the room.

They hug. I put my hands in my pocket.

"Everyone want prosecco?" yells my dad. "I just found an old bottle I can put in the freezer."

"Do we have any kombucha?" Ava yells back.

"That's a weird thing to drink out of champagne glasses," Dad says.

"You're not going somewhere, are you?" Ava asks me.

"Yeah, I am, sorry," I say. "I'll celebrate with you later. Take you out to dinner or something. Congratulations! I'm so proud of you!"

"But where are you going?" Ava asks, crestfallen.

"I have a date," I say.

My gaze is directed at her, but I'm watching Max, specifically the grimace on his face as I say that last syllable. I don't know why I said that. Two birds, one stone, I guess.

"*Whaaaaa?*" Ava asks. "Seriously?"

For a brief nanosecond I'm afraid I've hurt her just as much as Max. But then she grins and gives me a little push toward the door.

"Yay for you! You'd better tell me every detail."

I toss a "Later" over my shoulder and don't look back as I get into my car.

Today is cloudless, bitter blue, and cold. I crank the heat. It's not until I'm hitting the freeway that I let the quick interaction with Max there ring in my ears. It's like I just had my first fight with him or something, which is absurd, because we're not together and we didn't fight. We kissed once. I didn't return his calls after. Anyway, clearly, he's my sister's friend. I can't hurt her. I won't.

I let out the world's biggest sigh. I turn up, down, up the radio.

"I have to do this," I tell the rearview.

As I finally get off the freeway in Satterfield two hours later, my mind tired from the thinking and self-convincing, my eyes squinty and shrunken from forgetting sunglasses and staring into the sun over the highway, I can't stop the fire of questions in my head any longer. A pandemonium of hypotheticals has gone off, and I'm what-ifing at a rate faster than the speed of sound. What if he doesn't live there anymore? What if it's not even his house and Ava had it wrong? What am I going to say to him? What am I *doing*?

I just want answers. I want answers so badly. I want to see his face, learn why Ava won't let the world know about him. Maybe find out something about him that can take him down. Know my enemy.

I pass the long nothing-road dotted with windmills, a bus stop, a church with a marquee that says I LOVED YOU AT YOUR DARKEST, do a double-take.

It all looks so different in the daytime.

Tract housing. Bench. Plastic playground. I could drive this unfamiliar route in my sleep.

I park in front of his house. There's no one on the street. Trees cast shade on the sidewalks. Next door, a kid's bicycle left carelessly on a lawn. An airplane flies by, and it scares me that I'm so small they can't see me, that at this moment, no one can.

He could do anything to me.

My arms are noodley. Am I really going to do this? The doubt screws into my belly, sickening, and I have to will my every action to keep the momentum going. Step out of the car. Close the car door. Harden my face. Stand for a moment on the sidewalk staring at the rock lawn, thinking maybe I should pocket one of the more jagged ones in case he's dangerous. I lean down and pick one out. With enough force, I could slit his throat. I can't move for a moment as I stand there, fondling the innocent rock that just became a weapon that easily—with just a thought. I cross the rock lawn, steps scraping. Could I be a killer? Would the world be better with him dead? Am I truly here right now? Are you real or are you not, Vera? *Knock, knock.* Vera, I can't tell which you are anymore.

The door opens. It's a man.

My stomach pitches.

Everything behind him is not how I pictured it—a bird in a cage, some hung coats, a powerful stink of animal pee, a watercolor picture in a frame that says this, in block letters:

THE BEST THING ABOUT MEMORIES IS MAKING THEM.

I'm still thinking about killing him.

But of course I don't.

I suspect right away that this man is not him. This man's balding, white-haired, thinner than the forensic sketches. Then again, there are similarities. The blue-gray eyes. I don't know whom I'm looking for. This could be the face of my worst enemy or the face of a nobody. Every stranger wears a mask.

"Jonathan?" I ask.

My voice sounds so much smaller than I intended it—a peep, really.

"No—Pete," he says.

"Oh," I say.

There's been some mistake. I'm sinking fast. I think about turning around and going home, but then the man speaks up in monotone.

"I'm his brother. Jonathan passed away," he says. "I'm staying here handling some things for a few weeks. Can I ask who you are?"

The world melts into psychedelic slow motion for a second as those words, "passed away," echo in my brain and conjure up a meaning and that meaning turns to sick, nervous, angry, disbelieving relief.

"Uh . . . I'm sorry, he passed *away*?" I repeat.

"About a week ago," Pete says.

"Jonathan is *dead*? How did he die?"

"Overdose."

I clamp my hand over my mouth. Little does Pete know I'm actually fighting to keep myself from smiling. It's not a happy smile. It's a smile that is my face not knowing what to do with itself. Crocodilic.

"Holy shit," I say, taking my hand away.

I suck the air into my lungs the same way I have my whole life. But suddenly I can't get enough oxygen.

"I still can't believe it myself," Pete says.

"Was it intentional?" I ask.

I don't care if I seem heartless. I want to know exactly why he's dead. Guilt for what he did? Fear of getting caught? I'm glad he's dead, I am, but what a chickenshit. What an easy answer. He never had to face a single second in jail. Never saw a day locked away for what he did. Never faced the public.

I wish I believed in hell.

"We don't know," Pete snaps. "And excuse me, *who* are you?"

"No one. Never mind."

I head back to the car. My throat is so tight. I spin around again and stop to look at Pete.

"Your brother was a horrible human being," I say loudly. "I hope you know that."

I can see, even from ten or so feet away, his expression darken.

In my car, I catch a glimpse of a little girl now standing with Pete as he remains in the doorway and watches me drive away.

I drive into the eyeball-searing sunset, the sound of wheels purring. Moments later, I'm on the highway, hands shaking, tears sliding down my expressionless face.

Jonathan is dead.

There is no way I can break the news to Ava. She didn't even want him to go to jail, she certainly doesn't want him dead. What if this pushes her over the edge?

No. This has to be something I never tell anyone, not ever, that I force myself to never think about and erase from my own memory by telling myself a story that this never happened.

Breathe. It's okay. Pretend you're dreaming.

I sniff and dry my eyes with my sweatshirt sleeve.

The worst person in the world, who it sickened me to know was free, is dead. He is a corpse. He will never touch a little girl again. The world is better for his suicide.

Then why, why am I so filled with bizarre rage?

Nobody ever had the satisfaction of handcuffing his sorry ass. He never felt the spotlight of hatred, the cold walls of a locked cell.

Simply, very simply, it's not fair. It's. Just. Not. Fair.

I hate that his life was his to take in the first place.

I hate that I got what I wanted, really—That Monster is slayed—yet nothing is right.

Maybe nothing is going to be okay. Maybe it doesn't matter who lives or gets locked up. Maybe nothing, not even death, can undo the scars that decorate the people we love.

82

THE SECRET IS a ghost that sits at the table during dinnertime. The secret lies, invisible, between Ava and me in my bed at night as we brush each other's hair and watch laptop TV. The secret buzzes loud over the conversation when Max stops by one night and we stand on the porch as he fishes for a reason as to why I haven't wanted to see him. The secret weighs heavy on my lips and is the reason it takes physical exertion to smile. The secret is why I can't eat, I go to sleep early, I wake up late. The secret is the reason Ava thinks I've got "depression problems" like her and I should go talk to someone. But I would never talk to someone, because of my secret.

83

I GAZE INTO the bathroom mirror.

I know I'm a girl, a slight girl with poor posture in need of a haircut. But I feel like a dam about to break. I touch the circles under my eyes.

"You need to eat, lady," Ava says as she steps behind me and we stare at our reflections.

She's in chunky boots, her hair is enormous, and she appears taller than me right now.

"I know," I say.

My face tingles, aches, because it wants to shatter and it can't. It has to keep existing, being a face that looks normal to the world. I don't know how I can keep going sometimes. Knowledge can be a desert island.

"Whatever you got going on," Ava says softly, her voice behind me, sweet in my ear, "you can tell me. Don't be scared. Is it about me? I'm strong now. I can deal."

Maybe the world would be a smoother operation if we zapped the fakery and just let our truths fly free, even if they sting like bees.

"Ava," I say to the mirror.

The dam breaks. Water, water everywhere.

"What's going on?" she asks, alarmed.

"I can't tell you."

"You have to tell me," she says, voice climbing. She reaches out and moves my hand from my face, so I have to see her, so I have to see her wide, shining eyes. "Tell me, Vera. You're the one person in the world I trust. You have to tell me."

I don't want to tell her, though. I really don't.

"Tell me," she says again, in almost a shriek.

"Jonathan is dead."

Her expression doesn't change. She doesn't move. Mannequin sister.

I turn around. "I'm sorry, I didn't want to tell you—you seem so happy—Jonathan—it was apparently an overdose."

I swear, in two seconds, her color changes.

She disappears. I hear her go to her room and shut the door. I don't follow her. I don't knock when I hear the sobbing. For once, I just leave her alone.

84

I LET HER sleep in, but as soon as I hear Ava up, I go to her room and sit on the edge of her bed and make her talk to me. I tell her the story of how I found out the news. I say it's time she tells the truth about him—the man he was, his address, his ending. Time to share this info with my parents and the police and even the glossy, vomitous magazines. But Ava begs me not to mention it to anyone.

"I'm not ready," she insists. "I'm *processing*."

"The police are wasting time looking for a dead dude."

"Can you just give me a little time?" she begs, shrill, on the verge of perpetual tears.

So I give her the day. I focus on getting myself together. I eat three regular meals. I finish a personal statement for college applications it's too late to send. It gives me something to do.

That night, Ava and I settle back into the quiet peace of upstairs life. We go back to snickering at dumb TV together. The next day we go thrift store shopping, we try a new hike. Something in me has relaxed, has let go.

Look at my sister there, on the other side of the bed, a grown woman now with the bright, bothered face of a little girl. Think of all she's been through, the stories buried deep inside her. He's dead now. What's been done is irrevocable. Monsters live, monsters die, but survivors? They *survive*.

85

JUST TWO DAYS after the Jonathan news, my parents go missing.

Ava notices first when she's up early getting ready for a doctor's appointment. She's downstairs blasting pop music while making a smoothie and sees that my dad's basement door is open and he's gone. Odd, because he never leaves the door open. We guess he's out on a run. We check the master bedroom and find that Mom has vanished, too. Car still in the driveway. Well, maybe they went for a walk together—they do that sometimes. But we call their cells, leave messages, texts. Nothing.

"Maybe they're celebrating Valentine's Day," Ava says.

But there's doubt in her voice. Even Ava's seemed to pick up on the fact that our parents are not exactly the love story of the century. Also, who celebrates anything this early in the a.m.? I drop Ava off at her appointment, stop by the drugstore to pick up some shampoo, waste a half hour looking at hair dyes and then decide I don't want to be a redhead anyway, and at that point it's time to pick Ava up again. We go home. My parents are still gone.

Now it's noon and getting weird.

Mexico and Canada are whimpering and have no food. Which means my mom left today without feeding them. Not usual. I notice, in my dad's basement, he didn't turn off his computer and his wallet is sitting on his desk. Also not usual.

In the foyer, my mom left her makeup bag on the ground.

Shit, they've been kidnapped.

At first it seems like a crazy thought, but think about how high-profile Ava's case was, how many unbalanced people probably watched us on TV, how plenty of people know where we live and everyone in the neighborhood saw the paparazzi harassing us months ago. Maybe people think we have money and decided to kidnap my parents for ransom.

I say this out loud to Ava, and she pales.

"I don't understand—who are you saying could have kidnapped them?" she asks, pulling my jacket sleeve. "What are you saying?"

"I don't know."

"But he's dead, Vera," she says.

"Not him, obviously."

We have referred to him, since the secret news, simply as "him" and "he" and only in fleeting moments. We have silently agreed to not discuss it anymore. Together, we swallowed the truth, processed it separately, and moved past it in shared silence.

Oh, my dear sister.

The things we never say.

"I don't like this at all," she says loudly.

At 2:00 p.m., we're Googling how long we have to wait to file a missing person report (twenty-four hours). At 4:00 p.m., Ava and I get in the car and drive around the neighborhood at sharklike speeds, peering out the windows, calling their names as if they're lost cats.

"What if this is all just a joke on us?" Ava says hopefully.

"That would be a really messed-up joke, especially in this family."

"I texted Max. He says we should tell the cops we know. They'd probably rush it because of my case."

"That's true."

"Wait, is that them?" Ava asks, knocking her window.

Right now we're approaching a stop sign, a large church with a pointy roof on the right corner of the intersection. A bunch of overdressed people stand outside, spilling onto the sidewalk; a few even spill out into the crosswalk.

"Is who them?" I ask.

"They just went inside that church," Ava insists. "I saw them."

A car honks in back of me, and I weave around the people who seem to think standing in the street and talking is okay as long as you're into Jesus. I turn the car right, parking in a red zone.

"I would bet that Mom and Dad did not just run into a"—I check the rearview mirror to verify—"a 'community Baptist church.'"

"Why not? I saw them. I saw the backs of them. Mom was wearing that orange dress."

"Mom doesn't wear orange," I remind her.

"I saw them."

"Ava, you didn't see them. You know you didn't see them."

Ava's brow scrunches. She pulls her hair back in a tight bun on the top of her head.

"Something's really wrong lately," Ava says. "With you. I can feel it."

"With *me*? Because I don't think our parents ran off to a late-day church service today?"

"Not because of them," Ava says. "You know why."

I don't say anything.

The emotions I own lately, there aren't words for. It's sweet guilt, it's a disgusting sense of relief, it's barbed love I try not to touch.

"Yep," I finally respond.

"You just . . . feel far away."

"Yeah, I am."

I have covered myself in Teflon, Ava, since I learned your kidnapper and rapist is dead. Since I scoured the Satterfield obituaries and learned his last name, Kenneth, a stupid first name for a last name, a fat pharmacist who loved video games and stray animals and was once a failed art school kid. Since I saw his black-and-white photo and noted how different his real-life face was from the forensic sketch. You must have known that, Ava. You must have let it slide, nodded yes to that inaccurate picture and let it be circulated far and wide, his fake face pudgier and his facial hair more filled out, his eyes closer together, glasses, his hair too dark.

"I am far away," I say.

"How do I bring you back?" Ava asks softly.

"I want you to tell the truth."

She flinches at that, just a twitch.

Ahead, a streetlamp on the busy corner flickers on and off, making a passed-out homeless man appear and disappear, appear and disappear.

"Tell the police," I say. "This changes everything. He's dead now. Let's just move on, please. Let everybody else move on. Think of what it would mean to Mom and Dad—"

"I can't," she whispers.

"Why?" I ask, turning to stare at her.

Her eyes are lined in cat-eye swoops. Her cheeks have filled out these past few months, and I don't know if it's her neo-hippie diet or what but her skin has cleared up. She looks older, brighter than the Ava who showed up in the hospital at the end of the summer. She's different from the magazine pictures, too. It's hard to pinpoint what it is. I guess she just looks . . . normal.

She shakes her head. Her eyes are full. I don't push.

"I think we should go home and I should call the cops and ask if there's anything they can do for Mommy and Daddy," Ava says.

"You want the cops to help you?" I ask sharply. "Wow, isn't that new."

I start the car and drive toward home. We're close. The drive is so familiar I could be blindfolded right now and it'd look the same.

Great, now she's sobbing beside me.

"What?" I say, annoyed.

"Vera, I feel like I don't even know you right now," she says. "I'm stunned. This is stunning."

"Really?" I say in a sharp voice that's unbelievably my own. "Is this really stunning?"

"I didn't think you could be so *mean*."

"Oh, come on, you refuse to tell the police anything. He's dead and you're still protecting him. It's disgusting."

She looks like I smacked the air out of her.

"He was a kidnapper and a rapist!" I nearly scream. "He deserved to go to jail. And now that will never happen. Guess what, Ava? If you had been more cooperative, he'd probably *be* in jail right now."

"You sound like you hate me," she says.

I emit a short shock of a scream. "Come *on*."

Hold my breath. Bite my lip until there's blood. I'm not used to this feeling, the anger at her. I don't know how to stop. I keep driving down MLK, past our turnoff, because this conversation isn't over and I don't know where to go or what to do. Ava doesn't even seem to notice, she's so focused on me, studying me with worry I can physically feel as I keep my eyes on the dusk-gray streets.

"Max said you were depressed. I didn't realize . . ."

"Max can mind his own business." I look in the rearview at my swollen, dumb eyes. Then I look at Ava's. "I'm sorry."

"Me too." She dabs her eyes with her fingers. "I'm scared is all. And I can't believe he's dead."

"Yeah."

I've left our neighborhood and am creeping toward the hills. Then I see a street sign I recognize and park the car. We're right near Indian Rock, where Max took me last summer, which feels forever ago. Back when I was a girl with a future, a girl ready to run away from Berkeley and start over. That girl is gone.

"Why you stopping?" she asks.

"Want to get some fresh air?"

Our tired eyes match.

"All right," she says. "But what about Mom and Dad?"

"Let's clear our heads and then go home and deal with it. I called them both again and texted Elliott. Let's wait and see if they call back."

We climb up the stairs carved into the building-sized rock. Amazingly, no one is up here. The sky is inky and star-scarred, the Bay shining slick below it, the houses and streetlamps glowing.

"Wow," says Ava. "What is this place?"

"Indian Rock. Max took me here once."

"When?"

"Oh, before you came home."

"Huh." Ava rubs her temples. She pulls at her bun and lets her hair down, a crimped explosion. "So . . . was that our first fight?"

"Definitely not our first."

"First since I came back," she corrects herself.

"We get along pretty well."

"You're, like, the sister I always wanted."

My brow wrinkles. "I'm the sister you always *had*."

She doesn't respond.

"What did you mean by that?" I ask.

"If we got to choose our family, I'd still choose you to be my sister, Vera."

"I'd choose you, too."

"You really love me no matter what?"

"You need to ask?"

"'Cause there are things about me so ugly that I'm afraid if I told you, you wouldn't love me anymore."

I shake my head. "How many times do I have to say that you can tell me anything?"

"I don't believe you," she says, hugging her legs. "I know you believe yourself, but I don't believe you. Maybe someday."

I sigh, not knowing what else I can say to convince her.

"I hate feeling like there's something off between us," she says. "You know how important you are to me, right?"

I turn and we hug. Her shoulder, soft fur that smells like my own shampoo on a stranger. I close my eyes. *Jonathan's dead now*, I think. *At some point the truth about him will come out.* But it doesn't change anything. What I wanted was to kill the thing that hurt and forever changed my family and stole her from us. But that thing can't be killed.

We pull apart. Ava fixes my eyeliner with her spit-wet finger.

"It's gorge up here," she says. "You always know the best spots."

All the houses. They run together, same same same—dark squares with lit windows. I couldn't find ours if I spent an hour trying.

I check my phone. Nothing.

"We should go find Mom and Dad," I say.

"Just one more minute."

We sit, her head on my shoulder, watching the planes blink by in the sky, the freeway crawl with car lights like a candle river, and I remember again when Max took me here and how different the world seemed then, how I thought I knew what I wanted, how I thought I could escape my sister and the shape her absence gave me.

How wrong I was. How right it can feel sometimes to be wrong.

86

BACK AT THE house, Mom and Dad still aren't home.

Though I want to go into panic mode, I suggest Ava relax and take a bath upstairs. I'll call the local police to see what we should do. Adrenaline pumps; my heart is a techno throb. I walk around the rooms downstairs, turning lights on, doing one more search for my parents with my phone in my shaking hand. Mom's room is last. I stand over her desk. A stack of books about surviving sexual assault, a neat pile of printed maps of different areas of California with highlighter pens circling various areas, a yellow legal pad with indecipherable notes and timelines. An envelope from the police department sits on top of the recycle bin next to the desk. I sit on her swivel chair, grab it, and pull the letter out of it.

Words and phrases jumble together. *DNA testing. Cooperation. Final request.*

I try to make sense of what I'm reading.

I read it again and again and again.

The message is the same every time: Ava's DNA was never tested. The police are threatening to drop the case.

My stomach drops. I dig through Mom's recycling and find two more letters saying the same, with dates spanning the past couple of months. I read the first letter again. *Final request.* My vision blurs.

Why the hell wouldn't my parents comply?

I peek out the blinds in the living room and notice a car with lights on across the street: the police, sitting creepily in the dark, parked beneath an ash tree.

"Boo," Ava says, sneaking up behind me.

Her hair is wet and she's wearing my pajamas.

"Not funny right now," I say.

"Sorry. You're right. What are you looking at?"

I point through the window at the cops parked outside and Ava nods, seeing them, widening her eyes.

"Been a minute," she says nervously.

And it has. For a short period, we had something resembling normalcy—no media, no law enforcement, just our house with our cars parked in front of it. Black-and-whites used to lurk so constantly when Ava first got home that we barely noticed them. I close the curtain.

"You called them?" Ava asked.

"No. I don't know what's going on."

And it's true. I've never been so bewildered in my life. I look down at what I'm holding, a simple piece of paper with the power to put my whole world into question.

"What is that?" Ava asks, reaching for the letter.

I crumple it into a ball and drop it on the floor. "Nothing."

No use in scaring her. It has to be wrong. This doesn't make any sense.

Ava raises her eyebrow, glances at the ball on the floor, and opens her mouth as if she's trying to find the right word.

Someone knocks hard on the front door—twice—the way only a cop knocks.

Dread rises as we hurry toward the door.

"Something happened," I whisper.

I open the door. Two cops and—thank God—my parents stand there, all with stone-blank faces. In this handful of seconds, my blood pressure skyrockets. The inkling that something is wrong can only be described as "gross." Sudden and sickening as a roller-coaster plunge.

"Ava?" one of the cops says.

I don't recognize these ones.

"What's happening?" I ask.

"Ma'am, we're going to need you to come with us," the second cop says.

"Me?" I ask.

My chest is exploding, my knees have turned to jam.

"No—me," Ava says quietly.

I watch as one of them takes her by the arm, hard, pulls her outside to the front yard, and leads her toward the cop car. Ava looks back at me, eyes wide, like a girl who sees the flashing white tunnel of the end before her. She mouths something at me before she turns away: "Sorry."

"Wait—*wait*—" I yell.

Mom and Dad walk inside like a couple of zombies. They don't even turn around to see what is happening.

What is happening?

"The cops took Ava to their car," I tell them. "Are you seeing this?"

I step onto the porch. What is going on? It's dark except for a meager orange streetlamp, but the cops have her against the car and *are handcuffing her*.

"Stop!" I scream at the top of my lungs, so confused, so full of fire.

A hand grabs my shoulder, hard, and pulls me inside. I trip over my own legs. Stunned, I find my footing again. The door slams behind me. I face my parents in the foyer and that's when I know something is not just wrong, it's devastating. How do I know? Because my mom's makeup is skid marks along her cheeks. And my dad's eyes are so red there is no white.

"Ben, is she still out there?" Mom asks. "Ben, is she gone yet?"

"She'll be gone any second," Dad says in this wrecked voice.

My mother breathes loudly, her head nodding with a tremor like a woman who has officially lost her mind.

"Bad news," Dad says to me, his voice breaking.

I know "bad news" is a goddamn euphemism. I know whatever they are about to tell me is going to shatter my universe.

The moment hangs so long, I hear a distant BART train whirring loud and whiny as a high-speed ghost. I hear a freeway, a man yelling, a bicycle bell.

"Okay," I whisper.

"Ava's dead, Ladybug." Dad starts weeping loudly. It's not a weep. It's a howl. It's a vocal corkscrew and it makes me sick with hurt.

"She's dead. She's dead," Mom repeats, as if she's trying to convince herself. "She's actually dead."

"What do you mean she's dead?" I say.

My throat has shrunk to the diameter of a pin. I make a strange

322

laugh noise, although it's more like choking. I don't understand, I can't get air, I have never seen my parents like this, all spooky-eyed and pale and insane like this, and I'm afraid of them and afraid of the word "dead" ringing in my ears.

"She's right outside," I remind them. "With the cops."

"That girl out there is not your sister." Mom's voice sounds shredded. "Your sister is dead; they found her bones."

She dry heaves.

Dad squeezes his hands into quivering fists. Mom joins him, weeping. And now I can't see anything. Now the world has lost its lines and shape. I've lost my sight to tears.

"They found Ava's body?" I ask in sheer disbelief.

This also makes no sense to me, because Ava is outside, but my parents are breaking down in front of me and even though I don't understand what's going on I blink my tears out because I am watching my creators self-destruct.

"Yes," Mom says. "She was less than a mile away the whole time."

"Where?" I manage. *What?*

"It was Ozzie," she says. "He went back to the neighborhood where she disappeared again. He started back at the beginning. He got a warrant, searched a yard of a condemned house . . ."

It's like Mom's voice has left her. She keeps moving her lips, but no noise.

"A condemned house—across Ashby—they found her body when cleaning out the backyard—" Dad finishes.

"It was an accident," Mom says. "She . . . locked in an old refrigerator . . ."

We're all crying now, and hugging, and it's horrible.

"She was still wearing her angel costume," Dad says.

"It was a DNA match," Mom says. "That . . . person outside . . . is *not* my daughter."

With those three letters—*D-N-A*—all this information comes together in my mind in the worst possible way.

My voice is almost a whisper. "You already knew, didn't you?"

They don't answer.

"I found the letters in your room," I say.

They're silent, which is so much worse than any words they could possibly utter.

"You never confirmed her DNA," I say. "Why?"

"We were going to," Mom says. "We were going to so many times but . . ."

"We didn't . . ." Dad says.

"You didn't want to know," I finish, a mess of hot tears. "You didn't want to know."

"We *did*," he insists. "We were *going* to."

But he doesn't sound convincing. I'm not even sure he's convincing himself.

I'm so overwhelmed. I'm ablaze. I'm burning down. No. No. I close my eyes. Each breath becomes a boulder pushed up a hill. The words they've said to me unravel in all these directions—my sister, shrinking back into that tiny person in the angel costume, the one on all the flyers we saw for years, the one in old photographs. Then in another direction—this girl in her fur coat, my best friend, *Ava*, she's real, she's out there—how can she be two people? I can't make sense of this. It can't mean what they're saying it means.

"Even when they took her away just now," Mom says, "I wanted to hug her. But she's not mine. I want my daughter. *I want my daughter.*"

Mom runs to her room and we follow. She screams at the top of her lungs and punches her thighs. Dad has to pull her wrists and yell, "Michelle, Michelle, Michelle, Michelle," as I chant, "Mom, Mom, Mom, Mom," and finally she stops. She goes limp on the bed and Dad covers his face with his hands, seated next to her, a statue of defeat and anguish.

"Ava died over twelve years ago," Dad says so slowly, the words so heavy and foreign that for a breath I'm really not sure if they're English.

And the sadness rolls in, a permanent cloud, choking, black, stifling, thick sadness I swear I will never see through again. I was such an idiot. I was so taken.

"Then who is *she*?" I ask, pointing toward the direction of the front door.

"I don't know," Mom says with this blank, sheer horror that sends shivers up my arms.

"This is insane," I say. "No. You realize how insane this sounds? Someone made a mistake at the lab or something. Ava's alive. She's right out there."

"She *isn't*," Dad says, defeated.

"No," I say. It seems impossible, existentially impossible. "No, I can't—I can't accept this."

Can't. But *must*, somehow.

The truth is oppressive. It sucks the life out of us. But as the shock settles in permanently, the room quiets, and we all three sit there together stewing in the silence, something different is born. An ending, I guess, one that stings, but it is an ending.

My brain is a revolving door of strange, terrible realizations. Ava is gone. Ava is a little girl, forever gone, like I'd always suspected. An imposter was here in her place. The imposter is now gone. Anger, despair, no this can't be real, yes it's real, rinse, repeat.

"She's dead," we keep saying. "She's dead."

We try the words out as if we've just learned them for the first time. Truth is, we learned them a long time ago. We buried them in hope. There is something so horribly familiar about this night, about my parents' soul-wrenching despair, about the three of us grieving together as time bleeds and my mom's room grows quieter and quieter. A recurring nightmare. Déjà vu. My sister has been dead before. Now she's dead again.

They shouldn't ever call it "acceptance" when it comes to this kind of shattering, shape-shifting loss. It's only ever surrender.

In the drip, drip, drip of the minutes that pass. In the sharp breaths that suddenly never feel enough. In the forever of a night I spend with my parents in Mom's blood-lit room, in her soft perfumed bed, together, weeping, shuddering asleep and jerking awake with a yelp, to hug and be held, to mourn, to turn the television on, then off, in the ticktock of three heartbeats, broken but still keeping time.

87

WE KEEP OUR house's doors double–dead bolted, alarm set, curtains drawn. Next morning, the sun's hardly up but the vultures are back and they've multiplied. They have deployed a helicopter. They stand staring at our windows and if I look out at them, they get excited, flapping and squawking.

Elliott shows up super early. I hear him outside shouting, "Why don't you shove your stupid news story—" and I open the door, yell his name, and let him inside. My parents come running and shouting his name. It's a tearful, endless group-hug reunion.

My parents stay in their pajamas, practically comatose, sharing tranquilizers and making quiet phone calls to funeral homes and police. Elliott cleans the house, not knowing what to do with himself but wanting to help. I go out to pick up a food order at lunch, dressed like I live in Antarctica to hide myself. I break into a run the second my boots hit the pavement. A woman in thick makeup and two cameramen chase me for an entire block, yelling things like:

"Did you ever suspect it wasn't your sister?"

"Are you bringing charges against Anna Joplin?"

That last one makes me trip on the asphalt. Luckily I catch myself and am able to keep jogging away from the vultures toward the neighborhood Creole restaurant where I'm headed. I lose them after three blocks. Finally. Jesus space-invading Christ. As I slow down and catch my breath, the words "Anna Joplin" reverberate in my head.

Anna Joplin.

That's the first time I've heard her name. She was Ava to me. She's still Ava to me. I hate her, I miss her, I still don't get it.

I know the facts. Tell them to my heart.

I don't go home with the gumbo. I keep walking past my street, zombielike. I don't think it consciously, exactly, but my body knows where it's taking me. Down Ashby. To California. Neighborhood of ghosts and pain.

Besides the different vultures and the news vans double-parked on the street, there's what appears to be a rainbow mountain in front of the hoarder house. I squint my eyes and see dozens of bouquets, stuffed animals, candles. My eyes and nose sting. It's the type of useless drugstore merchandise you buy for a hospital visit. It's the cheap way strangers voice sympathy for tragedies they plain cannot understand. Tied to the fence of the hoarder house are Mylar balloons that catch the sunlight and blind my already burning eyes. I don't know what it is about that sight, the hive of unrecognizable people and vultures buzzing around it, the cheerful balloons, the fresh flowers in their plastic sleeves, the posters people made in memoriam with the ever-present first grade picture of my dead sister. But I get this wave of something blowing through me that I've never felt before. It's a quiet, sad nothing of a feeling I have no word for.

I turn and make the long walk home. I ignore the question-shouters and camera-stalkers and microphone-thrusters on the sidewalk and make it into the dim darkness of our house again, locking, double-locking, listening to the person outside say, "*Still* can't get a statement." Heels clicking away. Someone else yelling that they need an extra camera battery.

"It'll be over soon," I tell the empty room.

I catch my breath and realize what that feeling was back there. It's still in me, a subtle shift, a change in the air of me. It's relief. Because it *will* be over soon. Because we know the god-awful truth. Because nothing can really get worse. Because the whole world can come for us in a screaming mob, can open its jaws and swallow my sister, can make fools of us, but we're still standing.

We're Riverses. Keep trying, world. I dare you. You can't break us. I won't let you.

"Lunch," I say, entering the kitchen.

My parents are seated at the table with Elliott. Dad hasn't shaved. His eyes are permanently bloodshot. Mom's are like those of a different person, almost, her face unmade, puffy and shadowed with lines. Elliott is still as a statue, elbows on the table, chin in his hands.

"Let's try to eat," I say.

We open the to-go containers and slurp our lukewarm food in silence. I could tell them about the vulture infestation that has consumed our block, or how people built a memorial for Ava with shiny balloons and toys, or that the name of the imposter is apparently Anna Joplin. I'm sure they could relay details of the funeral arrangements or news from the police. We don't though. We just eat. After the meal's done, Dad stands and cleans up the table.

"Thanks, Ladybug," he says hoarsely.

"I wanted it to be her. I *needed* . . ." Mom murmurs.

"Mom," Elliott says, rubbing her shoulder.

She shakes her head.

Our day is dazed. I seem to have lost the ability to read. I sit staring at pages instead. Likewise, I see shapes moving on TV, I know what they're doing, but I don't understand them right now. My head is lost, parsing the same thoughts. Devastation that Ava died a little girl, that she died that way, trapped, gasping, frightened, alone. Despair that my parents are so wrecked. Relief that Ava at least wasn't the victim of some horrible serial killer. Guilt for feeling any kind of relief. Confusion as to who the pretend Ava was, and then Jonathan, her whole story—it makes no sense. Then I go through all those emotions and thoughts again. That's what I mean—my horrible revolving door.

I only break down and cry three times today. We go to bed early, in our own rooms, Elliott crashing on the couch. I can't seem to find comfort in my bed—the bed I shared with Ava—excuse me, Anna. I try to imagine where she is and what is happening to her. And why. *Why?*

"Brain," I say.

I finally drag my blankets and pillow to the floor. It's hard on my back. This is not going to happen. I get up and go downstairs, knocking on my mom's door.

"Mom?"

I don't wait for her answer. I go in and see, to my shock, my parents sleeping in the same bed together. We all slept in her room last night, but Dad had taken the chaise lounge in the corner and slept curled up, fetus-like. Tonight, he's holding her. Their eyes are shut and they snore. They look ashen. They look old. They look like pictures of themselves someone computer-engineered to age all of a sudden. I love them so much. I want to protect them from this forever hurt. I want to be everything for them. I want to resurrect Ava from the dead. I want a time machine to go back and make it so she never disappeared. I can't. I can't do anything.

I lie down at the foot of the bed and doze. It must be comfortable, because I only realize I slept when the sun is up and it's morning. And there's Elliott on the floor near me, wrapped in a blanket, sleeping soundly.

88

MY PARENTS DON'T really care about Anna Joplin right now. They're, understandably, grieving Ava with the help of professionals they should have sought out a long time ago. They're coming to terms with the fact that they should have moved on, but that they couldn't. Or wouldn't. We believe the things we want to believe, I guess. That's the horror they orbit in these days after the Monstrous Truth, these days spent hiding from the camera-ready vultures and planning Ava's memorial. But I think about Anna Joplin. Often.

The best friend I ever had was a big fat lie.

Her wig still sits on my dresser, her glitter still clings to my pillowcase, her computer with the stickers all over it sits in the corner next to the ukulele. She was here. She was real. But she wasn't Ava.

I've gone back and studied intensely; she looks *exactly* like the forensic projection of what Ava was supposed to look like. And she wasn't lying about Jonathan. She really was found in a Starbucks parking lot, and everything about her life in Satterfield was true. After the cops heard her story, they went and searched his house and found the attic. The boarded-up windows. The small TV. The crude letters written to Flora Daly in a child's scrawl. The pictures of flowers on the walls. It was exactly like she always told it. The drugs. The abuse.

What kind of sick world . . .

My sister—the old, I mean, the *young* one—died of an unthinkable, stupid accident. She snuck into some hoarders' yard, climbed into an old refrigerator, and shut herself in there, waiting for me, waiting to be found, sealed away in the dark. What a claustrophobic nightmare. Dying there in that backyard barely a mile away from our house.

Sometimes I ask myself, Why do we keep on living this horror show?

I visit the marina and watch a fiery sun sink into the cool jewel hand of the water one afternoon, right after the time change when the days feel longer. A seagull with one foot and missing feathers stands proudly on a jagged stone. The wind is mean, but she picks herself up and dives into the water. It must be so cold. She comes back up and does it again, again, into the water and out.

I take my old mood ring out of my pocket, studying its dull silver band, letting the glittery stone catch the light. It's green, whatever that means.

I throw it in the water.

89

I'VE ONLY BEEN to Max's house once, when we went to his Halloween party. It looks different now, half a year later, in the daytime. A bungalow painted blue and green, yard cluttered with defunct fountains, potted plants, and mismatched, half-painted patio furniture. I knock on the door and his mother answers, a small woman in tinted wire-frame glasses with curly gray hair who wears a tie-dye shirt and a neck brace. I haven't seen this woman in many years. She immediately wants to talk to me all about "the case," which is juicy again, trending hashtag everywhere in the news, and isn't a case anymore but a too-weird-to-believe true story, although really to me it's just my life. My life that I'm pretty tired of talking about at this point. Everything from my conversation with my bank teller to my revised personal statement for college centers around the Ava/Not-Ava tale. It's hard to find anyone who wants to talk about anything but.

Except Max, of course, who just texts things like, *feel you.*

here.

whatever u need.

As his mother picks me apart with hungry questions, Max comes out of his room and begins yelling, "Excuse me, no. No, Mom, I love you but stop, Mom. Mom, for the love of everything holy, *stop*."

We leave his house together, and he slams the door as his mother yells something at him about how disrespectful it is to raise one's voice. We walk west through the neighborhoods. His sunglasses are enormous and purple. He puts one arm around me. I haven't seen him in months, not since Not-Ava was still Ava. But he just puts his arm around me like we were always this thing and it was always this easy.

We talk about yesterday's rain. He tells me about how his mom has taken to wearing a neck brace because it feels more supportive. She's on a special no-gluten diet that is driving him insane. And she has put so much stress on herself with the diseases she thought she had over the years that she now has real heart problems from the stress.

"Super discombobulating," he says. "Now I'm all worried about her all the time. Like, actually worried, and not just worried about her being too worried."

"So you're sticking around."

"I have to take care of her. Are you sticking around?"

"I don't know. I don't have any reason really to be anywhere."

We're stopped at a crosswalk now, in front of a church. He presses the button, and we wait for the light to change. He pulls his sunglasses up and looks at me with such warmth that the blue sky behind him seems dim.

"Make a reason, then," he says.

"What? You?" I ask jokingly.

He's frozen, not smiling.

The light changes but we don't move.

"I love you, Vera," he says.

"Max," I say.

"I loved you, I am loving you, I will keep loving you."

"Stop," I say quietly.

"I keep thinking about all this completely *wacky* stuff that's happened to you. I mean, I'm grieving, too, over your sister. Both of them. At least—I know it's a penny in an ocean, I mean, believe me—but . . . some things are possible now."

"I feel so alone," I tell him. "Like, untouchably, indescribably alone."

He leans down and kisses me. The shock of tenderness seems to go farther than me, spilling out and reaching into the air around me. I put my arms around his neck and pull him in farther. I am falling. I am free.

When we pull apart, my eyes water as I laugh.

"What about now?" he asks.

I lean my head on his shoulder and hold his arm in mine. "I feel less so," I say.

"See?" he asks softly. "That easy."

I wipe my eyes.

I tell him I love him, because I do.

We cross the street. At the church behind us now, the lawn is staked with white crosses, one for every murder in Oakland this year so far.

Ahead of us, there's a cupcake shop that stinks of sugar.

90

THE VULTURES SEEM to have flown away from the neighborhood all at once. Occasionally I spot a news van. Funny how quickly the public grows bored with the Rivers drama. We have to live with it for the rest of our lives.

The night of the memorial service, Elliott asks if he can stay with us for a while. I kind of figured this was already happening—he hasn't left once since the morning he arrived. Elliott helps Mom dismantle Anna's room. He rents a truck and goes to Goodwill. I still have her things she left in my room in a bag in my closet.

He's also been sober, as far as I can tell, and super into using Mom's discarded gym equipment. He's looking fit.

I love that my brother is home. He's the only one I talk to bluntly about what happened, because Ava was his sister, too. We have the gravest conversations. When we revisit the truth, the sickening story of a little girl who wandered into the wrong place and died so alone, his bluster is gone. He's all sadness—honest, defeated, accepting.

"God, what that little girl went through," he says in a shaky voice. "I shouldn't have—"

But he doesn't finish his sentence.

I give him a hug. He can't quite muster forgiveness, but like the rest of us, he seems to have accepted his role in the unforgettable.

I catch myself more than once thinking to myself, *I can't wait to talk to Ava about all this.* Well, if that isn't a mental cul-de-sac.

Life, it keeps going. That's pretty much all it is when you boil it down: perpetual motion.

91

THERE ARE LOOPS I fall into, though, where the preoccupied feeling darkens everything, my brow constantly knit, my cheek chewed raw, trying to find a reason. Why did Anna Joplin, a foster kid kidnapped and kept in an attic in Satterfield, end up in our lives? How could this have ever happened at all? How on earth did we not know? Ozzie suspected it. It was why my parents cut him out. We've made amends with him. My parents invited him over for coffee, said they were sorry. Ozzie was sorrier.

We wanted her to be real. We made her real. We relived our old memories and told ourselves she was remembering, too. We were dazzled by how perfectly she fit the description. Her features, down to her cowlick, the mole on her cheek. My mom saw the mood ring and her lightbulbs went *ding*. We didn't stop to think about how we bought the mood ring from a drugstore chain. One of a million.

I should hate Anna Joplin more than anybody, because I loved her most. But it doesn't work that way. Hurt is prickly and love-barbed. I just want closure. Mom and Dad don't want to see her, and Elliott acts like he has no interest in her, but who knows. Maybe they will someday. She wasn't Ava, but there was a lot of truth to her.

People keep contacting me: strangers from high school, Madeline, old teachers saying they're sorry. Everyone wants to be my buddy and tell me they understand. Good-hearted liars, all.

I saw the long-form news article, shared in someone else's feed as if it had nothing to do with me, about Ava's found remains and the fake Ava living with us. Many of the people who used to protect us were quoted: publicists, lawyers, Shelly, experts of various shapes and sizes. Vultures. The first comment on the article just said, *WTF?? Dumbasses didnt figure out it wasnt her???* It made me mad at first, but then somehow I laughed. And then I stopped reading. I shut it off. They'll never know what it's like to be us. What it's like to want something to be true so badly, you are blind. Now FindAvaRivers.com just has Ava Rivers's first grade picture and the dates of the years she lived and died.

It's always going to be sad, but it gets more real by the day, and that's something.

My two twin pinholes of light in this dark time are Max and the acceptance letter I got to UC Berkeley for the fall.

Did you know it's one of the best public universities in the United States?

Not too shabby for a slacker like me.

92

I SPEND ABOUT half my nights at Max's these days. Max draws my portrait while I read books. I draw silly cartoons of him while he plays guitar. We watch old musicals, plan out imaginary trips to Europe. We have conversations dotted with long but comfortable silences. Together, we suffer the same simultaneous mourning of both a dead six-year-old and a fake teenage betrayer who we were pretty smitten with. I mean, he gets it. We occasionally stop to marvel about the times we spent with Ava-Anna and how we didn't figure it out.

"It was something like destiny," he says. "You know? To look that similar to the real Ava?"

"Yeah," I have to agree.

I still want to know why.

Every time I think about her being here and me getting to ask all the questions that worry my sleep in the wee hours, I don't know, I shut down. It halts me, the missing her, and makes me so ashamed.

Max's friend with the dolphin tattoo, Pilar, has two rooms open in her rickety purple Victorian near Telegraph Avenue. She lives with a sculptor, a theater student, and a professional weed grower. Max and I talk it over, go look at the rooms one day. Big windows that face a backyard with fruit trees and a fire pit. Someone's cooking curry and listening to jazz in the kitchen.

We smile at each other, dust dancing in the gold late-afternoon light, possibility a damn sweet high.

"Yeah," I say.

"Yep," he agrees.

93

MY PARENTS ARE surprisingly well.

It seems that the same way Ava's disappearance used to unite them into this productive team, Ava's death has spiraled them further into their own directions. It's for the greater good. Dad's training for a half marathon. Mom's got a part in a local one-act play. Elliott's landed a manager job at a frozen yogurt place he takes very seriously. We live parallel lives except for Saturday nights. Then, we laugh loudly and discuss the world with gravity. Silly accents have resurfaced—turns out the world can't take that away from us. We are bound, because we miss Ava. We know she's not coming back. At least there are still the four of us. You can trick us and break our hearts but we are still a family.

94

ONE NIGHT, MOM'S footsteps creak up the stairs; I realize how long it's been since I heard that noise and I ache.

On the floor, I'm packing again. My to-chuck pile is considerably larger than my to-keep.

"Vera," Mom says on the other side of the door. "You're home!"

"Come in."

She opens the door. It's the middle of the day but she's in her pajamas, men's pajamas, with transparent face cream on that gives her face a plastic glow. I used to never see her like this. Mom only came out of her room fully dressed, coiffed, jewelry twinkling.

"Wow, look at this," she says.

"I know." I stand up, uncomfortable in my own room like it's a half-painted set. I assume she's about to comment on the mess, but she seems to be studying the place. I hope I'm not breaking her heart by leaving. Come on, I'm not really leaving though. I'll be less than a mile away.

"Your bed used to be over there," she says, pointing to the other side of the room near the closet.

"I moved it so many years ago."

She sits.

"What's up?" I ask.

"I just wanted to be near you."

I sit next to her, rest my head against her head.

"I love you," she says. "I'm so sorry. You deserved so much more."

"Mom, it's not your fault."

"Yes it is," she says in a tight voice. "It wasn't supposed to be like this."

"I know."

I have to silently scream at myself to not crumble. I am a woman now.

She opens her mouth and makes a *hhhh* sound like she's trying to fog up a windowpane.

"So don't feel bad," I say. "Just—just let things be the way they are. It's okay."

"I wish I had given you more time," she says. "Instead of always chasing Ava's case or keeping so busy. Now I look at you and you're all grown up and I feel like I missed it."

When she begins to cry, years melt away and my mom seems to slip younger, younger, almost teenage.

"If you were a stranger, I'd still pick you out of all the moms," I tell her.

She sputters a laugh. It's what I used to tell her when I was a little kid. I loved her so much I'd choose her if I could.

Still would.

My small mountain of giveaways and puddle of keepers sit there on my floor, nearly sorted. I can tell you exactly what will be coming with me: clothes, books, a shelf, a box of keepsakes. Everything else will sit in the garage or out on the curb, waiting to be taken and loved by passersby.

"I can't believe you're going to move in with Max Spangler," she says, wiping her eyes.

"We're not moving in together like that. It's a big house. He's one of five housemates."

"Well, maybe I'll leave your room as it is for a while, in case you want to come back."

"Liar. You know you've already got plans for it."

"Never," she says facetiously.

I'll bet she has the whole thing picked out, down to the drapes and throw pillows.

"Are you going to stay here?" I ask.

"For now."

"You and Dad are . . . together?"

"It's hard to explain to you what all this—*everything*—has done to us," Mom says. "In some ways, your dad and I are bound; we have shared this . . . hell together that no one else will ever understand. But we're also different people because of it. We're not who we were before."

I hide my heartbreak with an understanding smile.

"I don't know what's ahead, Vera," she admits. "Except that I'm your mom, and I love you."

"I love you, too."

"Can I hug you?" she asks, almost shyly.

I nod. We come together and, as she hugs me, I feel her bones, her smallness. Like the last time we hugged this long and hard we were other people, me tiny, she a giant.

95

WITH A LOAD in my car, I'm gone.

I wake up in my new room every morning, hearing voices I only barely recognize out in the hallways and the living room, unpredictable music and swooshes of cars. Sometimes I wake up in Max's bed. Sometimes he wakes up in mine.

I sleep so well with him.

My parents and Elliott are still close enough to visit anytime.

My dad is doing a major spring cleaning. Boxes of books to the curb, yellowed papers filling the recycle bin. I even think I spotted that neon bandana, and damn my stupid, sentimental self for even getting sad about that. I go to say goodbye and he ropes me into helping him clean.

"You know, I'm glad you're going to Cal and sticking nearby and I can keep bothering you whenever I want," he says.

I smile.

"I am so proud of you."

"For what?" I say. "Taking the easiest road possible?"

"Vera, don't even pretend you've ever taken the easy road," he says, holding his foot ashtray over the garbage almost threateningly. "Yeah, you stuck around. You're a goddamn rock, and don't you forget it."

"Thanks for noticing," I say. "And yeah, you're right. I always wished I was a bird—but I guess I'm a rock."

"Takes one to know one."

"I'll take that ashtray."

He hands it to me.

In the silence, I think of Anna, as I often do.

"What if I wanted to call Anna and just talk to her," I say.

"I wouldn't even know where to direct you, Ladybug. We don't have contact. She's a very sick person. Talking to her isn't going to make you feel any better about what happened."

I pretend I don't care about his answer and pick up a pile of newspapers. Yes, my father is a clichéd eccentric drowning in newspapers.

"Recycle?" I ask.

"Sure," he says without looking.

I start up the stairs but look down and realize the page on top is folded neatly to OBITUARIES. And I'm staring at a black-and-white photo of six-year-old Ava May Rivers—the picture that I've seen so many times getting spit out of copy machines and hung up on telephone poles that it's become a kind of visual mythology. It doesn't even choke me up.

"Wait, Dad," I say, heading back down. "Don't you want this?"

He comes over to me, squints over my shoulder, and ponders it for a second. He shakes his head. "I don't," he says simply.

Stunned, I go upstairs and put the newspapers in the recycling. There's Ava's face, on top of toilet paper rolls and snack boxes, and though I know it's just a replica of a picture I've seen far too many times and it is so removed from the essence of the person it's supposed to represent, I know I shouldn't leave her there and walk away—but I do. Then I go downstairs and hug my father.

96

SNOW WHITE'S BEEN donated to a thrift store, and ever since I started my internship at a small press I've been rocking profesh-looking suit jackets and jeans. I cut all my hair off, pixie short, and Max can't keep his hands off me. I catch my reflection in the mirror often, struck by how grown-up and changed I look. For a fraction of a second, unrecognizable.

Sometimes I wonder what Ava would have looked like now. How different from the forensic sketch and how different from Anna. I stop thoughts like that pretty quickly, the what-ifs, because now I know she's dead. Grief trumps the wonder.

I stop by a diner and eat breakfast for late lunch after a day at the office. Alone. Well, not completely alone—I have a book to read. My window faces a parking lot and trees but the lights in here are so bright all I can see is myself, my stranger-for-a-second self. I check my email on my phone. There's one from Ozzie. Huh.

SUBJECT: Something for you.

Hello Vera, here's the address where Anna Joplin is staying. I'm not personally advising you to go see her. In fact, I think it's a bad idea. But your mother convinced me to give you the address. So here it is. She's in Santa Rosa.

I'm glad to hear you got into UC Berkeley and glad I could be of some help. You deserve it. Anyway, if you could let an old guy give you some advice: I know you're a special person. I know your life has been eclipsed. Don't worry. You've only just opened the door to the big fat world. There's a lot of joy with your name on it. Go get 'em.

And then the address.

Mother. I'm fifty miles from Santa Rosa. I'm a freeway and a bridge away. For a second, I almost believe in angels.

97

HOLY SPIRIT HOME for Troubled Teens is out in wine country. It's the end of the day and the sun's blaring its last hoorah orange, blinding over the vineyards I pass. I've got my sunglasses on, hands tight on the wheel, heartbeat a hundred miles an hour. As I see the address of Holy Spirit, I pull to the end of the long driveway and park on the road. It's a street with far-apart houses, so many trees, and long, thirsty lawns. It's a far cry from Berkeley, where the Victorians with funky paint jobs neighbor farmers' markets, liquor stores, and subway stations. For a second, I don't know why, I think of Portland. I think of the other somewheres in the big fat world, and I know someday I'll see them.

It looks like an ordinary blue house. I get out of the car and step up the driveway, double-checking the address on my phone. I was expecting something clinical, something halfway between a hospital and a prison. For a minute, the idea of fleeing back to my car seems like my best bet. What am I going to say to her? What if she is beyond-reach crazy and this is as hopeless as everyone seems to think? What possible answer could she give me that would ever make me feel better about the lies she told? But my finger is already pushing the intercom ATTENTION button. No turning back.

"Holy Spirit," the voice says.

The box, plastic and dirty in its speaker holes, has a TALK button. I press it and speak. "I'm here to visit someone," I say. "Av—Anna. Joplin."

"Visiting hours ended at 6:00 p.m., I'm sorry."

I check my phone. It's 6:30. The disappointment is nearly paralyzing. I swallow. "This is her sister. I drove all the way from Berkeley," I say. "Can I just see her for a minute?"

How easily that sweet word, "sister," rolled off my tongue just now.

The silence is so long I figure the lady is done with me. I'm going to have to come back another time, or maybe never come back at all. This could be a sign that it wasn't meant to be. But then I hear a beep.

"Come in," the voice says cheerfully.

Who knows—maybe we're getting special treatment because we're quasi-famous. Or maybe they're just bending the rules to be decent.

I walk inside. There's a long coatrack on the wall with so many sweatshirts and coats on it, a rack of shoes beneath. I spot the beat-up glittery Converse right away and get a flutter. The sounds of girls' voices laughing and popcorn in a microwave float into the foyer where I wait, reading inspirational posters in the hallway about the serenity to accept the things we can't change and God dancing on the day you were born. A couple girls walk by, gabbing, bowls of popcorn balanced in their hands. They don't seem like troubled teens to me. What makes someone *troubled*, anyway? Aren't we all?

After a short eternity, Ava—Anna—walks around the corner.

Her wild hair is up in a ponytail on top of her head with a little bow. She's wearing a shirt I've never seen with a kitten in outer space on it. She stares at the carpet between us, hugging her arms self-consciously. Her name might be different, but it aches how similar she appears. I have to remind myself our noses are not the same. We share no DNA. My twin sister is dead and not living in a group home in Santa Rosa, as much as I wish that weren't true.

"Oh, man," she says.

"Hi."

She still won't meet my gaze. I wait for my anger to come and flood me. But it doesn't. In fact, I fight the urge to touch her shoulder or even hug or something. It takes willpower.

"Um . . . you want to go to the visiting room?" she asks.

"Sure."

"Cool. Follow me."

I follow her through the living room, where about five or six girls are squeezing onto couches and beanbags to watch a movie—MGM lion roaring—and then to the back of the house. The visiting room is a sunroom, glass-walled, scattered with tables and chairs and mismatched furniture. It's awash with sunlight in the late afternoon. The backyard has a covered pool and a lawn with a volleyball net. It doesn't seem bad here. There's something alive and abuzz that makes the Rivers house back in Berkeley feel subdued. We sit at the table across from each other. We're the only ones in the room. My hands quiver in my lap.

"I really don't know what to say," she says, still not looking at me, picking at her fingernails. I can tell she's trying to keep herself together. "I never thought I would see you again."

"I still can't believe what you did."

The words seem to explode and take up the whole room.

"Why did you *do* that?" I ask.

"I don't know," she says, dropping her eyes.

"How could you *do* that to us?" I ask, voice rising.

She looks up at me.

"Can you imagine, for one sec, okay, that you had been a piece of trash no one ever wanted?" Her eyes meet mine finally and I see miles and miles of pain. "Abused, raped, manipulated, locked away with no friend but TV. And one day you wake up in the hospital with a head that feels like a block of ice and everyone tells you you're someone. And it seems familiar. Like déjà vu. You're like, okay, so this is my reality. To top it off you're surrounded by amazing people, with a house in a super sweet town where you're all taken care of, and loved . . . and everyone everywhere thinks you're a hero for surviving . . . which you did—survive—you survived your own horror story, you just had a different name—can you imagine, like, realizing you're not that person, slowly, over days, but then, like . . . like, convincing yourself? Like, squashing down the knowing and saying, I am this person. Saying it enough that you believe it and forget about who you really are. Can you imagine the freaking *miracle* of ending up there? Of looking exactly like the lost girl? Would *you* say something? Would you? Or would you roll with it and maybe even start believing it was true?"

I can't answer her question. I don't know what I'd do. I never will. "You really thought you were Ava, is that what you're saying?"

"Yes, at first, sort of." Her dust-blue gaze is teary and afraid, and some tightness in me goes sweetly limp. "It was all so mixed up, the real parts and the not-real parts, it started blending together. I hope you saw in the news it was all *true*. I mean, not the Ava part. Which I realize is a really big part. But I mean, everything I told you about the attic—and Jonathan—" She has to close her eyes for a second. "Shhhh. Wait. Wait."

Outside, a hummingbird lingers near the window, and then vanishes in a blink.

She opens her eyes back up again. "It's so brain-exploding weird. Ava looks *exactly* like me. I mean, that computer-generated picture of what she would look like today. And I wasn't pretending or acting when I was with you guys, you know? I fit in. I fit right in."

"You did."

"Sometimes I still try to think it out—like, I *could* be her."

"But you're not. You're not her. Ava is dead."

I put my hand over my face, tell myself to breathe, to calm down.

"I'm so sorry," Anna says. "I'm so sorry that she's gone."

She takes a deep breath. Now we're both trying not to cry.

"How screwed up am I?" she asks. "I'm super ashamed. I almost wish you weren't here right now because I feel so bad it hurts, it *hurts* all over. It's like, I can see this through your eyes—I must look so insane. But I am the same person I was when I lived with you— I'm just not Ava."

"No, you're not."

"I wanted to tell you. I thought about it sometimes. But—but I started thinking, how bad is this, really? If I'm not Ava, but I look just like her—if Ava's gone, and I'm here—I'm making everybody happy. You, me, the whole family, everybody."

"When we found out Ava was dead, it was basically like I lost two people at once. One real, one fake."

I grind my teeth. I push the soles of my feet into the floor. I will not cry. Anna breaks first, wiping her eyes before the tears can touch her face.

"I tried to tell you. I'm really sorry," she says.

"It's like, I knew Ava was dead," I say, my voice disappearing into my throat as I fight emotion. "I knew that for years. I figured she was dead and something terrible had happened. And that's awful. Life was so awful for so many years because of it. But then you came along and you made everything better—so much better—we were all so happy and so full of *hope* and that made everything so much worse."

She nods, unable to say anything, and covers her eyes with her hand.

"What were you going to do if Ava wasn't found?" I ask. "Just . . . pretend to be this dead girl your whole life?"

Anna wipes her red eyes. "All I know is I was never as happy as I was when I was Ava—when I was a Rivers."

It's like someone puts a fishhook through my heart and tugs, tugs, tugs. I can barely stand it. A part of me wishes she could have continued the lie forever, gotten old, spent dozens of holidays with the family—she's right, who would it have hurt? I wish I didn't know that my sister died in a freak accident involving an abandoned refrigerator and that this person in front of me isn't her. I really wish that. I wish it so bad it blazes.

A short-haired lady with a lip ring comes in and says our time is up. Anna gets up and so do I. The woman stands in the doorway. I don't want this conversation to end, but I'm never going to get the answer I really want. She isn't my sister. Plain as DNA.

We walk out to the foyer and I remember something.

"I have something in the car," I say to the lady. "Can she walk me out so I can give it to her?"

Anna turns to the woman standing with us. "I'm not going to run away, Leslie," she says. "Where would I go?"

"Go ahead. I'll watch from the doorway," Leslie says.

Anna follows me out to the car.

"How are you?" she asks. "I mean, besides all this?"

It's such a feeble question. How are you, besides the worst shit ever? But I say, "I'm actually doing pretty okay."

Because I am. I've even been seeing a therapist to work through and process everything, move forward with my life. Everything's looking up.

"I just moved in with Max," I tell her.

She smiles. I can tell she's genuinely happy for me and so relieved that I've shared a crumb of my life with her.

"That is so freaking cool," she says.

"Yeah."

I reach into the backseat of my car. The fur is soft against my hands. It seemed amazing, when I packed it up, that it wasn't really made from animals. I left the wigs and all her clothes behind. I put them out on the curb in Berkeley for strangers to take. But the coat, I don't know, I couldn't throw it away.

"Here," I say, handing it to her.

Anna looks down at the coat and her face falls. She hugs it and wipes her eyes. "Good times" is all she says.

We stand on the lawn, the short-haired lady in the doorway watching.

"It doesn't seem so bad here," I say.

"It's okay," she says. "They're nice. I miss you guys so much, though."

She buries her face in the fur coat.

"I got into school, too," I tell her.

The gush of sharing with her is such relief. Anna was the best friend I've ever had.

"Which school?"

"UC Berkeley."

"You're amazing."

"Thanks."

Her pink-rimmed eyes brighten and I can't help seeing traces of my sister in her even though I know it's trickery.

"Well," she says. "Congratulations. I hope you get everything you want."

"I won't."

"You can do it, girl."

Even breathing seems to hurt. "I hate myself for missing you."

A breeze blows her explosive ponytail. She wipes her eyes. "We're not sisters," she says with exhausted acceptance. "We're not twins." She puts the coat on and admires the sleeves. "But what if, in another way, we are?"

The wind dries my eyes to the point of pain. I sniff and shrug. I want to reach out and hug her. More than that. I want her to get in the car with me and for us to be a unit again. Because I know exactly what she means. In fact, nothing has ever felt more real than her being my sister, and nothing, not even the truth, can erase that.

"Anna, you're pushing it," yells Leslie from the doorstep.

"I gotta go," Anna says. "I can't say enough sorries, Vera."

I stand on the lawn, unable to move or say anything.

"Good luck," she says.

We wave, sad-eyed, hair blowing, a funhouse mirror.

She turns to go. I watch her run up to the doorstep, and Leslie gently puts her arm around her. Everything gets blurry. The wind seems to have infected me, crawled inside my nostrils and my eyelids, taken over my throat and lungs, and the sting is everywhere.

"Anna," I yell.

She turns around. So does Leslie.

"You have my number, right?" I go on.

Anna's face falls. She covers her mouth and nods. Leslie pats her back.

"Don't be a stranger," I say.

She flashes me the peace sign—a two-fingered V—before turning back around again.

They go inside and close the door. I get in my car and drive south again. Freeway. Fast lane. My phone buzzes in the passenger seat. Berkeley gets closer, the Bay to my right a glimmer. How perfect this place would seem if it were new. What if a person can transform enough internally that a place can transform externally, can be reborn? Wouldn't that be something?

The sky deepens and the blue-chunk moon sharpens. Wheels beneath me hum.

Max texts me. Our housemates made lentil salad and chickpea burgers. They're about to watch a documentary on beekeepers. Even though it's been hours, Max says he's "jonesing for a Vera fix."

Isn't it the best thing—that love is a kind of magic that turns strangers into family?

In a shock of enlightenment speeding toward home, I get it: This now couldn't be without everything terrible that happened before it. This beautiful now.

I think it might be possible to love what I wish had never happened.

I get the world's mean pain and sweet, warm lips.

I get it's not an either/or deal.

I forgive you, life.

I forgive.

ACKNOWLEDGMENTS

First, thank you to my agent, Claire Anderson-Wheeler, whose patience and vision helped bring this manuscript from its messy beginning to these polished pages. Not only is she this book's strongest supporter, she also had a huge hand in shaping it. I owe so much to her.

Thank you, Tiffany Liao, for first falling for my book and giving it a wonderful home at Penguin. Your early edits were so influential and my only regret is that I didn't get more time to work with you.

Thank you, Jessica Harriton and Ben Schrank, for your editing expertise. Jess, your advice and advocacy have been invaluable throughout every stage of this publication process and I appreciate all you do so much.

Thank you, Lauren Hougen, for your careful copyedits, Samantha Hoback for catching all my typos, Rachel Porter for your sensitivity reader wisdom, Samira Iravani for a gorgeous cover design, and everyone else at Penguin who lent their expertise to this book.

Thank you and virtual hugs to brilliant authors Amber Smith, Kerry Kletter, and Kathleen Glasgow—I'm humbled that you took the time to be my early readers.

Thanks to my best friend Ramona Itule-Patigian, who sat down with me and talked through my book early on, treating my characters and story like real things. We're not sisters. But in another way, we are.

Thanks to my wonderful family full of my favorite humans: Mom, Dad, Matt, and Denese, and the North Carolina crew, Jackson and Katie, and Micaela.

I'm so grateful every day for my dear husband Jamie, who lets me rattle on about worlds that don't exist and stare at my screen for ridiculous amounts of time and loves me anyway. For our astounding little daughter Roxanna Tulip, who was such a perfect baby she let me write the whole first draft of this book on maternity leave. And for Zora Firelily, the sequel.